RAVES FOR JOAN HESS
and
THE MAGGODY MYSTERY SERIES

"SUCCESSFULLY COMBINES MURDER AND MAYHEM with the most bizarre goings-on east of the Rockies." —*Library Journal*

"FUNNY AND FAST MOVING . . . I ALMOST SPLIT A GUSSET. . . . Joan Hess has a true ear for dialogue, a sharp eye for setting a scene, and a compassionate affection for her characters. . . . More power to her pen!" —Charlotte MacLeod

"DOWN HOME FUN . . . Hess' lively wit and well-crafted plot stand up smartly to all the kidding. Check it out." —*Kansas City Star*

"The loony inhabitants of Maggody are at it again . . . amiable, mildly raunchy fun, with a telling edge . . . another easy-to-take chapter in the ongoing saga of Maggody." —*Kirkus Reviews*

"TO CREATE LIVING, BREATHING CHARACTERS TAKES TALENT. To create a whole town inhabited by such characters borders on genius—and this is what Joan Hess has done with M_____ _____ Maggody and eve_____ _____ everybody) in it.

MUCH ADO
IN
MAGGODY

AN ARLY HANKS MYSTERY

JOAN HESS

AN ONYX BOOK

ONYX
Published by the Penguin Group
Penguin Books USA Inc., 375 Hudson Street,
New York, New York 10014, U.S.A.
Penguin Books Ltd, 27 Wrights Lane,
London W8 5TZ, England
Penguin Books Australia Ltd, Ringwood,
Victoria, Australia
Penguin Books Canada Ltd, 10 Alcorn Avenue,
Toronto, Ontario, Canada M4V 3B2
Penguin Books (N.Z.) Ltd, 182–190 Wairau Road,
Auckland 10, New Zealand

Penguin Books Ltd, Registered Offices:
Harmondsworth, Middlesex, England

Published by Signet, an imprint of Dutton Signet,
a division of Penguin Books USA Inc.

First Onyx Printing, September, 1991
10 9 8 7 6 5 4

 REGISTERED TRADEMARK—MARCA REGISTRADA

Printed in the United States of America

PUBLISHER'S NOTE
This is a work of fiction. Names, characters, places, and incidents either are the product
of the author's imagination or are used fictitiously, and any resemblance to actual
persons, living or dead, events, or locales is entirely coincidental.

To Priscilla Ridgway,
who, perhaps more than anyone else,
makes me laugh. I take back all
those things I said about you.
Really.

ACKNOWLEDGMENTS

I would like to acknowledge the gracious assistance of the following: John Leonard, who shared his knowledge of banking practices, both licit and illicit; Ray Reynolds, who answered my legal questions without too much laughter; and Captain Larry Poage and Lieutenant Terry Lawson of the Fayetteville Fire Department, who spent a great deal of their valuable time explaining the intricacies of arson investigation.

1

I am not going to start off bitching and whining about how nothing ever happens in Maggody, for two reasons. One is that the premise is getting as stale as day-old bread. The other is that it doesn't appear to be all that valid anymore. That's not to say a lot of what happens in Maggody, Arkansas, isn't on the mundane side. We're talking about outsiders running the single traffic light or putting the pedal to the metal in the school zone. Dogs being stolen. Good ol' boys brawling at the pool hall on a regular basis. Marijuana and moonshine. Among Maggody's 755 residents, someone's always stirring up minor headaches for yours truly, Arly Hanks, chief of police extraordinaire. I've got a real live badge and a box with three bullets in it to prove it.

And there have been some bizarre incidents during my official tenure, which began when I submitted the only application for the position. Calling them crimes of the heart seems too romantic for this neck of the woods; they're more like crimes of the bowel. But if on a given day you were to cruise through Maggody (observing the speed limit signs, we'd like to think), you'd be hard pressed to find anything seething below

the surface. You might see a couple of good Christian
folks in tight white patent leather shoes, gabbing out
in front of the Voice of the Almighty Lord Assembly
Hall; a grizzled sort in well-worn overalls shuffling
into the tiny branch bank to see if Miss Una can help
him make heads or tails of some new-fangled com-
puterized bank statement; the Emporium, run by a
bunch of aged hippies who still sit around in the nude
behind their house and hum through their noses, to
their neighbors' alarm. Earl Buchanon, in particular,
keeps muttering about communes, Communists, and
how a backside of birdshot's too good for 'em. Not
everybody's into mantras in Maggody.

There's a line of stores, the windows decorated with
yellowed newsprint and strips of peeling tape. A red
brick building, the police department, that gives me a
place to while away the hours swatting flies, drinking
coffee, taking potshots at the roaches with the radar
gun, and wondering why in hell I ever came back to
Maggody. Okay, I came back because I wanted to lick
my wounds after a tacky divorce. I had no intention of
doing so for more than a few months, but I was still
licking away two years later, mostly because I'm not
double-jointed and therefore can't twist my leg back
far enough to kick myself in the rear.

Moving on, there's the Suds of Fun Launderette and
the Kwik-Stoppe-Shoppe on the left, followed by some
shabby houses and enough weeds to drown a toddler
in. On the right, however, is our local attempt at glitz:
Ruby Bee's Bar and Grill. It's painted a peculiar shade
of pink in deference to the sign out next to it that
proclaims the availability of accommodations at the
Flamingo Motel. The neon flamingo looks a little

motley, and the V CAN Y sign hardly draws a crowd, but the parking lot in front of Ruby Bee's is usually filled with pickup trucks. The beds of the trucks are guarded by emaciated, gunky-eyed hounds wishing they were out chasing coons instead of snuffling dust and growling at potential truck thieves.

I won't extol the virtues of the Pot O' Gold Mobile Home Park, the skeletal remains of Purtle's gas station, the Dairee Dee-Lishus across from the high school, or even the bucolic bliss that reigns all the way to the Missouri state line. Prevarication's more of a winter sport, and the thermometer had been pushing triple digits for nigh on to a week.

I was fiddling with the window unit in the PD when the door banged open and Johnna Mae Nookim stomped into my sanctuary.

"Holy cow," she said as the heat hit her. "This place is worse than an oven, Arly. I swear, if you had a mind to, you could bake buttermilk biscuits in here."

"I realize that. In fact, I'm seriously considering tacking up a sign outside that offers free sauna sessions. Our first health club."

Johnna Mae gave me a puzzled look as she settled her hefty bottom on the chair across from my desk. She had seriously bleached hair, a round, tomato-colored face, and the beetlish brow and yellowish eyes of the Buchanon clan. She was wearing a prissy white shirt, the armpits of which were getting wetter by the second, and a miniskirt that made no concession to her pudgy thighs, dimpled knees, and thick ankles. God knows how the spike heels supported all of the above, but one had to presume they did. After all, she hadn't crawled into the PD. Then again, if the air conditioner continued to balk, she darn well might find herself crawling out—with me clinging to her ankle.

"I don't think this is all that healthy," she muttered, fanning herself with a piece of paper. "I'd be more inclined to say it was downright unhealthy, if you get my drift. You ever thought about getting a fan or something, Arly?"

I twitched a knob or two and banged my fist on the top of the damn thing. I had drawn back my foot to bust it when a cool breeze drifted out. It wasn't anything arctic, but I took it as a conciliatory gesture and reluctantly lowered my foot. Once I was sitting behind my desk, I said, "Hear you had a baby, Johnna Mae. Congratulations."

"Seven pounds, twelve ounces, and enough red hair to make a wig for an Irish setter. He is the sweetest little ol' thing imaginable, and the spittin' image of his daddy. That's not to say I didn't have a spot of trouble convincing little P.J. to make the trip, of course. He wiggled around so much the last couple of weeks before his birthing date that he was about as cattywampus as a baby can get. My first two slid out just as easy as you please, but this one had to be taken out by a cesarean section, where the doctor makes this slit right across the front of you and reaches in and pulls the baby out. Putter like to have passed out cold in the delivery room. He still turns a little green when I talk about it, but he's always had a delicate side most people can't see."

"Sorry to hear that," I said before I was given further graphic description of each and every minute of little P.J.'s arrival. "But you look like you've bounced right back."

Johnna Mae's brow lowered until she could barely see from under it. "I have regained my good health, yes. Now, I was only intending to take off a few days of maternity leave, but the C section changed all that. Dr. Herkmeyer insisted I stay a whole solid week in the hospital, and then he told me I couldn't go back to work, I had to stay home for another five weeks. I must admit I wasn't feeling all that chipper. Putter was real good about taking care of the kids and seeing to the housework, and I just kind of stayed on the sofa and watched my soaps while I recuperated."

"Great," I murmured, wondering why she was sounding madder and madder as she described a six-week session of sofa vegetation.

"That's fine and dandy for you to say, Arly. None of it was my fault, you know. Not even Dr. Herkmeyer could see that little P.J. was going to give me such a troublesome time during and after. Anyway, long about last Wednesday I decided I'd better get my rear off the sofa and get back to work at the bank. Due to Putter's disability he's been unemployed for nearly three years now, and we were feeling a pinch most everywhere. I called Mr. Oliver and told him I'd be in. I managed to squeeze into panty hose and a jumper I'd worn during the confinement, then I had Putter drop me off in front of the bank just like he's done for eleven years. I breezed through the front door, hollered a greeting to Miss Una, and headed straight for my locker in the back room. Well, that's when the shit hit the fan, if you'll pardon my French."

"Oh," I said, nodding wisely. I had no idea where she was heading, and I wasn't overly enthralled by the narrative. If the truth must be made known, my brain was drifting down the highway toward Ruby Bee's, where there might be a plate lunch with my name on it. In capital letters.

Johnna Mae gripped the arms of the chair and leaned forward. "That locker has been mine for the last six years, since Mr. Oliver decided to spend all his time at the main bank in Farberville and I assumed the position of head teller at the branch." She paused for a moment, just in case I wanted to get her autograph or some such fool thing. I didn't twitch. "Being head teller isn't like being executive vice president at the main bank, but it involved a right nice little raise and a certain amount of authority. I don't want to crow on my own fence, Arly, but I did a mighty good job of it for six years."

"And now you're no longer head teller?"

"You hit it square on the head. In my absence, this damn fool college smart-ass youngster was brought in and given my position, not to mention my locker and my desk. Why, you'd like to have thought he'd been there for years from the way he'd thrown out all my little efforts to make things homey at the bank. Miss Una managed to save my philodendrum from the garbage can, but my African violets just went everywhere. He took my photographs of my family and put them in a box and then proceeded to put the box in the dampest corner of the back room. There was mildew on the backs of them by the time I fished them out and wiped them off. I want you to do something, Arly."

"About the mildew?" I said, mystified.

"About this smirky youngster who took not only my position, but my desk and my locker and my personal belongings." She took a tissue from her purse to mop her forehead, and leaning so far over the desk I could feel her breath, she said, "I want you to arrest Sherman Oliver and have him put in jail!"

"Wait a minute, Johnna Mae. I thought you were talking about some newcomer to the branch, but—"

"Mr. Oliver is the one who gave Brandon Bernswallow all those things I struggled for and slaved for and earned through good, honest sweat, not to mention eleven years of dedication to the bank. Now this Bernswallow fellow sashays in, and Mr. Oliver gives me some cockeyed story about how his father is on the board of directors of the bank and how Bernswallow was sent to our branch to learn the ropes so he could end up being president some day down the road."

"I can't arrest him for playing politics," I said, holding up my hands and wishing the air conditioner would blow hard enough to do something about Johnna Mae's tuna fish breath. "If the main bank sent in a scion to learn the business, that's for you, them, and Sherman Oliver to work out. There's nothing criminal about it."

"But there is! Last year when I was visiting my older sister and her good-for-nothing husband what live down near Pine Bluff, she dragged me to this seminar about women's rights in the workplace. This woman with a hyphenated name was right eloquent, even though I must say I never did understand about the hyphen. Do you know what I learned there, Arly? Do you?"

"Not right off hand," I admitted as I picked up a scratch pad and tried to ward off the attack of the killer tuna sandwich.

To my heartfelt relief, she sank back and sighed.

"Well, for one thing, it is illegal to harrass women in the office. That means some jerk of a hotshot executive is not supposed to play grab-ass with his secretary unless she doesn't mind. And if he does it anyway, she can file a complaint with some office at the state capital and they'll make him regret the day he even thought about grabbing her ass or pinching her breast or making lewd remarks."

"You're not telling me that Sherman Oliver was trying anything with you, are you? He's at least sixty if he's a day, and hardly the sort to chase anyone around the desk like a silver-haired satyr."

"I wouldn't know what that happens to be," she said with a sniff. "And I am not accusing Mr. Oliver of having lustful thoughts in his heart, or the wherewithal to catch me, or even Miss Una, if'n he did. He has been nothing but a gentleman for all my eleven years at the bank. He is a deacon at the Voice of the Almighty Lord and has been teaching the men's Bible study class on Sundays since God made little green apples. His wife is the president of the missionary society and does a Sunday school class herself. She's the only one who'll even go into the room with the seven- and eight-year-old boys on a regular basis."

My stomach made a suggestive comment about the possibility of fried pork chops and peach cobbler. "That's a real comfort to know, Johnna Mae," I said as I gazed longingly at the door. "I'm glad to know you have such respect for Mr. and Mrs. Oliver. However, there's nothing either of us can do about this interloper. Give him a few months and he'll be gone, and then you can have your position back, along with potted plants and photographs on your desk. Now, if you don't mind, I have to—"

"I want you to arrest Mr. Oliver and have him put in jail."

"We just went over that, and I explained that whatever happened was not a criminal matter."

"Sexual discrimination is against the law, Arly Hanks. In that you've sworn to uphold the law in Maggody, it's up to you to do something. If Putter hadn't been unemployed these last three years due to a ruptured disc in his back, it wouldn't be quite so serious. But we just can't pay the rent on the mobile home, make payments to the doctor and the hospital, keep our children in shoes, and put food on the table every night if I'm making minimum wage. How'd you like to feed a family of five on three dollars and thirty-five cents an hour—before withholding and all of that?"

"You were dropped to minimum wage after eleven years at the bank?" I asked despite myself.

Her eyes filled with tears. "That's the honest to God truth, Arly, and you know me well enough to realize I'm not some sniveling crybaby who ran to the teacher any time a boy snapped my bra on the playground. But I learned at this seminar that it's illegal to demote a woman because she takes maternity leave. Women are supposed to have babies. That's why God gave them wombs."

"It might be a violation of the Civil Rights Act, but it's still not a criminal matter, Johnna Mae. I agree that you've been treated shabbily. I wish I could do something to help, but I can't. You need to find a lawyer who specializes in this kind of discrimination."

"Now, how am I supposed to find some lawyer,

much less pay him, when I can't feed my family meat more than once a week?"

I didn't have a good answer for that one. We talked a while longer, then I gently shooed her out the door and walked down the highway to Ruby Bee's, where at least it would be dark and cool. To my delight, it was also deserted, except for one comatose character in a far booth. Several empty pitchers both explained and attested to the depth of the coma, but I didn't even raise an eyebrow. Too hot for facial aerobics.

I perched on a barstool and allowed the lovely breeze to wash over me. I was still evaporating when the proprietor came through the kitchen door and shot me a beady look.

"I suppose you want something to eat," Ruby Bee said in a most unfriendly voice.

"I was hoping."

"And you didn't stop to think for one minute about how I'd have to stand over a hot stove to fix it for you, did you? Didn't think about how the vents in the kitchen don't work and it's hotter than a fire in a pepper mill, did you? All you think about is your innards, missy. If you paid half as much attention to other folks, you'd think twice before insisting on someone having to slave and perspire so's you could gulp it down and prance away without so much as a thank you kindly."

Did I mention that Ruby Bee is my mother?

I pondered my options for a moment. "I am always most grateful when you make such sacrifices for your only child," I said meekly, sucking in my cheeks and widening my eyes in true Oliver Twist fashion. "I'd have gone over to the Dairee Dee-Lishus for a cheeseburger, but your cooking is the best in the county. However, I cringe to think of all that slavery going on over a hot stove, so I'll just head back down the road."

"Haven't I taught you anything about eating well-balanced meals?" she snapped, looking pissed enough to come across the bar and turn me over her knee. It would make an amusing scene, to say the least. To begin with, I'm five foot ten and she's five foot period. She has brassy blond hair, courtesy of her friend Estelle Oppers, owner and sole operator of Estelle's Hair Fantasies. Despite the waves of pink eye shadow and the inch or so of powder, Ruby Bee resembles everyone's granny, from her angelic smile to her clean white apron and support stockings. If the woman knocked on your door, you'd invite her in to make cookies in your kitchen. You'd beg her to watch the kids while you ran out for a package of chocolate morsels. Truth. Then again, there are a lot of smirky, smart-ass rednecks who've learned the wisdom of backing off when Ruby Bee gets a certain tightness to her mouth.

So had I, and I was backing off fast, although in a metaphorical sense. "I'll do whatever you want, Ruby Bee. I'll eat here. I'll eat at the Dairee Dee-Lishus. I'll trot home and eat a can of chicken soup. I won't eat anything at all."

"You already look as scrawny as a heifer what's caught the eye of the resident bull. There's no way you're ever going to find yourself a man if you don't put on a little weight."

"And it wouldn't hurt none to do something with your hair," Estelle contributed as she came across the tiny dance floor and sat down beside me. "Wearing it in a bun like that isn't exactly the fashion rage these days. I keep thinking that a delicate auburn rinse might bring out some highlights, Arly. Then, with a perm and a few wisps to frame your face, you'd look just like a June bride." This from a woman with a foot-high beehive of fire-engine-red hair, which gave her an overall upright dimension of six feet plus.

Ruby Bee clasped her hands to her bosom and gave me a misty look. "Why, I can just see you in a lacy veil, all trembly with excitement, waiting at the top of the aisle while some sweet little girl scatters rose petals in your path."

"Ruby Bee right there in the first pew, wearing her blue silk dress," Estelle added in a husky voice. "I'd be sitting beside her in my aquamarine suit with the seed pearl buttons, just dabbing like crazy with a hankie while the tears streamed down my cheeks."

"Your aquamarine?" Ruby Bee chewed off a quarter inch of lipstick. "I do believe it might clash with my blue silk. How about that pale pink suit of yours? It's dressy enough."

"The aquamarine enhances my complexion. Why don't you wear that beige linen if you're so all-fired worried about clashing?" Estelle countered.

"Because it's my flesh and blood getting married, that's why."

"And I'm supposed to look all sallow? Is that what you want, Miss Selfish Mother of the Bride?"

I reminded myself that the PD was about as warm as an August day in Manhattan. I listened to my stomach rumbling. I envisioned a heaping plate of pork chops and creamed potatoes. And a square of peach cobbler with vanilla ice cream oozing over the edges. All washed down with a big glass of icy cold sweet milk, the droplets condensing on the outside of the glass like seed pearl buttons.

All that kept me occupied until the two stop squawking long enough for me to hop in. "But I'm not getting married," I said brightly. "I tried it once and I didn't much like it."

Ruby Bee rolled her eyes. "That's because you married that awful man and went to live in Noo Yark City. If you'd married some nice young fellow from these parts, you wouldn't be wearing a gun or hiding behind a billboard to arrest speeders. You'd be home where you belonged, raising my grandchildren and keeping house and cooking well-balanced meals for your husband so he could have supper when he came home from work every afternoon at five o'clock, regular as clockwork."

"Like Johnna Mae Nookim?" I said with a sweet smile.

Ruby Bee was blinking in confusion, but Estelle intercepted the ball and ran with it. "Isn't that the most awful thing you ever heard of? I can't imagine what came over Sherman Oliver to do such a thing to that nice girl what has to support her husband and three children. Putter can barely get around these days, much less go back to roofing. Elsie McMay says she saw him going into the Emporium just the other day, and he was moving so slowly she couldn't help but think of Ike Wiggins after his hemorrhoid surgery."

"Johnna Mae came by to discuss it with me," I said, trying not to stare at a wedge of cherry pie under a glass dome. "It sounds like a pretty nasty business, but

I can't do anything to help her. I hope she can find a lawyer."

Ruby Bee snorted. "Lawyers ain't good for a blessed thing except spouting jibberish at each other so they can run up a big fat bill. Someone ought to round 'em up and put 'em on a desert island where they can sue each other till the cows come home." She let rip another snort, then calmed down enough to push a glass of sherry across the bar to Estelle. "Do you recollect how big Johnna Mae's baby was, Estelle? It seems to me it was on the scrawny side. I hope this awful heat's not too much for the little thing."

"Seven pounds, twelve ounces," Estelle answered promptly. "According to Joyce, who heard it from Earl's wife, who has a cousin who works at the hospital in the records department, when the doctor started grabbing around inside Johnna Mae's privates, Putter turned greener than a bowl of spinach and they had to hold his head between his knees the whole time."

I slid off the barstool and wandered off to make myself a can of chicken soup, thus saving my mother from all the slavery over a hot stove, Estelle from all those wild notions about my hair, and yours truly from what was likely to be a marathon of medical mis-information.

Carolyn McCoy-Grunders dug her fingernails into her thighs and ordered herself to count to ten. Long about three, however, she heard herself say, "Did it occur to you to mention this four and a half months ago, Monty? Perhaps before you came by to drop off a legal brief and ended up dropping your designer briefs on my bedroom floor?"

It came out calmly, with a satisfying hint of iciness that rather surprised her. She picked up her martini and took a long drink, then set it down without so much as a tiny clink.

"Now, Carolyn," Monty murmured, reaching across the table to pat her hand as if she were some mindless dog in heat, "we're both adults. We both consented to the seduction, which was delightful, and you were fully aware of my delicate situation at home. I never promised or even implied that, at some time in the future, I might divorce Elizabeth. Although I care very deeply about you, I must consider the consequences. What would happen to the poor woman should I ever leave her?"

Carolyn downed the martini and curled a finger at the waiter, who was hovering nearby on the off chance he might overhear one of those incredibly amusing conversations. "Another of these, Roberto, and screw the vermouth." Once Roberto had moved away, she propped her elbows on the table and gave Monty a sultry smile. "Oh, yes, I'd almost forgotten how responsible you feel for the poor woman, whose father, coincidentally, is a senior partner at your law firm. Why, you were so considerate that you called her every night from our hotel room in Acapulco, didn't you? And all those nights you were supposedly slaving away at the office while in fact you were indulging your carnal desires in my bed, you never once forgot to call and let her know you'd be late. You are a prince, Monty."

"Carolyn, Carolyn, don't work yourself up into such a lather. We both knew this was to be a brief encounter,

as if we were but ships passing in the night. Two souls
inexplicably drawn together for a moment of ecstasy."

Roberto swooped in with a martini glass on a silver
tray. "Here you are, darling. And how about your
friend? Would he care for another drink? I would be
simply thrilled to bring it to him *tout de suite.*"

"Perhaps a towel," Carolyn replied. "I do believe
he's drowning in bullshit, and we don't want him to
have to go to court looking untidy."

Monty's smile slipped. "Stop it, Carolyn. This is
between you and me. Neither one of us wants to have
our reputations maligned in the kitchen by a swishy
waiter and a hairy dishwasher."

Roberto stalked away to find Carlton and repeat
every last word of the conversation between the two
lawyers. Carolyn folded her napkin and put it beside
her plate. She stood up, tucked her briefcase under
her arm, and went around the table to stand next to
Monty.

"You're so right, dear," she said, noting with
malicious pleasure that they had the attention of almost
every diner in the restaurant. She accordingly raised
her voice so as not to disappoint anyone under the
ferns. "How naive of me to assume you were any
different than all the other sleazy, bullshitting, cock-
sure married men in this city. Lies spring to your lips
the instant your pitiful little pricks spring to life. The
pricks shrivel and die, but the lies just keep getting
bigger and bigger. Too bad the inverse isn't true."

She took his glass of water and poured it into his
lap. As she walked through the room, she threw a kiss
to Roberto and a hirsute sort in the kitchen doorway.
She made it all the way to her office at Woman Aligned

Against Chauvinism in the Office before she burst into tears. Her mood did not improve when she found an invitation to her ex-husband's wedding. And by the time her secretary, one Staci Ellen Quittle, came into the room with a stack of telephone messages, Carolyn McCoy-Grunders was sorely pissed at approximately fifty percent of the world's population.

2

A few days later I decided to drop by the branch bank and see how Johnna Mae was doing. I wasn't feeling especially altruistic, but the damn window unit at the PD was feeling downright hostile. The air conditioner in the police car was a work of art—minimalist art, that is. The fan in my apartment had given up the ghost in a miasma of burnt rubber and acrid smoke. There was no refuge to be taken at Ruby Bee's until the kitchen vents were fixed and certain people's good nature restored, and the repairman was holding the whole damn county hostage. I'd had to stop Ruby Bee more than once from offering to cater a lynch party.

I parked in the bank's gravel lot and went inside, praying that all that money could produce coolness. The branch wasn't up there with Chase Manhattan. It had a small lobby, a pseudomarble counter with two windows for tellers, a few plastic plants, and a wonderfully frigid air about it that won my heart and soul in a New York minute.

Miss Una Corners glanced up to make sure I wasn't a drug-crazed lunatic in a ski mask, then returned her attention to Raz Buchanon, who was scratching his head and grumbling like a chicken truck going up a steep hill. Miss Una was a frail little thing with wispy gray hair, half-moon glasses, and a pinched frown that was getting more pinched by the second. Raz, on the other hand, was a smelly, stubbly, beer-bellied, tobacco-chawin' pain in the neck. And that's a charitable description.

"That is not your balance," Miss Una said patiently. "That is your account number. Surely you don't think your balance runs to eight figures, Raz. That would mean you have in excess of eleven million dollars on deposit with us."

"But it sez right there that—"

"That's the date of the first transaction," Miss Una continued, tapping the crumpled paper with a pencil. "This is the deposit. This is the balance for the end of the reporting period, less the minor charges you're supposed to tally yourself. This is your account number. You do not have eleven million dollars."

Raz peered over his shoulder at me, no doubt worrying that I'd leap on him with a marriage proposal if I found out the extent of his family fortune. Ruby Bee's face might match her blue silk if she saw that apparition waiting at the altar for her flesh and blood. "How much does I have then, Miss Una?" he asked in a hoarse whisper.

"This is your balance," she hissed. The pencil was now tapping like a woodpecker going for a juicy bug in a rotten log. "This number less customary charges."

Johnna Mae came out of the back room before I could scrounge up a poptop ring and spring the question. She climbed up on a stool, pushed a pencil to one side, and attempted a smile. "Hey, Arly, how's it going? Can I help you?"

"I came by to see how you were," I murmured as I moved in front of her window.

"Peachy keen. The dentist over in Starley City says Earl Boy needs braces afore too long, P.J.'s got the colic something awful, and Putter's back started acting up so bad last night I had to drive into Farberville long about midnight to get his prescription refilled. It costs forty-seven dollars, and sometimes he just has to gobble them pain pills down like they was the world's most expensive M&M's."

"Sounds tough," I said. "I wish I could do something."

"Ain't nothing anybody can do, I guess. I called this lawyer fellow in Farberville, and he wanted fifty dollars just to hear me out. He wasn't about to make any promises that he could help, although he was as itchy as a patch of poison ivy to take my fifty dollars."

The door to the office opened and a youngish man in a shirt and tie strode out. "Mrs. Nookim," he began, stopping to appraise me as if I were a particularly questionable piece of real estate. "Excuse me, miss. Please continue your transaction. Mrs. Nookim, I'd like to have a word with you when you're free." He turned and went back into the office. The door closed with a click.

"Is that the newcomer?" I asked.

Johnna Mae stared at me for a long time, no doubt underawed by my deductive prowess. "Yeah, that's the hotshot head teller. Lord, I'd give anything if just one time he'd sweat. He takes off his jacket every morning when he comes in, but he keeps that tie around his neck like it was the only thing holding his head on. He never rolls up his sleeves. Mr. Oliver never wears a tie, and one time he even came by in

Bermuda shorts on his way to the golf course in Farberville. Miss Una like to have had a stroke when her eyes lit on his bony knees."

At the next window, the alleged witness stiffened. "I would never presume to look at Mr. Oliver's knees, Johnna Mae, and you know it." She shoved the grimy paper into Raz's hand and firmly sent him on his way. Then, after a nervous glance at the office door, she joined us. "Mr. Bernswallow is simply doing his best to familiarize himself with his family's banking business. I realize that he can be difficult to deal with, but we must make allowances. He is inexperienced. I've learned after sixty-three years that it will accomplish nothing to yearn for the good old days. We must adapt to change, not whine and complain."

Johnna Mae's eyebrows lowered. "Miss Una doesn't think I ought to report Mr. Oliver for doing this terrible thing to me. She says I should just turn belly-up and accept a demotion and a cut in pay. Of course, Miss Una's going to retire in two years, and she doesn't have a family to feed and clothe and put braces on."

"But I have my hungry little kitties," Miss Una said, tittering. She settled her glasses halfway up her nose and studied me. "Aren't you Ruby Bee's girl? How is she doing these days? We go to different churches, so I hardly ever have the good fortune to run into her. I'd drop by for a nice visit, but I'm afraid I just wouldn't be comfortable in an establishment that serves alcohol. My mother was most adamant in making me swear on the Bible while I was still in pigtails that I'd never set foot in that sort of place."

It was not a major loss for the clientele of Ruby Bee's Bar and Grill. I told Miss Una that my mother was fine, thank you, and that I'd be delighted to pass on a small greeting. Once Miss Una trotted back to her window and opened a black ledger, I looked at Johnna Mae. "Why didn't she get promoted ahead of you?"

"She refused the promotion, saying she was happy doing what she's been doing for twenty years and didn't want to have to take on added responsibilities at her age. She enjoys visiting with the customers, and she has the patience of Job when someone like Raz or Hiram starts pestering her. I didn't mind one bit, since we needed the money. She has three cats to feed. I have a family."

The office door opened and Bernswallow again appraised me. This time the door closed clicklessly.

Johnna Mae picked up the pencil and snapped it into two pieces. "I don't reckon I can stand this much longer, Arly. He's all the time spying on us like he thinks we're taking people's money and stuffing it down our blouses like call girls. For three nights running he's made us work late to make the over-and-long account balance to the penny. When I was head teller, we didn't worry about a few extra pennies in somebody's cash drawer; I just figured it'd even out over the duration."

"What does Mr. Oliver think?" I asked.

"The good Lord gave him a brain, but he may have forgotten to plug it in. Mr. Oliver comes in every morning to see how we're doing, then says he has to go into the main bank to work there. He used to be an officer before he became the branch manager out here in Maggody. He still does something about the portfolio, which conveniently keeps him from bothering us. He doesn't care a rat's-ass about what goes on here."

Johnna Mae took a tissue from her cash drawer and noisily blew her nose under Miss Una's disapproving scrutiny. I was fresh out of anything to say and had reluctantly decided to face the outside world, when Bernswallow again came through what seemed to be a revolving door.

"May I trust that the service was satisfactory?" he said. His tone managed to imply that he would be more than amazed if it had been.

"I use a different bank, in Farberville. It gives me an opportunity to travel."

While he digested that, I did some appraising of my own. He was still young enough to have a plum-colored pimple or two on his chin. His hair was styled rather than cut, and his expression conveyed muted arrogance, from his clear blue eyes to the slight tilt of his jaw. I'd seen millions like him on Madison Avenue, all striding along while visions of power lunches danced in their heads. I would have wagered a year's ration of cherry pie that he owned the dark green Mercedes I'd noticed in a shady corner of the parking lot outside. Okay, so maybe I'd recognized Miss Una's ancient Crosley and Raz's pickup truck. All those months at the police academy honing my powers of observation had not been in vain.

"I'm sure your bank in Farberville provides good service," Bernswallow said with a condescending smile, "but we'd like to think that a local branch can provide more personal service to the citizens of Maggody. I hope that you'll consider us should there ever be anything we can do to help you, Miss . . . ?"

"Hanks," Johanna Mae muttered. "Arly Hanks, chief of police."

Bernswallow's eyes lit up as though I'd introduced myself as the sole heiress of Howard Hughes. He came around the edge of the counter and extended his hand. "How nice to meet you, Miss Hanks. I'm sure your diligence is what's kept our little branch safe all these years."

I shook his hand. "I would imagine it's the lock on the door. None of the locals are clever enough to figure out how to get past it."

"Ah, certainly. In any case, please feel free to call on me if there's ever anything at all we can do for you. The First National Bank of Farberville will be delighted to serve you. Now, if you'll excuse us, Mrs. Nookim and I have a small situation to discuss in my office."

Johnna Mae may have loosed a remark as she stomped through the door, but it doesn't bear repeating. Miss Una gave me a twinkly smile and a little wave. I could almost smell the lavender water as I forced myself out the front door and into the swampy steam of Maggody.

I was working up the courage to touch the car door handle when yet another product of Buchanon inbreeding came around from the back of the building. Buchanons dot the county like ticks in a blackberry patch. Since very few folks are dumb enough to want to marry into the clan, they've been obliged to mate and consummate among themselves, until not one of them needs a costume on Halloween. Intelligence is out of the question; animal cunning is about all any of them can aspire to. This particular specimen, Kevin Buchanon, had no aspirations.

"Hot enough for ya, Arly?" he said, shuffling his feet in the dust until I almost choked. Although he had defied the laws of nature and graduated from high school a year or two back, he was still battling puberty. His voice cracked on every other word and his Adam's apple was enough to mesmerize the unwary. Had there been a breeze, his ears would have flapped like sheets on a clothesline. As it was, they sagged like the chickweed along the highway.

"Yes, it's hot, Kevin. It's so hot I'm afraid I'm going to get blisters if I try to open the car door."

"Yeah, it sure is hot. It must be hot enough to fry an egg on the sidewalk, don'tcha think? 'Course we'd haft to go all the way to Farberville to try it, in that there ain't any sidewalks in Maggody." He guffawed at that bit of wit, then scratched his ear and frowned at me. "You been in the bank?"

"That's why my car is parked out here."

"I dint know you were a customer here. Did you know I'm an employee now?"

"I didn't know that, Kevin, but I'm pleased for you." From his expression I could see that more was expected of me, and that I wasn't going to escape until I bit the bullet and complied. "And what is it you do for the bank? Loan officer? Executive vice president in charge of bullion shipments from Fort Knox?"

He would have stuck his thumbs under his suspenders and popped them, had he been wearing any with his dirty white T-shirt and scruffy blue jeans. "I'm the night security guard, Arly. Ever' night I come in at nine and don't set foot outside until Miss Una arrives the next morning."

Despite the heat (which was pretty tough to overlook),

I felt a shiver run down my back. "You're the bank's security guard?"

"That's right. Once I've mopped down the floors and cleaned the rest rooms and emptied the trash cans and generally tidied up, I'm supposed to make sure no one sneaks in to steal any money. I have a special chair in the back room by the door so's I can hear any suspicious noises. Once I heard something that I thought was going to be a bank robber, but it turned out to be a couple of stray cats doing it with each other."

"Then you also have custodial duties," I said, returning to reality with a major sigh of relief.

"Yeah, and cleaning, too. But now that I have a regular job, I'm getting up my nerve to ask Dahlia if she wants to get married. Do you think I ought to ask her, Arly? I mean, we could get us a mobile home over at the Pot O' Gold and save all our money right here in this bank so we can have a little house some day with a garden and a porch swing and a washer-dryer. Why, we might even have children when we can afford it. What do you think, Arly? Do you think she'll have me?"

"If anyone will, she will," I said, retreating from his enthusiasm. I was steeling myself to open the car door when Johnna Mae marched out of the bank, slamming the door behind her in the process, and took off down the edge of the county road, her jaw flung so high she was in danger of slipping in the loose rocks and ending up in the ditch. Miss Una's shadow flitted across the door, then faded into the dimness.

"Wow," Kevin said, twisting his head to follow Johnna Mae's retreat. "She looks madder than a coon in a poke. Wonder what got her so all-fired hot under the collar?"

"She's been having problems with Mr. Bernswallow."

"Him? I think he's a right slick guy. He always compliments me on the shine on the commodes and the sinks, and one time he gave me a sack of shirts with crocodiles on 'em. Said they was real expensive."

"He sounds like a jewel, Kevin." I watched Johnna Mae swing through the rusty arch of the Pot O' Gold. I toyed with the idea of driving down to her mobile home to make sure she was okay but reminded myself that there wasn't anything I could do beyond making sympathetic noises and admiring the baby. I told Kevin to keep the bank safe from Bonnie and Clyde, opened the car door, wincing, and drove back to the PD to work on the sauna sign. If my crayons hadn't melted.

"Ain't this amazing, just amazing?" Estelle demanded, shoving the letter across the bar to Ruby Bee. "You could have knocked me over with a snake feather when I opened the envelope this morning just before Elsie came in for a shampoo and set."

"Is her hair natural?"

"What transpires between a cosmetologist and her client is confidential, as you well know. How'd you like to lie in bed every night wondering if half the town knew the truth about your hair color? You'd be deeply offended if I went around telling folks how your hair's grayer than seasoned barn wood, wouldn't you?"

Ruby Bee went over to the cash register and punched a key or two while she tried to grab hold of her temper, which was as riled as a swarm of hornets. "My hair may have a silver tint to it," she said, avoiding Estelle's eyes, "but you have no call to say it's the color of barn wood."

"How would you know? You haven't seen it natural since before Hiram Buchanon's barn burned, and that was twenty years if it was a day. But I don't have the time to squabble with you, not with Perkins's eldest coming in for a perm in a while. Just unruffle your tail feathers and read this letter."

Ruby Bee relented and took the proffered piece of paper. Once she'd read it, she gave Estelle a bewildered look. "I don't recollect you mentioning that you borrowed money from the bank."

"That's because I never did. I considered it once when Jaylee was planning to study cosmetology, thinking I might expand the salon so she could have her own station right there with me. I was going to knock out that wall above the hydrangeas. But I haven't even thought one second about it since Jaylee was murdered a couple of years back." She stopped to wipe a smudge of mascara from under her eye, then cleared her throat and added, "What do you think this means, this letter?"

"I haven't got a glimmer," Ruby Bee admitted.

"Well, those folks at the bank in Farberville are riding mighty high to say that I'm late making a payment on a loan I never took out. I've got a mind to march right in their fancy bank and slap this letter down on some snippy banker's desk and demand to know what in tarnation they think they're doing."

"It might do some good," Ruby Bee said, smiling to herself as she envisioned the scene. "What'll you wear?"

"What difference does it make? The point is that they've got no cause to send innocent folks nasty letters, and I'm going to tell them so. I'm going to give them a piece of my mind like they've never heard in their fancy bank. Let me tell you, they'll be mighty sorry when I'm done with them!"

"I reckon they will." This time Ruby Bee had to turn around, aware that any trace of amusement would not sit well with Estelle. All that stuff about red hair and hot temperament was the gospel truth, she thought smugly, although she had sense enough not to say it out loud.

"If I didn't have Perkins's eldest in less than ten minutes, I'd do it right this minute," Estelle continued. She narrowed her eyes as Ruby Bee turned back. "I'd like to hope you're not making that smirky face because you think this is funny. It ain't funny."

"I never thought it was funny, Estelle. I was making that face because of this bodacious heat. In fact, I think I'll call that good-for-nothing repairman again so he can tell me how he's busier than an ant at a Sunday school picnic and I can tell him how my brain bubbles every time I have to stand over the grill in the kitchen. We know the conversation by heart, but at least it passes the time of day."

Estelle wasn't convinced, but it was time to give Perkins's eldest a perm. She curled her lip to let Ruby Bee know she wasn't anybody's fool and sailed out of the bar without so much as a see you later.

Ruby Bee picked up the letter and reread it. It was a puzzlement, to be sure. But everybody knew that the bank was always right, so Estelle must have slipped up somewhere and forgotten about taking out her loan. Still, Ruby Bee thought, sticking the letter in a cabinet under the bar where it'd be safe, it wasn't like Estelle to do something more befitting one of those dumb Buchanons. Not like her at all.

*   *   *

"Not now, Staci Ellen," Carolyn McCoy-Grunders said, covering the mouthpiece of the telephone receiver with one hand. "I told you to hold all my calls. If you would bother to move that mane of hair from your face, you would see that I'm still on the telephone."

"She says it's long distance," Staci Ellen said, not bothering.

"And I told you to hold my calls." Carolyn glared until Staci Ellen closed the door, then sank back in her chair and said, "So what, Monty? You may stay in Las Vegas until hell freezes over, but I'm not going to be there with my snowshoes. Why don't you invite poor Elizabeth to go with you? That way you won't have to worry about her."

She sat and listened while he argued, but she felt no flicker of remorse. Monty had had his chance, but he'd blown it. He was nothing but pond scum. He— and all the other pompous pricks in the world, including her ex-husband and his flat-bellied, sorority girl bride— could rot in hell, for all she cared.

When Monty stopped to take a breath, she told him as much and banged down the receiver with a venomous frown. Men wanted only one thing. As soon as they got it, they started looking over the fence to see if the grass was greener and the asses tighter. Chauvinist pigs, every last one of them. And lawyers were the worst of the miserable lot. She'd survived the asshole professors in law school, but she'd discovered immediately that she couldn't stomach the genial condescension of a paternalistic law firm.

Thank God she'd applied for the position at Women Aligned Against Chauvinism in the Office. It paid a pittance, but at least she wasn't forced to simper at some disgusting old man simply to be assigned a case. Here she was her own boss and could pick her cases as she pleased.

She was contemplating a wedding present for the little couple—and wondering if there were a postal regulation concerning the interstate mailing of coral snakes—when Staci Ellen tapped on the door.

"What is it now?"

"That same woman called again," Staci Ellen said cautiously (and wondering if her boss was in the throes of PMS and therefore unlikely to allow an early departure on Friday afternoon). "She keeps saying she went to one of your seminars last year, and that you're the only one who can help her."

Carolyn snatched up the nearest file and opened it. "Tell her I'm too busy to talk to her. If she wishes, she can give you her address and you can mail her the initial complaint forms. I'll look them over when I have time, but it may not be for several months. Doesn't she know we're absolutely swamped with complaints?"

Staci Ellen dutifully went away to repeat the instructions from high. Carolyn shoved the file away and took out the telephone directory. "Pet stores," she said under her breath as her fingers did the walking.

3

Toward the end of the week I was still sitting around the PD, although I'd roused myself long enough to run into Farberville to a travel agency in order to pick up a handful of brochures for Alaskan cruises. I had them spread across my desk so I could see glaciers from every perspective. The heat had pretty well sautéed my brain, and I was idly considering the wisdom of knocking off the branch bank to finance my cruise. With Kevin Buchanon as the security guard, I figured I could be in and out in a matter of minutes. No one would be the wiser—especially Kevin.

I was having such a fine time that I was a little irked when I heard footsteps outside the door. Irk turned to out-and-out irritation when Mrs. Jim Bob Buchanon opened the door and actually set foot in my office. Mrs. Jim Bob is my least favorite resident. She's prim and self-righteous, even when she's preparing to screw somebody with a ten-inch screwdriver and a twelve-inch screw. Her beady yellow eyes glitter, and her tight little mouth snakes up at the corners in a pretense of a smile. I know better; I've seen the expression on cats playing with half dead chipmunks or bloodied bunnies.

She is, however, the mayor's wife, and the mayor controls the police department purse strings—and my salary comes from within that purse. A while back we'd had an amusing incident in Maggody in which Hizzoner the Moron was shown to be the hypocritical sleaze I'd always known him to be. But it was too hot for witty repartee, so I settled for a flip of my hand and a bright, "What do you want, Mrs. Jim Bob? Looking for a place to bake buttermilk biscuits?"

She blinked at me for a moment, then decided I was being a smart aleck and perched on the chair across from my desk. Once she'd crossed her ankles, settled her purse squarely on her lap, and folded her hands neatly across it, she said, "This place is disgraceful, Arly. I don't know how you expect citizens to file complaints when it's so hot in here." She pulled a church bulletin from her purse and began to fan herself with ladylike fury.

"I do believe you're right," I said through a yawn. "Maybe Brother Verber can drag the congregation down here on Sunday to extol the perils of hell. Thirty minutes in here would put the fear of God in every last soul who survived."

"I do not care for that kind of talk. You'd better watch that mouth of yours if you plan to continue being chief of police."

"Okay, I quit. Just give me a minute to knock off the branch bank and I'll be on the road to Fairbanks and points north. Maybe I can meet a well-endowed Eskimo dressed in skintight sealskin, and we can rub noses until they fall off from all that exotic, erotic stimulation. You know, I've never before considered my nose as a sexual organ, but—"

"That is quite enough, Arly Hanks. I did not come in here to listen to your trashy language or your pornographic carryings-on."

"That's mighty comforting to know, Mrs. Jim Bob. If that's all, I was getting ready to oil my gun and draw up a map of the bank. I don't suppose you have an old ski mask I could borrow, do you?"

Her eyes narrowed so much I was surprised they didn't implode. Her fingers twitched for a minute, as if feeling themselves wrapped around someone's neck, before returning to her purse. "Are you finished with all this mouthy talk, Arly? If so, I'd like you to do something about that disgraceful situation up at the bank—and I mean right this instant. You *are* the chief of police. You have an obligation to the town council and the citizens of this community to get off your fanny and do something!"

"What did you have in mind, Mrs. Jim Bob?" I asked through another yawn. "I've already explained to Johnna Mae Nookim that there's nothing I can do. However, if you're going to get all huffy, I suppose I can run Sherman Oliver over to the county jail and have him locked up for a few hours."

"Sherman Oliver? I swear, this heat has addled you. Truda Oliver happens to be one of my dearest friends, not to mention president of the missionary society at the Voice of the Almighty Lord. Not that you'd know that, of course, since I don't believe I've ever seen you in the house of the Lord. Jim Bob and I haven't missed a service in twenty years, and that includes Wednesday prayer meetings, Sunday evening potlucks, and every single night of the annual revivals."

"Is that right? By the way, how are Jim Bob's

illegitimate children doing these days? Did you ever decide what color to paint the nursery?"

"Perkins's eldest sees to them after Bible school every morning until bedtime, but it is none of your concern, Arly Hanks. What is your concern is that vulgar display going on at the bank this very moment. If you're not willing to do something, I'm going to have to telephone Jim Bob all the way in Starley City, where he's pricing some used washing machines for the launderette, and have a word with him about your aversion to doing your sworn duty."

"What's going on at the bank?" I asked, wearying of the lack of challenge. Baiting her was as difficult as finding a cab in Manhattan—on a pleasant, sunny day when you're not in any kind of hurry and really don't mind the chance to window-shop. The cabs swoop in like a flock of starlings.

"That Nookim woman is causing a ruckus. I want you to arrest her and lock her up tighter than new shoes on a heathen. She is an embarrassment to my dear friends, Sherman and Truda Oliver, not to mention that nice young man who's doing his best to carry on his family's upstanding tradition of service to the community, and all the God-fearing good people of Maggody." Mrs. Jim Bob stood up, brushed at a wrinkle in her skirt, and started for the door. I was holding my breath, but it didn't do one damn bit of good because she stopped and glowered back at me. "You are still sitting there, Chief of Police Hanks. I thought I just told you to go over to the bank and arrest that woman."

"I have no idea what she's doing."

"And you anticipate coming to a revelation by staying glued to that chair and looking at shiny pictures?"

I thought of a few diverting remarks but let them slither away. "I suppose I could mosey down to the bank," I said, losing the battle to yet another yawn, "but it's awfully hot. Why don't you tell me what Johnna Mae Nookim's doing?"

"Why don't you just mosey down there and have a look-see for yourself!"

The door slammed behind her. I waited for a minute, glued and ready for her to barge back in, but she didn't. I took the car keys out of the middle drawer and grudgingly forced myself out to the police car. I didn't have the energy to conjure up any theories about what Johnna Mae was doing, and I wasn't excited about taking anyone to the county jail, unless it was Hizzoner or Mizzoner—or both, if I could get them a double cell. Twin bunks, however, so Hizzoner wouldn't get any filthy ideas.

The sky was a bleachy blue. The sun did its best to bake me as I drove down the highway. I braked to let a scruffy hound wander by, waved at a dust-streaked child in a saggy, baggy diaper, and wondered if a six-week cruise would be too brief. I had about decided that ten weeks would be dead minimum when I got my first view of the bank.

Johnna Mae was pacing along the edge of the highway, a sign propped on her shoulder. Bernswallow and Sherman Oliver stood in front of the bank, their arms crossed over their chests, and Miss Una's face could be seen hovering through the glass doors behind them, as if she were trapped in a murky aquarium. Milling nearby were several upstanding citizens, including Raz Buchanon, Elsie McMay, someone's mother, someone's mother's friendly cosmetologist, a few neckless hulks from the pool hall, and Mrs. Jim Bob herself.

I parked on the far side of the highway and tried to figure out what the hell was happening. As Johnna Mae reeled around, I caught a glimpse of the crude printing on her posterboard: SHERMAN OLIVER IS A CHAUVINIST PIG AND HATES WIMMEN.

Sherman Oliver certainly looked as if he hated one woman in particular. Under a shock of white hair, his eyes were slits. His nose was on the purple side, and his cheeks were blotchy. His jaw was quivering like molded gelatin. He seemed to be muttering to Bernswallow, who was also looking rather displeased. Everybody else, with the exception of Mrs. Jim Bob, was observing the spectacle with varying amounts of interest/amusement.

"Yo, Johnna Mae," I called as I walked across the road.

"The Bank of Farberville discriminates against women! Take your business elsewhere! Sherman Oliver hates women! Don't bank here—take your money to another bank!" She broke off to catch her breath, then snapped her sign up and took off in the opposite direction. "This bank cheats women! Don't trust them with your hard-earned money!"

"About time you got here," Ruby Bee said out of the corner of her mouth. "This could turn right ugly."

"Elsie said that Johnna Mae said she was going to bash Sherman Oliver smack on the top of his head if he so much as laid a finger on her," Estelle added out of the corner of her mouth. The two of them watch way too many gangster movies, along with their daily diet of police and private eye shows.

"I can't see this crowd turning any uglier," I said out of the middle of my mouth. "How long has this been going on?"

Ruby Bee kept her eyes on Johnna Mae. "Estelle and I just heard about it ten minutes ago. Dahlia came in to work and said something about a commotion. I stuck the Closed sign on the door and we trotted right down here to see what was happening. What do you aim to do about it, Arly?"

"Why should I do anything about it?"

"I don't know. I just think there's gonna be trouble if you don't do something pretty quick."

"I doubt it," I said, glancing at the crowd. "Johnna Mae'll get tired of all this parading after a while, and everybody will wander off to get out of the heat. I don't want to hurt Johnna Mae's feelings, but this isn't all that exciting."

"Hussy!"

I looked over my shoulder at the character stomping across the street. Mizzoner held the number-one spot on my list of least popular, and now we had the first runner-up in our midst. Brother Verber, spiritual leader of his fuzzy flock, defender of the faith, and beacon of sanctimony carried a Bible in one hand as he charged into battle with the devil. His nose was aglow with righteous indignation, and droplets of spittle dotted his lips.

"Hussy," he panted, pointing the finger of retribution at Johnna Mae, who'd paused in mid step to stare at him. "Don't you know what the Bible says about women? It says they're supposed to be obedient, not loud-mouthed and vulgar."

Mrs. Jim Bob nodded. "That's right, Johnna Mae.

You're supposed to stay home and take care of your family, not march up and down in the street and make accusations against good Christian folks like Sherman Oliver."

"Maybe she can't afford to stay home," Ruby Bee muttered. Mrs. Jim Bob spun around to glower, but Ruby Bee stood her ground and glowered right back. Estelle managed a glimmer herself. I settled for a comradely wink.

Brother Verber mopped his shiny forehead. "That is not the issue. The Bible says women were made out of a man's rib, so they're supposed to be subservient and do what-all they're told. They're supposed to be modest, not vulgar. It says in the vows of holy matrimony that women are supposed to obey their husbands, and I think we can safely conclude that they therefore ought to be obedient all the time. This woman is making a disgrace of herself. Where's your husband? He ought to drag you home this minute and teach you how to behave."

Johnna Mae's fingers tightened around the stick of her sign. "My husband is home with the kids. Just who do you think you are, you pompous old fart, telling me how I ought to stay home and keep house? I'd like not to have to work, but I'd like to put food on the table every night, too."

"A woman's place is in the home," Brother Verber countered.

Several of the pool hall hulks nodded, although I would have bet a week's salary that all of their wives were plucking feathers at a poultry plant in Starley City or waiting tables in Farberville. Someone had to pay for the custom pool cues and the long-neck beers.

To my astonishment, Ruby Bee went to stand next to Johnna Mae. "Yeah, how's she supposed to feed her family and new baby if she stays home?"

Estelle completed the triumvirate. "Everybody knows her husband's disabled. You have no call to stand there and say that sort of thing about a woman who's trying to take care of her family."

"She's tempting the devil," Brother Verber replied smugly, if inanely. Mrs. Jim Bob scurried right over to him, her expression that of a hen anticipating an attack on one of her chicks.

Sherman Oliver cleared his throat. "I don't see why this needs to go any further. Why don't we all just go about our business?"

"Chauvinist pig!" Johnna Mae shouted at him.

"This is an outrage!" Mrs. Jim Bob shouted at me.

"Hussy!" Brother Verber shouted at Johnna Mae.

"Old fart!" she shouted at him.

"Go home and diaper your baby!" someone shouted from the crowd.

"Who's supposed to pay for the diapers?" Ruby Bee shouted in the general direction of the last participant.

"Sherman Oliver is unfair to women!" Johnna Mae shouted.

"He is not!"

"Stuff it!"

"An abomination in the eye of the Lord!"

I could assign all this dialogue, but it doesn't much matter who was shouting what because all of a sudden everybody was shouting at the top of his or her lungs and the noise level was rising faster than Boone Creek after a thunderstorm. Elsie McMay was nose to nose with Raz, busily telling him how Johnna Mae was doing the right thing by bringing home a paycheck. Ruby Bee was doing the same with one of the hulks, while Estelle was shaking a finger and shrieking at another. Johnna Mae was exchanging remarks with Brother Verber. Mrs. Jim Bob was getting in her two cents' worth every other second or so.

Cars and trucks were crawling past now, the passengers in danger of terminal rubberneck from twisting to catch every bit of the scene. Kevin Buchanon almost lost his life to a camper when he stopped his bicycle in the middle lane to goggle. The hippies came out of the Emporium and stood on the porch, shading their eyes with their hands and poking each other when someone let out a particularly idiotic remark.

Sherman Oliver was turning more purple by the moment. He stormed over to Johnna Mae and began to bellow at her, which of course sent Ruby Bee and Estelle right back to Johnna Mae's side to bellow in her defense. Which isn't to say that she wasn't bellowing real well herself.

You might be wondering what the upholder of law and order was doing during all this. Nothing. Not a blessed thing. I suppose that I could have fired my gun into the air to stop everybody, but I hadn't thought to bring a bullet along. I was pondering the possibility of trying to make myself heard, or going inside the bank where it was bound to be cooler, when that which had been threatened took place, to wit: Johnna Mae Nookim grasped the broom handle of her sign with both hands, raised said sign above her head, and slammed it down on Sherman Oliver's bald spot.

Despite the fact that the sign was primarily posterboard,

he stumbled backward and might have sprawled in the shrubbery had not Brandon Bernswallow caught him. "Arrest that woman for assault!" Oliver sputtered.

"And battery!" Mrs. Jim Bob added as she rushed forward to play Florence Nightingale.

I felt obliged to intercede. Johnna Mae had the sign reared back to bust him again as I grabbed the corner of it. "Hold your horses," I said. "You can't do this."

"Why can't I? He damn well was asking for it. I have every right to express my opinion, because this is the land of the free and we are guaranteed freedom of speech." She tried to tug the sign out of my grasp. "Hell, Arly, he's a pig. Lemme have one more swing."

All the combatants had quieted down by this time and were crowding in around us. Faces were still red, however, and the breathing was heavy. A few hands were curled into fists, including one of Ruby Bee's. "What about freedom of speech?" she demanded.

"You have to do your duty," Mrs. Jim Bob said, tapping me on the shoulder in case I didn't know to whom she was speaking. "This is a clear case of assault and battery, not to mention outrageous behavior on the streets of Maggody."

"And a sin against all of mankind," Brother Verber rumbled piously. "The Bible says that woman should obey man, and—"

"Calm down, Johnna Mae," I said, ignoring everybody. "You can't bash people on the head, no matter how justified it seems to you. Why don't you let me have the sign and go on home and cool off?"

Brandon Bernswallow got Oliver steadied, then he came over to peer down his nose at me. "There has been a criminal act, and we intend to press charges.

This woman, in front of witnesses, attacked Mr. Oliver with the intent of causing him bodily injury. I demand that you arrest her."

Sherman Oliver looked uncomfortable as all eyes turned on him. "Well, now, I wouldn't say there was any bodily injury, Brandon. She whacked me with a piece of cardboard, not a two-by-four. If she'll promise to stop this childish nonsense and stay home, I think we can forget about this."

"Okay, Johnna Mae?" I said.

"No, it is not okay. I am not some worthless person who can be demoted like I was trash or hadn't spent eleven years working at this bank. Mr. Oliver and this fellow think they can cheat me, but I ain't going to roll over and play dead just because they say so."

"Right on," came a low voice from the crowd.

One would like to think one's mother was not a seasoned agitator, but one would find oneself in error. I glared over my shoulder, then turned back to give Johnna Mae a grim look. "I understand your frustration, but you cannot cause a riot on the street or attack someone simply because you're unhappy with your position. Mr. Oliver is entitled to file charges against you. Now, he's said he'll forget this if you'll promise to stop protesting."

"I won't stop," Johnna Mae said as her eyes filled with tears. "I got to do what I got to do."

"Please," I hissed at her.

"No, Arly. There's no reason for me to go home and watch my children eat beans and corn bread until the money runs out. I have plenty of free time on my hands now that he"—she scowled at Bernswallow—"has relieved me of my duties. I might as well be here

as lying on the sofa in front of the television, especially
since they'll cut off the electricity before too long. I'm
going to be right here every day from nine until five,
just like it was a regular job. If he doesn't like it, he
can lump it."

Bernswallow clearly didn't like it. After a hushed
conversation, he announced that Mr. Oliver would
press charges once he'd had an aspirin and a few
minutes to rest. He then took the branch manager's
arm and led him into the bank. I pulled Johnna Mae
aside and told her that she would have to come back
to the police department so that I could do the necessary
paperwork.

The crowd drifted away, leaving Ruby Bee and
Estelle in one corner of the metaphorical wrasslin'
ring, and Mrs. Jim Bob and Brother Verber in the
other.

Mrs. Jim Bob leapt into the lull. "I must say that I
am sorely disappointed in you, Rubella Belinda Hanks.
I never once thought you were one of those women's
libbers who burn their bras and mock the church and
turn into lesbians if they're not careful."

"Nobody's a women's libber, Barbara Buchanon
Buchanon, and you know it. You can stand there and
spout all those pious things about a woman staying at
home, but Johnna Mae has to work."

"Well, it's not right for her to boss men around,"
Mrs. Jim Bob said, bristling at the very idea.

"That's right," Brother Verber added. "Women
weren't created in order to run the world and tell men
what to do. Adam came first, not Eve. She was put in
the Garden to be a helper, to bear children and fix
supper."

Estelle put her hands on her hips. "And we all know what God made man out of, don't we? Dirt. That's the gospel truth and you know it. Man was made out of your common variety of dirt."

That didn't sit well. I could see we were on the verge of a tag-team event, so I took Johnna Mae's arm and got her into the police car before the actual violence broke out. She was sniveling by this time, and big, plump tears rolled down her cheeks to plop into her lap. As I turned around in the bank parking lot, I saw a tableau that did nothing to ease my conscience one bit: Putter Nookim, a black-haired scarecrow in faded denim overalls, stood in the shade, a blanketed bundle in his arm. Behind him were two small figures, clutching his legs and peering out from either side.

I hated my job.

Lottie Estes sat behind her desk in the home ec room, rereading the letter for the tenth or maybe the twelfth time. No matter how much she squinted at the words, they still seemed ominous. Lottie Estes had never been late in her life. She'd been born on schedule, and she wasn't the sort who'd ever missed the previews at the picture show, the opening hymn at the Assembly Hall, or even the very first notes of the theme songs of her favorite television shows. Never once in her thirty years of teaching had she not been the first in the classroom or the first in the cafeteria for a teachers meeting. Whenever a friend had a baby shower or a small gathering, Lottie was there in time to help set the food out while the hostess finished dressing.

But now this letter was telling her that she was late. What's more, she couldn't have avoided this accusation because she didn't know she'd ever borrowed money from some bank in Farberville, much less missed a payment. It didn't make one whit of sense.

"Miss Estes?" said a timid voice from the doorway. "We're ready to start the Future Homemakers of America meeting. Heather wants to know if we should go ahead and read the minutes or wait for you."

Lottie Estes stuffed the letter in a drawer and hastily rose. "Please tell Heather I am on my way, Grace Ellen. I have never arrived late to a meeting, and I do not intend to do so today."

"No, ma'am—I mean, yes, ma'am," Grace Ellen murmured, properly abashed.

Carolyn McCoy-Grunders threw down the file and picked up another from the stack. Except for her inner sanctum, the office was dark and quiet, which was the way she preferred it when she was not in a good mood. Carolyn was in a foul mood. And it wasn't her fault: Monty had had the nerve to take his wife to Las Vegas and had made sure everyone in the county bar association heard about it at the last luncheon. He'd known Carolyn would be there, of course, and that certain bitches would be sure to tell her the news. And just when she was trying to be mature about her ex-husband's marriage to that little slut young enough to be his daughter. Or kid sister, anyway. Carolyn dearly hoped the newlyweds drank the water in Acapulco and got their just deserts. And she didn't mean tortillas dipped in brown sugar.

She tossed aside the file and snatched up the next. Maybe Monty would lose his BMW at the blackjack table; God knew he had trouble counting to twenty-one unless he took off his shoes and socks and dropped his pants. She glanced at the complaint form.

"So we think we were passed up for promotion, do we?" she said, dropping the file on the floor and taking yet another. "Maybe we ought to stop whining and expecting people to rush over and wipe our noses."

She almost threw the last file in the pile. The handwriting was laborious, almost illegible, and in pencil. Carolyn preferred forms written in ink, if not typed neatly and with a minimum of corrections. This one was smudgy. The spelling was atrocious. The complainant had managed to cover almost every bit of the white space with her long, tedious gripe about maternity leave and demotion and how much the baby weighed, for pity's sake. Carolyn had no use for babies. Or crybabies, for that matter.

With a martyred sigh she settled her glasses on her nose and squinted at the form. Some idiotic little podunk town nobody had ever heard of, much less had any interest in. Some two-bit branch bank. God, who'd want to be head teller of such a vile little operation?

It was about to join the pile on the floor when Carolyn spotted a familiar name. It was very much as if she'd inserted one of her manicured fingertips into an electrical socket. Once she'd stopped waggling her jaw and blinking, she leaned back and began to reread the complaint very, very carefully, her lips curling upward in a smile.

4

I got Johnna Mae settled in the PD, centered her lethal weapon on my desk, and proceeded to tell her all sorts of things she wasn't real happy to hear, such as the fact she'd committed a class A misdemeanor that carried penalties of as much as a thousand-dollar fine and a year in jail. In my best cop voice, I recited the Miranda warning and took out an arrest form.

"I can't go to prison," she wailed. "Who's going to take care of Putter and the kids? Who's going to get him his prescription from Farberville? How's he going to pay for Earl Boy's braces or P.J.'s first pair of hightop shoes?"

"Very possibly not the person who refused to go home and forget about picketing the bank every day from nine until five," I said, slapping down the pencil. "You should have thought of that earlier. Sherman Oliver was willing to forget the whole thing, you know. All you had to do was shut up and go home."

She held out two pudgy wrists. "Arrest me and drag me off to prison. Will they let Putter bring the kids when he comes to visit on Sunday afternoons?"

"We haven't quite gotten to that stage, Johnna Mae. I'll fill out the complaint, release you on your own recognizance, and then go over to the bank to talk to Mr. Oliver. He may not want to appear in front of the municipal judge any more than you do, and he may agree to tear the complaint up and let things slide—if I can assure him that you're sorry and that you won't come back to the bank to picket."

"He ain't a bad fellow," she allowed with a drawn-out sigh. "We've gotten along real good all the years I've worked at the bank. His wife always sends over a fruitcake or a plate of cookies around Christmastime, and she even dropped off a little baby present for P.J. It's that Bernswallow guy that's causing all the trouble."

"Why'd he fire you?" I asked curiously.

Johnna Mae's martyred expression vanished in a blink, although I didn't know how to interpret its replacement. After a moment of studying the floor, she gave me an innocent look and said, "He just told me a bunch of stuff about how my attitude was poor and how I was all the time making errors in my drawer. He acted like a few cents off in the long-and-short was some kind of federal offense. I reckon I said some things back. He got puffed up worse than a horny bullfrog and told me to clean out my work area."

"Did he offer any severance pay?"

"No, he said I'd already missed so much work I was lucky he wasn't sending me a bill. Then he said get out and I got out."

"Did you try to discuss this with Mr. Oliver?"

"Yeah, I did. I even went over to his house and tried to explain that I was upset about losing my position. Mr. Oliver got all squirmy and apologetic, but he said that Bernswallow was in charge of personnel matters. He was pretty nice about it, so I guess I shouldn't have hit him on the head like that. What I should have done is run Bernswallow down in the truck. Over and over again, until he was flatter than a tabletop and too dead to skin. The highway department would've had to scrape him up with a cake spatula."

"Don't say things like that, Johnna Mae," I said, rubbing my face and wishing I were on the road to Juneau. Or the Emerald City. Or a nice padded room with bars across the window. "You're in deep enough trouble as it is. Let's fill out the complaint and then I'll try to talk Mr. Oliver into ripping it up for old times' sake. But I want you to promise me that you'll go back to the mobile home and stay away from the bank."

Her lower lip went in and out for a long while. "And I get to leave on my—what'd you call it? Recognizance? How much is that?"

"All it means is that I'm trusting you to stay in town and out of trouble. Okay?"

"I suppose," she muttered.

We made it through name, address, and various tidbits. I asked her if she wanted a ride home, and she said the walk back to the Pot O' Gold Mobile Home Park might help her cool off. I didn't point out that the temperature was in triple digits, and after eliciting one last promise from her I let her go. I did not allow her to take her picket sign.

I drove to the bank, thinking all the while that I was spending so much time there that I ought to open an account. Then again, Kevin Buchanon would be protecting my zillions of dollars. Not a comforting concept, to say the least. I parked next to the slinky

Mercedes and went through the glass doors into the charmingly cool air.

Miss Una stared at me from her window. "I must admit, Arly, that in my opinion you might have taken action to prevent this dreadful tragedy from happening." Her voice was a good ten degrees cooler than the inside of the bank.

"I'm not sure we're up to the level of dreadful tragedy," I said. "Johnna Mae's sworn to stay away from the bank, and I'm hoping Mr. Oliver will agree to drop his complaint. Is he in his office?"

"Mr. Oliver has gone home to lie down. The poor man was most disturbed about being attacked in front of half the town. What's more, he has a lump where Johnna Mae whacked him, and I imagine he'll have a bruise before morning. I am as fond of her as I am of my kitties, but we can't have that sort of unseemly behavior at the bank. It's undignified. I didn't know what to think when I saw her smack Mr. Oliver. She could have caused a serious physical injury."

"Posterboard can be deadly," I said soberly.

At this moment Lottie Estes came out of the back office, an envelope in her hand. Brandon Bernswallow followed her. "We at the Maggody branch will clear this up," he said in a voice oily enough to do a lube job on a tractor trailer. "We're committed to community service."

Lottie beamed at him. "You have been most helpful, young man. It's such a relief to have this taken care of by someone with nice manners. As I told you earlier, it has preyed on my mind since the moment it came in the mail. I have never before been accused of such a ridiculous thing, and I was floored. As if I would borrow five hundred dollars! I have always paid cash for my purchases. My father used to say that credit was the work of Satan hisself."

Brandon gave me a quick look as he placed his hand on Lottie's shoulder. "Your attitude is what makes banks like ours work for the community. You just keep building up that savings account, and I'll deal with this mistake."

He turned and retreated into his office. Lottie came to Miss Una's window, nodded vaguely at me, and said, "He is such a nice young man, Una. He'd be a perfect catch for some Maggody girl, who could see that his shirts stay ironed and his shoes polished." She leaned forward and lowered her voice to a whisper. "Is it true what I heard in the teachers' lounge about Johnna Mae Nookim chasing Sherman Oliver down the middle of the highway with a broom? It's not the least bit difficult to believe. I had her in several of my classes fifteen years ago, and I always suspected she cheated on the small appliance final. One of my better students swore Johnna Mae had the blender manual taped to her thigh."

Miss Una bobbled her head. "She attacked poor Mr. Oliver right out there in front of the building. She was frothing like a rabid dog and calling him all kinds of terrible names."

I departed before I heard further escalations. The Olivers lived in the Maggody version of a subdivision, which meant there were twenty-odd houses jammed together in the middle of a flat, treeless cow pasture. I drove past the high school and the Dairee Dee-Lishus, turned across from the football stadium, and found their house at the end of an honest to goodness cul-de-sac (we used to call 'em dead ends, but the developer wasn't having any of that). Their house was larger than those surrounding it, but hardly imposing enough to qualify for "mansion" or "palace."

Clutching the complaint in my sweaty little hand, I parked in the driveway and walked up the sidewalk to the front door. Before I could knock, ring, or holler, the door opened. Mrs. Sherman Oliver seemed startled momentarily, but she regained her composure. "Arly Hanks, isn't it? Ruby Bee's girl?" she said.

Anonymity, not to mention life itself, is tough in Maggody. "Yes," I said. "I'd like to speak to Mr. Oliver if it's convenient."

She came out onto the porch, carefully closing the door behind her. She was an attractive middle-aged woman with tidy hair, soft brown eyes, and fluttery hands. She fluttered them for a moment, then said, "I'm afraid Mr. Oliver isn't feeling well. He is deeply distressed by what happened earlier. He came home, took two aspirins, and told me he would prefer to be left alone in the den until supper time. Perhaps you might come back tomorrow?"

"I'd like to get this settled as quickly as possible. Johnna Mae is rather distressed herself, especially by the possibility of being sent to jail for a year over this silly little incident."

Truda smiled sadly. "It is silly, isn't it? I told Sherman as much, and I think by tomorrow he'll be willing to forget about it. Brandon can be a bit of a hothead, but Sherman really prefers to avoid any kind of conflict. He says it throws off his golf game."

"I can see how it might," I said, trying to maintain a

sympathetic tone. "When would be a good time for me to return?"

"Sherman goes to the main branch every morning. He's still in charge of the portfolio purchases, even though he requested the transfer out here in order to enjoy the tranquillity of country life. He'll leave at nine or so. He usually plays golf in the afternoons, but he ought to be home by supper time."

"I'll try to catch him before he leaves," I said. We exchanged pleasantries and then I drove back to the highway, feeling enormously relieved. I certainly had no desire to see Johnna Mae behind bars, even for a few days. In my professional capacity, I wasn't supposed to enjoy watching one citizen batter another. At a more personal level, however, I'd found the incident most amusing. Cheap thrills. More exciting than when Hiram Buchanon's barn burned.

There I was, smirking and grinning and having a right good time as I pulled into the gravel lot of Ruby Bee's Bar and Grill. I parked next to an unfamiliar subcompact, but you never know when some unwary tourist is going to make a serious mistake and stop by for cold beer and sparkling conversation with the locals. It only takes one time to learn better.

The Closed sign was still hanging from a thumbtack, but I ignored it and was reaching for the door when it flew open. Jim Bob Buchanon would have stomped right over me if I hadn't jumped back at the last second.

"About time you did something," he growled at me. He seems to growl at me a lot, but it's appropriate in that he reminds me of a bulldog. He's got the infamous clan features, along with a stubby gray crew cut and a soft belly cantilevered over his belt. As far as I can tell, his upper lip stays glued in a perpetual sneer.

"About time I ate lunch," I said. "And what's better than Mom's home cooking? Ruby Bee fixes the best fried okra in the county."

"That is not what I meant, Chief of Police Hanks. I heard what happened earlier at the bank. It seems to me there was a clear case of dereliction of duty. You should have been down there in the first place, and you should have put a stop to that crazy Nookim broad's 'protest' before things got out of hand."

"Is that what I should have done? Gee, Jim Bob, I guess I was confused. I thought I was supposed to protect the constitutional rights of the citizenry. Silly me."

"Mrs. Jim Bob gave me a damn earful about how you refused to do anything to prevent the incident from getting way out of hand. This is something that will be discussed at the next town council meeting. You may find yourself out of a job, Arly. Then you can sit around all day thinking up smart remarks. You and Ruby Bee can have yourselves a fine time."

"Don't tell me, don't tell me. Ruby Bee said something that didn't go down real well with you. That woman is crazier than the Nookim broad. Maybe we can figure out how to have the both of them shipped off to the state prison farm, or even better, to a penal colony off the coast of South America. That's what we ought to do, Jim Bob—unless you'd prefer I just shoot 'em dead in the street?"

"What I'd prefer is none of your damn business." He stalked across the parking lot toward the Kwik-Stoppe-Shoppe, a.k.a. Kwik-Screw, muttering all kinds of things under his breath. I noted for the first time that he was slightly bowlegged, unless his jeans were a shade too tight. Poor baby.

I went on into the bar, which was dim and noticeably unpopulated except for a woman perched on a stool at the end of the bar. Ruby Bee is an excellent cook and usually has a mob at every meal. The current situation was downright eerie, I decided as I picked a stool and climbed onto it. The unfamiliar woman glanced up incuriously, then returned to a file spread out in front of her.

I'd pretty well decided she was a sales rep when Ruby Bee came out of the kitchen, snorted in my direction, and joined the woman at the end for a whispered conversation. They were both shooting veiled looks at yours truly, who was merely mystified and hungry.

"Is it possible to get a grilled cheese sandwich?" I asked.

"We're closed," Ruby Bee said. "Didn't you read the sign on the door? Closed means not open, as in come by later if you want something."

My mother gives me hives. I would have stalked away in a huff, but my stomach was pleading for me to stick it out and find out what was going on. "But you've got a customer," I pointed out nicely, "and I ran into Jim Bob leaving a few minutes ago. What's going on—selective service? Do I have the wrong-colored hair or what?"

The woman, who appeared to be in her late twenties and way too well-dressed for this neck of the woods, gave me a cool smile. "I am not a customer. I stopped here to ask directions and am simply eliciting some further information before I continue."

Ruby Bee gestured at the woman to hush and said, "And Jim Bob Buchanon was told that the bar and grill is closed, no ifs, ands, or buts about it. He got testy, but I made it clear I wasn't about to serve the likes of him for a month of Sundays and then some. Now this person and I got things to discuss, so why don't you slide off that stool and wander away to pester other folks?"

"Why are you closed?" I persisted.

"Because I put the Closed sign on the door, Miss Have to Know Everything. You most likely remember what curiosity did to the cat, but if you need a refresher course, I may be willing to oblige you."

"I'm not curious. I'm hungry," I said, wondering what on earth was wrong with Ruby Bee. She'd pulled this conspiracy nonsense once before, and it had ended with a murder, a couple of kidnappings—Ruby Bee being among those snatched—and a great deal of Maggody's dirty laundry being waved around for the entertainment of the masses. I thought about reminding her as much but decided there wasn't much point in it. Ruby Bee is not known for profitting from experience.

"Well?" she said, watching me through narrowed eyes.

I was working on a snappy retort when Estelle came through the kitchen door. "I called over there, but Putter said she wasn't—" She stopped with a gulp as she spotted me.

"Arly's leaving right this minute," Ruby Bee informed her, although I suspect the information was aimed at other ears.

"Are you hunting Johnna Mae Nookim?" I asked.

Ruby Bee and Estelle started fidgeting like a pair of toad frogs. The woman glanced at them for a moment, then turned to me and said, "Do you have information concerning her whereabouts at this time?"

"Yep," I said.

There was a long silence. Ruby Bee leaned across the bar to whisper to the woman. After a great deal of hissing, she straightened up and said, "This is Carolyn McCoy-Grunders. She's from WAACO."

"Wacko?" I echoed blankly. "Did you mean to say Waco, as in Texas, or wacko, as in crazy?"

Carolyn gave me a frigid look. "WAACO is the acronym for Women Aligned Against Chauvinism in the Office. We're committed to fighting sexual discrimination and injustice through education, self-awareness, and legal support. Ms. Nookim sent in a letter concerning her treatment by the bank, and I feel there is merit to her accusation."

"I'm impressed you came so quickly," I said, still fighting back a grin.

"The legal system grinds exceedingly slow in these matters. I will assist Ms. Nookim in the preparation of a formal complaint for the Equal Employment Opportunity Commission, but it takes as long as four months to get any response from them. They are overworked and understaffed, or so they claim. We of WAACO are dedicated to immediate action. We demand the injustice be rectified, and we're willing to do whatever is necessary until our demands are met."

"I hope you're willing to baby-sit," I said. "I still haven't had a chance to talk to Sherman Oliver about dropping the battery charge. If you get Johnna Mae riled up again, she may end up in the county jail. Someone will have to pick up her husband's prescription and drive the baby to the shoestore."

"Sacrifices must be made for the betterment of society," Carolyn said smoothly. "We cannot allow personal inconvenience to cloud our purpose."

"Right," Ruby Bee said, although she didn't sound real happy. "So where is Johnna Mae, Arly? You didn't lock her up, did you?"

"She left the PD a couple of hours ago to walk back to the mobile home park. She's had time to get to Hasty and back by now. In any case, now that I'm no longer a pariah, how about that sandwich?"

Estelle put her hands on her hips. "I swear, all you ever think about is food. If you don't watch out, you're going to end up like Dahlia O'Neill, and then you'll be sorry."

On that bright note, I slid off the stool and went on my merry way, leaving the three of them to fight chauvinism, battle injustice, and make all the personal sacrifices they could think of. I was more interested in chicken noodle soup.

Brandon Bernswallow sat at his desk at the bank, his hands clasped behind his neck as he gazed at the ceiling. It was obvious that the embezzlement scheme had been going on for years, and with great success. In truth, he rather admired the way it was operated— very quietly, very discreetly. No large sums that might attract a bank examiner's attention or alert the IRS. Just lots of small sums juggled like shiny silver balls.

However, he thought with a smug smile, the juggler was having a problem keeping the balls in the air.

Nothing had crashed yet, but the possibility was very real, now that he had uncovered the scheme. What to do, what to do. He could, of course, expose the embezzlement and demand the perpetrator be prosecuted unmercifully. Betraying the trust of the community. Depriving honest citizens of their hard-earned money. All that crap. He spent a few pleasant minutes imagining himself being interviewed on television, his expression a delicate combination of outrage at the heinous crime and pain at the idea that a bank employee could betray the institution. His father might be impressed enough to transfer Brandon back to the main bank, where he would have a tastefully decorated office, a new desk, martinis for lunch, and a secretary with enormous tits.

Then again, his father was an asshole who spouted off at every opportunity about working one's way up through the system, honest labor, earning one's position, etc. Which was why Brandon was stuck in this miserable little town in this vile branch with dim-witted coworkers and a piddling salary that wasn't going to cover the damn car payment much longer. His father was more than capable of leaving him to rot for years.

The secretary's tits shrank until they resembled the deflated bags on Miss Una's chest. Her firm buttocks spread until they were as wide as Johnna Mae Nookim's rear end. Her bright eyes turned to Sherman Oliver's vaguely unfocused gape. The glare of the television lights went black.

He could expose the crime, but he was likely to get no more than a pat on the head and a notation in his file. The loan company would get his car. There was a second option. The perpetrator had been stashing away money for a very long time. Perhaps it could be shared—with the one person who knew exactly what was going on and was willing to stay quiet as long as he could drive his Mercedes and dress well.

It wouldn't do to be overly demanding. But it would do quite well to be firm about it, to make it clear that the embezzlement would remain a secret only as long as he was willing to keep his mouth shut. Once he'd decided he would prefer weekly payments, Brandon picked up a pen and began to compose a letter. It was definitely not the sort one dictated to a secretary.

5

The Closed sign stayed on the door of Ruby Bee's Bar and Grill for five days straight. In the beginning, a few of the good ol' boys strolled in just like always, and promptly found themselves right back in the parking lot, their ears stinging and their faces hotter than a bushel of red beets. Not one of them tried it twice.

Which isn't to say all was dark and empty within the hallowed confines. Not by a long shot. All sorts of activity seemed to emanate from the pink building, causing the good ol' boys to scratch their heads and wonder what the hell was goin' on and how they were supposed to have a beer and a plate lunch if the bar was closed, God damn it.

Carolyn McCoy-Grunders's car stayed parked by the door for the most part, although at midnight or so it might be seen around back in front of unit 2. Dahlia O'Neill waddled across the road to the Kwik-Screw every now and then, clutching a shopping list that included such odd things as peanut butter and masking tape. Ruby Bee came and went, as did Estelle (when she could get away from the demands of the beauty parlor). On the second day, Elsie McMay was spotted marching through the door, along with Joyce Lambertino,

70

whose husband Larry Joe was the shop teacher at the high school and also a member of the town council. But when he was asked what was going on, he could only shrug and mumble something about how he and Joyce weren't exactly talking to each other these days. Or nights, for that matter.

Johnna Mae Nookim was rumored to be in there too. The two hippie women from the Emporium started coming by in the evenings. Earl Buchanon's wife, a.k.a. Kevin Buchanon's mother, may have been there, but when anybody tried to ask him if she was, Earl was meaner than a snake with a knot in its tail. Millicent McIlhaney and Edwina Spitz were seen at the door, along with Millicent's daughter Darla Jean, who reputedly looked a little pissed about being dragged along. By the third day, all sorts of mothers, daughters, wives, widows, and spinsters were showing up at various hours. It was starting to look as though half the womenfolk of Maggody were spending a goodly amount of time there—and they were refusing to say one word about what they were doing.

Lottie Estes told Miss Una that, in her opinion, whatever was going on in there was the work of Satan hisself. Miss Una felt it prudent to agree, although she wasn't real sure Lottie wasn't experiencing those hot flashes again, when she went on and on about how every man in the county was scheming to rape her. Miss Una always found that pretty darn difficult to believe.

Mrs. Jim Bob was obliged to stop by the Kwik-Screw several times a day to pick up a few things, but no matter how long she stood by the cash register staring across the road, she sure couldn't figure out

what they were up to in there. She went so far as to
ask Brother Verber if he thought they might be forming
a coven to practice witchcraft and sacrifice goats and
dance around buck naked. He was so disturbed by the
suggestion that he thudded to his knees like a load of
topsoil and offered a prayer right then and there for
the salvation of any souls in need of it at the moment
or in the future while they were dancing. Mrs. Jim
Bob thought he was being a might melodramatic over
what she'd meant to be an idle question, but she didn't
say anything and left as quick as she could.

The chief of police was aware of parts of the above,
since she was being bombarded with questions about
the situation. The PD could have used a revolving
door those days, and the linoleum would never be the
same. And said person had not one tiny theory about
it.

Not that it was keeping me awake at night, mind
you. In that Ruby Bee's was the sole nightspot in
town, there wasn't much to do except sleep. I'd run by
Sherman Oliver's the morning after the picket sign
incident, and he'd assured me that he wasn't about to
file a complaint. We smiled, shook hands, and left it at
that. I called Johnna Mae to tell her the news, and
Putter said he'd give her the message. The dreadful
tragedy was thus averted, at least for the time being.

I will admit I was wondering about this mysterious
gathering, however, and growing increasingly concerned
about my nutritional requirements. Canned soup is
fine in a pinch, but it doesn't hold a candle to pork
chops and cobbler. And cool beer on a sizzling
afternoon, even if one had to listen to witty dialogue
about hawg prices at the sale barn and the inconve-

nience of having to go all the dadburned way to the co-op in Starley City to get layer grit (don't ask; it has something to do with chickens and that's all I know).

Therefore, out of nothing more than pure and unadulterated selfishness, I went so far as to wave down Kevin Buchanon one afternoon when he peddled by the PD on his bicycle. "How's it going at the bank?" I asked with incredible slyness, ready to manipulate the conversation at will.

"How's what going?"

"Your job, Kevin," I said patiently. "You do still work at the bank, don't you?"

"Yeah, sure, I still work at the bank. It's just great, Arly. How're things going with you?"

"Just great. Have you popped the question to Dahlia yet?"

"What question would that be?" he said, his Adam's apple bobbing like a salmon fighting its way upstream. "Like, how's it going at the bank or something like that? Dahlia doesn't work at the bank, you know. She's a barmaid at Ruby Bee's. She has been for a long time, and I don't recollect she ever worked at the bank."

I took a deep breath and reminded myself that my goal was information. "I know that. What I wanted to know is if you'd asked Dahlia if she wanted to get married."

He gave me the look of a faithful old hound that'd just been kicked across the room. His eyes began to water. In a ragged voice, he said, "I mentioned something to her about it, but do you know what she said?"

"I don't suppose she shrieked with joy."

"She said—" He broke off to wipe his nose on his sleeve. "She said that marriage was like being chained up in a dungeon. She said she wasn't about to get herself chained up like that because she was a human being and ought to be treated like a man. I asked her why she wanted to be treated like a man, in that she ain't one to begin with and never was, and she just gave me a real mean look and walked off. I like to have cried."

"Oh," I murmured, touched by his emotionalism if not his eloquence. "Does this have something to do with whatever is happening at Ruby Bee's the last few days?"

"What's happening at Ruby Bee's?"

"That's what I was hoping you could tell me. I thought Dahlia might have given you a hint or let something drop."

He screwed up his face while he tried to think. I could see it was a painful and unfamiliar process, and I ordered myself not to rush him. After what must have been five minutes, his face eased and he gave me a grin. "Now I remember what she said. She said they was mad about something and were going to turn themselves into men, or something like that. I still don't understand why Dahlia keeps harping about being a man. She's the finest figure of a woman what ever walked the earth. Her cheeks are like peaches and her lips are like cherry cough drops. She's so soft and marshmallowy sweet I could just gaze at her all day long." He sniffled at the image, and pretty soon we were back to watery eyes, a drippy nose, and noisy gulps.

You may have gotten the wrong impression from

Kevin's ravings. Dahlia weighs three hundred pounds, at the least. Her cheeks may be the color of peaches, but they're the size of watermelons. The cough drops pass through her lips, along with everything else she can find. She has chins too numerous to count and massive breasts that sway back and forth like a pair of tire swings when she walks. Her expression is that of a bewildered bovine, and she's about as witty as her boyfriend. Or ex-boyfriend, I supposed.

"So what should I do, Arly?" Kevin said piteously.

"Beats me. I would imagine that she'll get over whatever's bugging her at the moment and take you back. I wouldn't take the treat-me-like-a-man thing too literally and offer her a chaw of tobacco or anything. Just try to listen to her and nod when you don't understand her."

"Gee, Arly, do you really think she'll take me back? What about marriage being chains in a dungeon? I thought we could live in a mobile home. I don't reckon there are any dungeons around these parts anyhow. I wasn't going to make her wear chains, unless they was those nice yellow gold ones with a locket or a pearl."

I considered trying to explain the philosophy of feminist thought to Kevin Buchanon while standing in hundred-degree heat on the edge of the highway. We could be there for days, if not weeks. Months. It occurred to me that I was already brainbaked to toy with the idea of explaining anything to Kevin Buchanon, much less a concept or an abstraction.

"Buy her one of those gold chains with a heart-shaped locket," I said. "Maybe that'll win her back. What about your mother, Kevin? Has she said anything about what's happening at Ruby Bee's?"

"Gosh, no. She hasn't said more than three words all week, and none of them was very nice. This morning she was ironing me a shirt when Pa yelled down at her to get his breakfast on the table. She told him to cook his own damn breakfast. Pa liked to have choked himself on his suspenders; he's never cooked in his whole entire life. He told Ma that that's why he got married, so he'd have a wife to cook and keep house. Ma's voice got colder than a well digger's ass and she told him to take his bacon and stuff it where the sun don't shine. I don't think I've ever seen Pa quite so mad," Kevin concluded in an awed tone. "Or Ma, neither."

"Must have been real entertaining," I said. Kevin pedaled away and I went back into the PD to ponder all that. It was obvious that Carolyn McCoy-Grunders, the woman from WAACO, was stirring up the distaff side of the community. They were hiding out in the bar while they plotted whatever it was they were plotting, and I had an icy feeling in my stomach that it was going to be a doozy of a plot.

Not that I had any objections to a little enlightenment in this last bastion of the dark ages. Earl Buchanon certainly deserved to be told to cook his own damn breakfast and to find an anatomically improbable place to stash the bacon. Johnna Mae had been treated unfairly by the bank. The majority of the women in Maggody considered themselves property of their husbands, to be abused, neglected, beaten, or ordered about like slaves. It wouldn't do any harm for them to raise whatever consciousness they possessed.

However, I was worried about Johnna Mae's potential involvement. Sherman Oliver might be more than a little irked if she started in again picketing the bank and shouting rude things about him. I decided to go over to her mobile home and see if I could convince her that a year in the pokey would be seriously inconvenient.

I drove to the Pot O' Gold and parked in front of her mobile home. A dark-haired child in shorts and a misshapen T-shirt was throwing a ball against the metal wall in a desultory rhythm. He stopped momentarily to gaze at me, then returned to his activity. I went to the door and knocked.

Putter Nookim opened the door. He stared at me as he wiped his hands on a dingy dish towel. A television blared from behind him, and somewhere in a back room a baby began to cry. "Hey, Arly, you looking for Johnna Mae?" he said without visible or vocal enthusiasm. "She ain't here."

The tennis ball made a thwacking sound near my ear, but I held back a wince and said, "Do you have any idea when she'll be back?"

Thwack. "No, she's off with those women at Ruby Bee's. She been there all the time for most of a week now and I don't know when she'll come home." *Thwack.* "She says it's real important what they're a-doing. She says it's for the cause." *Thwack.* "I jest wish she'd come home."

"I'm sure you do," I murmured, eyeing the stained apron he wore over his jeans. "How's your back, Putter?" *Thwack.* "Any chance you can go back to work soon?"

He shoved his hands in his pockets and shook his head. We looked at each other for a moment—*thwack*—and then I said I'd try to catch Johnna Mae at Ruby

Bee's—*thwack*. He closed the door. I went to the future major league pitcher and offered him a dollar for his ball. He snatched the ball out of the air and hightailed it around the mobile home, no doubt to commence his game on the other side.

Although it was late in the afternoon, the sun was still blistering the road and doing its best to peel a couple of layers off everybody and everything. The upholstery in the police car crackled as I eased onto it, and I could feel it through my clothes. I decided I could put off a confrontation with the conspirators long enough to stop by the Dairee Dee-Lishus for a cherry lime ade, but as I reached the intersection with the highway, I saw that which is not seen in Maggody more than once a decade.

Two of them, actually. One was a boxy white wagon with a television station logo painted on its door. The other was a cream-colored van with a television station logo painted on its side, and they were parked in front of the Voice of the Almighty Lord Assembly Hall. A man and a woman were chatting at the edge of the lawn, while two men armed with portable cameras were fiddling with their equipment on an individual basis.

The lawn was otherwise uninhabited. As I sat at the intersection, blinking like a toad in a hailstorm and wondering if the Goodyear blimp would show up shortly, Brother Verber and Mrs. Jim Bob came out of the white frame building and joined the man and woman. Much gesturing ensued. At one point Mrs. Jim Bob shaded her eyes with her hand to peer down the highway. Brother Verber took out a handkerchief, blotted his glistening forehead, gustily blew his nose, and stuck it back in his pocket, all the while talking and frothing at the two unknowns, who seemed bemused but not impressed. Mrs. Jim Bob stalked back into the Assembly Hall, her buttocks aswish with indignation.

Things got even more intriguing when a sheriff's deputy drove into the bank's parking lot and pulled in beside me. He gave me a little wave and got out of the car as yet another deputy appeared from the opposite direction and pulled into the lot. The two walked to the edge of the highway and began to talk.

Fascinating, I told myself, wishing I'd purchased the tennis ball so I could throw it at them to get their attention. I was about to flip on the siren just for the hell of it (it hardly ever works, but you never know) when another car pulled up behind the television van and a man with a camera around his neck got out, accompanied by a dowdy woman with a notebook. They joined the circle on the lawn.

Sweat was dribbling down my back and dripping off the end of my nose, but I couldn't seem to snap into action, mostly because I wasn't sure which action to snap into. I had about to decided to ignore the whole thing in favor of a cherry lime ade when I heard shrill voices in the distance. I inched the car forward until I could see around the corner of the old drugstore.

Parade time in Maggody. Estelle's station wagon was coming right up the yellow line in the middle of the highway, creeping along at a turtlish pace. Crepe paper streamers flapped from the roof and the door handles; a poster was taped on the door, but I couldn't read it from my vantage point. Following behind it was a wall of women, their arms linked and their mouths moving in unison, twice as fast as Estelle's station wagon. Some of them were decorated with sandwich boards and crepe paper, while others carried signs. They were all familiar.

I cut off the engine and scrambled out of the car. The television people had whipped to attention and were aiming cameras at the protesters. The newspaper photographer was in the middle of the road, snapping away. The two deputies had moved into the shade under a wilting crab apple tree beside the bank, but they were watching intently.

"Down with the Maggody branch!" came the battle cry.

The door of the pool hall opened and the neckless wonders wandered out to stare as the procession moved regally past them. Roy Stivers came to the door of the antique store, his thumbs hooked in the straps of his overalls. His cheek puffed out with a wad of tobacco, Perkins could be seen staring through the window of the barbershop, as could Earl Buchanon and Jeremiah McIlhaney. Lottie Estes scowled from the porch of the Assembly Hall.

"Sherman Oliver discriminates against women!"

The accused and Brandon Bernswallow came out of the bank. Bernswallow tapped one of the deputies on the shoulder and began to talk insistently into his ear. Sherman Oliver folded his arms and waited impassively, although I could see his eyelid twitching and his face getting redder by the second. His foot was tapping hard enough to eradicate an entire colony of ants.

"We shall stand together!"

Mrs. Jim Bob scurried across the lawn, her jaw leading the way, and took her position next to Brother

Verber, who was mopping his face and working on a full-scale expression of righteous outrage.

"Down with the Maggody branch!"

The protesters passed the Emporium and stopped long enough for the television cameras to catch them in their finest hour. Estelle flashed a smile for all those unseen viewers, wiggled her fingers at me, and began to drive slowly toward the bank parking lot. There were at least three dozen women in three rows, and I didn't even have to squint to find Rubella Belinda Hanks smack dab in the middle of the first row, with Johnna Mae on her left and the WAACO woman on her right. Where else would the chief of police's mother be—home baking cookies?

"We shall overcome!"

I wasn't sure what they intended to overcome, although it was probable we would all be overcome with heat before too long. Or tension, which was as smothering as the humidity and twice as thick. In that the women were squarely in the middle of the road, we were developing a small problem with traffic flow. We don't normally have a steady stream through town, but we have a smattering of pickup trucks and your occasional tourists out in search of bucolic bliss and cheap antiques. By this time, we had collected several of each species both coming and going, although obviously nobody was doing much of either at the moment. Some of them were, however, beeping their horns or shouting out the windows of their vehicles.

"Unity for all women!"

One of the deputies was scratching his head, the other his ass. Neither one seemed to have any idea what to do, understandably enough. The television people were still filming away and the reporter was trying to elicit a few words from the outer edge of the row.

"Sisterhood forever!"

Mrs. Jim Bob jabbed Brother Verber, who sucked in a breath and strode out to the yellow line. Everybody swung around to see if Estelle would brake, and from her expression I could tell it was on the iffy side. With no more than two or three inches to spare, she did, causing a collective sigh of relief to stir the air.

Her head popped out the window of the station wagon. "Git yourself out of the way."

"What you're doing is sinful, Estelle Oppers, and all the rest of you women," he intoned, clasping his hands in the classic supplicative pose and half closing his eyes. "I want all of you to go home to your husbands, get down on your knees, and beg, yes, I say *beg* their forgiveness for the terrible thing you're doing this very minute."

"Old fart!" Johnna Mae called. She freed her arm long enough to shake her fist at him, then slipped it back through Ruby Bee's and added, "Paternalistic pig! Who does he think he is anyway? Moses?"

"Pride goeth before a fall," he shouted back, earning a moment of puzzled silence from the crowd. "A woman's place is in the home. The Bible says you're supposed to glean and reap in your husband's field, not block traffic and make spectacles of yourselves."

"Go reap yourself up a tree!" came a comment from within the ranks.

This elicited responses from the crowd, which was swelling like a pregnant sow's belly. Those in the cars and trucks were scrambling out now, either to escape the sun or to hope for a chance to appear on the nightly news. The spectators along the street had gathered too. The deputies were looking decidedly unhappy, but neither had moved out of the shade.

Brandon Bernswallow came at me, his forehead so deeply creased the lines might have been etched with an ax. "You have to stop this right now, Chief Hanks," he barked. "This is illegal, and you damn well better do something immediately. This kind of publicity can do permanent damage to the bank's image in the community. God knows my father'll have a stroke when he sees this on the news. He'll have some crazy idea that this whole thing is my fault. Now do something, and do it now!"

I was about to point out that I would have more than a small amount of difficulty doing much of anything when I heard a thud. I looked over Bernswallow's shoulder. Brother Verber was now spread-eagled across the hood of the station wagon, roaring at Estelle through the windshield and splattering it with spittle. She rolled up her window and turned on the windshield wipers. Mrs. Jim Bob was clinging to Lottie Estes, who was fanning her with a tissue and screeching at the protesters.

The television cameras descended on me. A woman with immaculate hair stuck a microphone under my chin and said, "We're talking with Arly Hanks, chief of police in Maggody. Chief Hanks, how do you intend to deal with this escalating crisis? Do you feel you and these two deputies will be able to prevent violence as more and more people gather here on the road to seek equality for women?"

I flapped my jaw, but before I could respond, Bernswallow nudged me aside and said, "The Bank of

Farberville is deeply concerned about this minor yet distressing incident. We have always dedicated ourselves to—"

Carolyn McCoy-Grunders nudged him aside. "I'm the official spokesperson for Women Aligned Against Chauvinism in the Office, and we'd like to go on record as—"

Brother Verber nudged her aside. "The Bible admonishes women to cleanse the temple and honor and obey, not carry on like common sluts. Furthermore, in my experience as pastor of—"

Johnna Mae nudged him aside. "I was employed at this branch for eleven years. Just because I had a C section and had to stay home for six weeks while the scar healed up is no reason—"

Even the television people were getting tired of the nudging and interrupting. The lights went off and they headed toward the women milling about in the parking lot. The deputies rallied themselves and began ordering the crowd to disperse and get back in their cars or go inside or whatever if they didn't want citations for blocking the road.

"Just who do you think you are?" Bernswallow snapped at the woman from WAACO. "Around these parts we don't think real highly of tight-assed women who're too damn big for their britches and come into town to stir up trouble."

That set off a conversation I preferred to pass up, at least for the moment. I left them snarling at each other and went to Sherman Oliver's side. "Johnna Mae must have changed her mind," I said with a shrug.

"So she did, so she did. I'm sorely disappointed,

and I suppose I should have heeded Brandon's advice and filed the complaint against her." His already red face turned a deeper hue. "Now what in tarnation are those damn fool women doing?"

What in tarnation they were doing was unloading the station wagon in the middle of the parking lot. We're talking aluminum patio chairs, coolers, grocery bags, casserole dishes covered with plastic wrap, and gallon jugs. Some of them, anyway. Other busy little bees were propping up posterboard signs, none of which was complimentary to the branch bank or its manager. The television crews were delighted with this display of industriousness and centered on someone's mother as she taped a particularly offensive sign to the crab apple tree.

Brother Verber, Mrs. Jim Bob, and a whole passel of husbands were observing from the lawn of the Assembly Hall. The deputies had the traffic moving, but those on the far side of the road were motionless. Grim. I'd never seen so many clenched jaws, rigid lips, and narrowed eyes in my life—and I used to take the subway in Manhattan when it rained.

"Arrest those women," Sherman Oliver said, his jaw pretty damn clenched itself. "They are trespassing on private property."

Brandon snorted a final insult at Carolyn and stalked over to us. "That's right, Chief Hanks. The parking lot is private property. I don't know what the hell they think they're doing, acting like they're settling in for a little picnic over there, but we won't stand for it."

Carolyn joined our jolly group. "Oh, yes, please arrest all those gray-haired, middle-aged housewives and throw them in jail. Won't the bank look just dandy when the story hits the news? What a wonderful way to express all that dedication to serving the community, by locking up half the population in some filthy jail cell. Do you have enough handcuffs to go around? You'll most likely have to drag them into the police wagon, since we've all agreed to react with passive resistance."

"Arrest those women," Bernswallow said, sounding a shade petulant.

Sherman Oliver held up his hand. "Let's put that on hold for a minute. We don't want to get all carried away before we've thought about this." He chewed on a hangnail and stared at the parking lot, which was beginning to resemble a terrace party, now that card tables had been draped with tablecloths and set with paper plates and plastic tableware. Someone had thought to bring mason jars as vases, and each now held a small bouquet of flowers. Estelle and Elsie Buchanon were uncovering dishes on the tailgate of the station wagon. Dahlia O'Neill hovered nearby, licking her lips at each unveiling.

"Good grief," I said, mostly to myself. I raised my voice and added, "Let's find out what the game plan is before we do anything rash."

Carolyn smiled. "It's really quite simple. We intend to stay here until Johnna Mae Nookim is restored to her rightful position as head teller of the branch, with full back pay for her maternity leave and for the days she was wrongly unemployed. She also deserves compensation for the pain and suffering brought on by the discriminatory actions of this man." She pointed a red-tipped finger at Bernswallow. "And, of course, he'll have to be fired."

"What?" Bernswallow sputtered. "You've got knots in your panty hose, honey, if you think you can make those wild demands and expect to get away with them. My grandfather founded the bank, and my father's chairman of the board. Nobody's firing this boy."

Sherman Oliver looked at Carolyn. "He's right about how his family owns the bank, young woman, but I think we can find a solution. This picnic in the parking lot won't harm our reputation in the long run. As long as you girls promise to clean up after yourselves before you go home tonight, I think we can just forget this whole mess ever happened."

"We're not going anywhere tonight, buddy boy, unless our demands are agreed to in writing. I've done a rough draft already. Perhaps you might care to look it over?"

"You bra-burning bitch," Bernswallow snapped. "What's with you, anyway? I'll bet you're one of those lesbians who hate men because men don't find them attractive. Couldn't you get a date to the prom, princess? Did you have to stay home and lick cunt?"

"Stop this!" I said, jabbing him in the chest. When he retreated, I turned around to Sherman Oliver and said icily, "You tell him to keep his mouth shut. This is difficult enough without a bunch of wise-ass remarks being thrown about. There's got to be some way to resolve this."

Oliver looked at the parking lot. He ran his hand through his hair and shook his head. "We cannot tolerate a lot of bad publicity. A bank survives on goodwill and community support. I guess I'd better go call Mr. Bernswallow and see what he wants us to do."

Brandon flinched. "Maybe I ought to call him."

"That might be better," Carolyn said sweetly. "Let him hear the news from his little boy who bullies women when he's not pulling wings off butterflies or using his masculine wiles to rape sorority girls."

"That's it, bitch!" Brandon said, moving toward her with a malevolent expression.

"Oh, Carolyn," trilled a voice from the parking lot. "It's time for supper. We want you to sit at the head table."

I wished I'd brought a bullet, if only to send it into my own head.

6

I pleaded with the sheriff's deputies until they agreed
to stay for a while to maintain a semblance of order,
and then I went to find Ruby Bee. She was sitting at a
card table with Estelle, Johnna Mae, and Dahlia. As I
approached, she made a great show of shoveling in the
chicken salad, but I wasn't buying.

"We need to talk," I growled.

"Howdy, Arly," Dahlia said through a mouthful of
green bean casserole, a Maggody favorite, done with
cream of mushroom soup and canned onion rings.
Ruby Bee always fancies it up with pimentos, claiming
the addition of color gives it a festive air. Ruby Bee
has the soul of an artist.

"Hi, Dahlia. I talked to Kevin earlier today, and he
seemed pretty upset." I paused for a moment, both
for dramatic effect and to allow her time to jump-start
her brain, and then coldheartedly added, "In fact, he
was so broken up he could hardly speak. He was in
tears."

Her fork stopped midway to her mouth, possibly for
the first time in her life. "He was? Gee, mebbe I'd
better talk to him."

Estelle shook her head so hard a red curl popped

loose to dangle in the middle of her forehead. "Now, Dahlia O'Neill, we already agreed that ain't none of us going to quit just because the menfolk try to pull this crap. We are doing this not only to help out Johnna Mae, but also to improve the lives of women across the country. They are our sisters, and we aim to see they are treated equally like men, not like some oppressive minority. You are not going to throw in the towel just because Kevin got all misty in front of Arly. He probably had a gnat in his eye."

"He has a terrible time with bugs when he rides his bicycle," Dahlia said, brightening enough to propel the fork into her mouth. "He like to choke himself silly on a June bug one time. I had to pound him on the back until I was afeared he would go flying on his face right in the dirt. Who made the green bean casserole? Was it Elsie McMay? I surely would like her recipe."

Ruby Bee poked a pile of the stuff with her fork. "Why, I declare, this has water chestnuts in it. Who'd have thought of such a thing? I'll speak to Elsie myself about it, then copy it on one of my personalized recipe cards for you, Dahlia."

"I was right on the verge of saying they were slices of celery," Estelle said pensively.

"No, they're water chestnuts," Johnna Mae said, not looking at me. "I sort of like the crunch myself."

I took a deep breath, counted to ten, and said, "I find it difficult to understand how you expect to improve the lot of American women by exchanging recipes in a bank parking lot. And according to the WAACO woman, you're all determined to stay here until wrongs are righted and justice prevails. Don't you think such lofty ideals will pale long about midnight, or did you bring kerosene lanterns so you can play canasta all night?"

Ruby Bee turned up her nose at me, which took quite an effort since she was sitting down and I was looming over her. "We brought everything we need, including lanterns, and we intend to occupy this lot until our demands are met."

"This is not Columbia University, and you are not sixties college students," I pointed out as calmly as possible, considering. "Nobody may give a rat's ass where you sleep, but what about you, Johnna Mae? Are you planning to desert your husband and children for the duration?"

"I already explained to Putter, and he was real sweet about it. He understands this is the only way I can get my job back."

"What if Mr. Oliver decides to reinstate the battery complaint?"

"Carolyn says that we'll get national media coverage that will show how oppressed we pink-collar employees are. She says that once he hears the extent of her media resources, he won't have the balls to do it. She says if we stick it out, we will rid ourselves of the shackles of sexism."

"What has she been doing all week, lecturing on the proper rhetoric for confrontation?" I said, noticeably less calmly than before. "Did you all have vocabulary quizzes every evening after supper? Did she take off for spelling?"

Carolyn touched my elbow. "Arly, I hope you aren't feeling pressure from the paternalistic powers that control the town. We're doing this for the betterment

of all the women in Maggody, and we'd like to think
you'll support us. We're not the enemy. I'd hate to see
you aligned with them, and therefore, against us."

"And your own mother," someone said under her
breath.

"I am not against you. I agree that Johnna Mae
deserves to get her old job back and receive some
compensation for maternity leave. The problem is that
you've breezed into town and stirred up a veritable
hornet's nest, and these women are likely to be the
ones who ultimately get stung. You've created a lot of
animosity between husbands and wives, employers and
employees, and mothers and daughters. Once this mess
is resolved, you're going to breeze away, leaving these
women to deal with the residual problems."

It was a stirring speech, I thought, but Carolyn
merely gave me a supercilious smile and went to the
adjoining table to congratulate Elsie McMay on the
success of the damn green bean casserole.

I glowered at Ruby Bee, who was still prodding the
goop with her fork. "Did we bring our sleeping bags?"

"And our cots," she replied serenely.

I was about to inquire about pajamas and toothbrushes
when Earl Buchanon burst out of the group across the
street and stalked to the line in the middle of the
highway. "What about my supper?" he yelled.

Eilene Buchanon put down her napkin and stood
up. "You can cook it yourself, or you can starve. It
makes no matter to me."

"Listen up, woman, and listen up good. You're
making a fool of yourself, you and your friends. You
all are acting like those yellow-bellied Communist
hippies did during the Vietnam war. I want you to git

over here right this minute, unless you want me to come over there and git you!"

Conversation concerning water chestnuts and double-fudgecake brownies stopped abruptly. All of the women looked at Eilene and then at Earl, as did the deputies, Oliver and Bernswallow, who were still by the door of the bank, and the chief of police, who was praying for a semi to come barreling around the curve at eighty miles an hour.

Millicent McIlhaney's husband joined Earl on the broken yellow line. "You, too, Millicent," he called. "You and Darla Jean stop this foolishness and git over here. If you know what's good for you, you'll have my supper on the table damn quick."

Brother Verber strutted forward. Rocking on the balls of his feet, he folded his hands over his belly and said, "We all can see this is the work of the devil, particularly if you're intending to get naked and slaughter farm animals and rub their blood on your bodies and dance. Your very souls are in peril of eternal fire. Yes, I said in peril of eternal fire that'll lick at your feet and singe your skin until you cry for mercy. I am sorry to have to tell you that the Bible says there won't be any mercy. If at this very moment one of you rips off your clothes, I can pray for you but I can't be responsible for your soul."

"Old fart," Johnna Mae muttered.

Ruby Bee wrinkled her nose at Estelle. "Why on earth would we want to get naked and rub blood on ourselves? I don't recollect hearing anyone suggest that."

"I think I'd remember," Estelle said, equally bewildered. Both of them looked at Dahlia, but she was preoccupied with a molded gelatin salad (lemon Jell-O, pecan pieces, and coconut).

A fourth figure found courage to come forward, although he almost tripped on a particularly sly bit of gravel. "Dahlia," he yelled, "I want you to give up this tomfoolery. We aren't married like these other folks, but we've been keeping company for a long time and I'd like to think you're bespoken for."

"Why, Dahlia," Estelle said, "I hadn't heard that, but I'm thrilled to pieces for you. When are you two planning to get hitched?"

Dahlia's cheeks puffed out and her lower lip protruded. "You can think whatever you like, Kevin Fitzgerald Buchanon," she yelled, "but I am not bespoken for and you got no call to say such a thing, especially in the middle of the road and in front of everybody."

"And I ain't going home," Eilene Buchanon said loudly.

"Neither am I," Millicent said. Other protesters echoed the phrase, and Johnna Mae snuck in another "old fart," this time loudly enough to elicit a harrumph from the old fart himself.

Ruby Bee got up and went to the edge of the road. She placed her fists on her hips and produced the expression that had cut short many a potential barroom brawl. "Now it's your turn to listen and listen up good, Earl Buchanon, and the rest of you. I happen to be a widow, so I don't have to take orders from some chauvinist anymore, or scurry around trying to get supper on the table exactly at five o'clock or stay up till midnight ironing overalls or get up at six every blasted morning to make biscuits from scratch. But I did it for right at twenty years, because I was brought up to think that was the way married life was, that it didn't matter one hoot if I wanted to sleep late or go to a matinee at the picture show in Starley City. Well, no one should have to do those things unless she wants to, and none of us wants to anymore. Not Eilene or Millicent or Elsie or Dahlia, if and when she gets hitched, or any of us here in the parking lot."

She was working up to a Verberish pitch when a car came around the curve, braked momentarily, and stopped at the edge of the lot. Truda Oliver got out and came over to the table where I was still looming. "Johnna Mae, I have thought about how the bank treated you after you took that time off to have a baby, and I have decided that you deserve better from the institution you have been loyal to all these years." She fluttered a hand at her husband, who was clinging to Bernswallow like a baby possum hanging on to its mama. "Sherman, I am going to stay here and support this protest until you agree to undo all the wrong things done to this woman. As for your supper, it's high time you figured out how to work the can opener."

Carolyn rose to her feet and began to applaud in a slow, measured rhythm. One by one, her followers stood up and joined in until each clap seemed louder than a firecracker. Sherman Oliver stared uncomprehendingly at his wife, who had a hand on Johnna Mae's shoulder and a smile that surpassed simple martyrdom by a long shot. The noise drove those on the yellow line back to the far side of the road, where they muttered to each other and shuffled their feet in the gravel.

The noise also drove Oliver and Bernswallow back into the bank. The deputies merely drove away, and after a moment of thought I went back to the police car and did the same. I may have been grinning just a tad, but it didn't matter because nobody could see me. Cherry lime ade time.

Staci Ellen Quittle put down her paperback novel and picked up the telephone receiver. "Women Aligned Against Chauvinism in the Office office," she said, utilizing her tongue to ease the wad of gum to the other side of her back molars, out of the way. After listening for a moment, she added, "No, I'm afraid she's out of the office this week. She's on a case in some place upstate named Maggody and doesn't know when she'll be back. Do you want me to take a message?"

Sighing at the affirmative response, she found a pencil and a discarded envelope. It turned out not to be the kind of message that she took on a regular basis. Most of the words contained exactly four letters, luckily for her, since her spelling wasn't all that good. Although Staci Ellen would never dare use those words herself, having been raised to have a healthy respect for the taste of soap, she was familiar with them because her boyfriend made her go watch him bowl every Thursday night, Thursday being league night, and the language got pretty rough after the boys downed a few beers. Once she'd tried to beg off with the excuse she had to wash her hair, but he'd come by the house and almost literally dragged her out to his car anyway. And that was the night his team rolled against the body shop on Pipkin Avenue, and all the girlfriends knew from experience that the body shop (not to mention their slutty girlfriends) used the worst language of anyone. Once Wanda said that in her opinion it was gutter talk, and Staci Ellen laughed so darn hard a tear ran down her leg and she had to wash out her panties in the ladies' locker room and dry them under the machine that blew hot air.

"I'll be sure and tell Ms. McCoy-Grunders when she checks in," Staci Ellen said, "and thank you for calling the Women Aligned Against Chauvinism in the Office office." She hung up and reached for her book. A thought intruded. If she couldn't say out loud all those four-letter words, how was she supposed to relay the message from the potty-mouthed man in Las Vegas? She wondered if she could sweet-talk her boyfriend into hanging around the office until Ms. Hotshot With a Hyphen called, but decided it wouldn't work because Bruno all the time kept harping on how he didn't even like the idea of her working for a woman lesbian and that was why he never picked her up after work and she always had to take the bus and sometimes didn't get home until after dark, which was on the unsettling side because of the neighborhood and all the high school dropouts in tight jeans who stared at her and used some of those four-letter words right out in public.

She freed the gum and chewed it while she thought some more. A few ideas came to mind, including the straightforward approach of just wadding up the envelope and throwing it in the trash can. Or closing the office early, and if caught, saying she'd been overwhelmed by PMS—but that wouldn't work because she'd used it last week and Ms. Hotshot With a Hyphen had sympathized, that being the politically correct posture at WAACO, but at the same time most likely had jotted the day and time in her notebook just so she'd know if Staci Ellen tried it again one teeny tiny minute too soon.

At last Staci Ellen decided she could spell out each word over the phone. That way her vocal virtue wouldn't be compromised and she could still avoid being accused for the ten thousandth time of losing a message, which she found both an exaggeration and an insult. She picked up the book and found the scene where the count with the slate gray eyes and the dueling scar on his cheek was holding the raven-haired, penniless governess (who was in truth a wealthy heiress but wouldn't find out right until the next to last page) against her will and kissing her so hard it bruised her lips even though secretly she found herself strangely drawn to him and therefore unable to keep her breasts from heaving against his chest and herself from feeling a wave of heat in her loins that threatened to consume her.

It was Staci Ellen's favorite scene, especially after she'd looked up the word *loins* in the Women Aligned Against Chauvinism in the Office office dictionary. But not when Ms. Hotshot With a Hyphen was there. Staci Ellen Quittle sure as heck wasn't born yesterday, as she was fond of telling herself and sometimes Bruno, assuming he let her get in one little word when all he ever wanted to talk about was handicaps and seven-ten splits and changing the color of his team's shirts or adding a picture of a skull and crossbones on the back.

A flicker of irritation crossed her face, and she glanced over the top of the book at the calendar. Thursday. Darn, darn, and double darn.

Once it was dark, I drove up the road to the bank to see if the protesters were burning dollar signs on the

lawn or doing anything else worthy of my professional
attention. There were at least a dozen pickup trucks
parked on the Assembly Hall side of the road, and
twice that many men leaning against the trucks, their
arms folded and their expressions mean. I presumed
they hoped to intimidate the protesters with their silent
vigil, but it wasn't having much effect on the occupants
of the lot, who were drinking out of plastic cups and
chattering to each other. A few lanterns had been
placed in strategic corners, and a foursome was actually
playing cards at one table. I couldn't tell if they were
playing canasta, bridge, poker, or go fish. In that
Dahlia was one of them, I figured it was the least
demanding of that list.

Eilene was shooting quick looks across the road,
however, and so were several others. Off to one side
of the lot, Truda Oliver was fluttering her hands and
talking intently to Johnna Mae. Ruby Bee, Estelle,
and Elsie McMay were engaged in battle with a pile of
army surplus cots, no doubt debating the wisdom of
defying tradition (and the Baptist Women's League
recipe pamphlet, *Blessed Be Thy Suppers*) by the
inclusion of water chestnuts. Carolyn McCoy-Grunders
was bouncing around to supervise the activities.

They were extremely well organized. It was obvious
that Carolyn had led more than one protest in the
past. I considered stopping to tuck everyone in and
wish them all sweet dreams but increased my speed
and headed for Farberville to see if a certain amiable
state trooper might be willing to offer me a glass of
wine in exchange for an incredibly clever recitation of
Maggodian current events. Any port in a storm,
although personally I prefer burgundy. Hee, hee.

*   *   *

Brandon Bernswallow grimaced as he remembered his father's scathing comments, all of which were totally unfair. It wasn't as if Brandon could have done anything to save the bank from the unfavorable publicity—and there had been a shitload of it on the six o'clock news. A long scene of the protesters coming down the middle of the highway, for starters, and then the interviews with the feminist bitch (who, no matter how wonderful she thought she was, still had to squat to pee, by damn), the Nookim broad, himself, dopey Oliver, and even the idiotic windbag of a preacher from across the street. Which was where Brandon was in the process of parking his car. He'd driven into Maggody on the county road from Hasty and cut off his lights before coasting in behind the Assembly Hall. His presence at this hour needed to remain a secret, and a hefty percentage of the locals were on one side of the road or the other. There was a light on in the mobile home back there, but the curtains were closed and he didn't see any shadows moving inside.

The Emporium was dark. Brandon cut across the area behind it, alarming the rats chewing holes in the plastic garbage bags, and continued through the weeds until he was far enough away from the bank to risk a brisk dash across the road. He then repeated the manuever to come up behind the bank, where the damn fool women couldn't see him enter through the back door. As if they'd stop gabbing and stuffing their faces long enough to notice anything, including a nuclear explosion, he thought as he flashed an unseen yet nevertheless obscene gesture at them.

He unlocked the door and slipped inside, reminding

himself not to lock it behind him; he was expecting company and it would be downright inhospitable and even insulting to his guest, who then might vanish. The back room was darker than the inside of a cow. He headed for his office, his hands out in front of him to avoid any injury to his admittedly attractive face. Had the sorority girls been hot to kiss his silky lips or what, he thought with a smirk. He had laid more dames than any of the guys at the frat house, and been ribbed about it day and night. College had been the best years of his life, what with the beer busts and girls' busts and that crazy luau party when he'd gotten into the purple passion about noon and was drunker than a skunk by the time he picked up his date at the Delta Omega house (better known to his brothers as the doghouse, but that was an in-house joke). He must have had a gallon of Shanson's wicked brew that afternoon. Not that that'd impaired his renowned prowess, of course. Why, he'd made Luci Hunnicut lie across the front seat and give him a blow job while he drove back to the house, only going up on the curb one time. Some party that'd been. Purple puke everywhere.

"Stop or I'll be obliged to shoot you," croaked a voice from the darkness.

Brandon stopped and he did it damn fast. His heart was thudding so loudly he could hear it, and a sour taste flooded his mouth. His fingers were frozen in the dark. He managed to get his raised foot down to the floor and to bring his arms to his sides. "Who's there?" he managed. It came out in a gurgle, but it was the best he could do.

"Don't make me have to kill you. I have this big, enormous gun aimed right at you."

Brandon frantically tried to recall if there was anything in the back room he could use for a weapon. The metal wastebasket didn't seem real lethal, nor did the dusty ledgers piled in a corner. "Stop or I'll debit your account" wasn't going to intimidate the prowler. He sucked in a breath and tried for a more authoritative tone. "I am the branch manager, buddy, and I have every right to be here. I also have a rifle and I've killed enough ducks and squirrels to feed your favorite African nation."

"Oh, yeah? Let's see some identification."

"You can't see anything, hairball. It's pitch black in here, or haven't you noticed?" Brandon said, feeling brave enough to risk taking the offense, it being, as Coach Grebes used to say in the locker room during halftime, the best defense. The remark had always puzzled Brandon, but he'd loyally memorized it just the same.

"I know as well as you do that it's dark in here," the voice retorted, clearly offended. "But how am I supposed to know if you're really Mr. Bernswallow or if you're a bank robber who's pretending to be Mr. Bernswallow to trick me? What if I turn on a light and you shoot me with your rifle?"

Brandon recognized the voice now, but perversely decided to see how far he could push the security guard, who had cotton for brains and not enough of that to make a tampon for a mouse. "Yeah, you'd feel pretty dumb if I shot you between the eyes, which is where I always shoot squirrels and rabbits and rats out at the town dump. Ka-boom!"

"Uh, how about we both put down our weapons?"

"Sounds like a good idea to me—but wait a minute.

If I'm a bank robber lying about being this Bernswallow guy, how can you be sure I won't lie when I say I put my rifle down?"

There was a long silence while the security guard chewed on that one. "Well," he said at last, "mebbe after you say you put your rifle down, you also say 'Cross my heart and hope to die, stick a needle in my eye'?"

"Yeah, that ought to do it." Smirking so hard it almost hurt, Brandon quickly recited that which was requested of him, even kicking the metal wastebasket for sound effects. Then he said, "Turn on the light, Kevin, presuming you know how the switch works. Unlike yourself, I've got more important things to do than to stand around in the dark."

Kevin turned on the light with a hand trembling worse than a palsied widow woman. His eyes were round, and his mouth was dangling open. "Gee, Mr. Bernswallow, I didn't know it was you or I wouldn't have acted like I was a-goin' to shoot you like you was a bank robber. I'm real sorry."

"You sure are." Brandon brushed past him and went into the dark front room. Through a side window he glowered at the damn bitches out in the lot, then closed the blinds and ordered Kevin Buchanon to go away.

"But I'm supposed to guard the bank, Mr. Bernswallow. You know that, don't you? After all, when you hired me to clean the toilets and mop the floors, you said I was supposed to hang around the rest of the night in case some bank robber showed up and broke down the door to steal—"

"Go away, damn it. I have an important piece of

business to conduct, and I don't want you slobbering over my shoulder when I do it."

"I wasn't going to slobber over your shoulder, Mr. Bernswallow. I was going to sit on a folding metal chair by the back door the way I always do. It's so hard on my buttocks that I can't fall asleep, even if I wanted to."

"Just get your buttocks out of here," Brandon said through clenched teeth. "You can come back in an hour and sit on your damn folding chair until your buttocks atrophy, for all I care."

Kevin smiled, exposing uneven teeth and a hunk of spinach from supper (which had been consumed at the truck stop outside of Starley City, 'cause his pa sure as hell wasn't going to fix it). "Speaking of trophies, I was admiring that big one you got in your office. You know the one, don't you? It's the gold cup what has handles on either side and that real nice plaque on it. How'd you win it, Mr. Bernswallow?"

"It's a loving cup from my fraternity brothers. That's all I'm going to say about it. If you value your job, and perhaps your life, you will take your ass elsewhere for the next hour."

Brandon waited until Kevin stumbled to the back door, then went into his office and sat down behind his desk. The trophy Kevin admired was indeed a large one, worthy of anyone's admiration. Brandon had told his parents it was for fraternity spirit, which was a hoot, since he'd been known to drink spirits from it. If his parents had learned the truth, they'd have dragged him to the damn doctor's office to be tested for every known sexually transmitted disease in the western hemisphere.

Snickering under his breath, Brandon took out the page he'd worked on earlier and lovingly studied his calculations. A lump sum, payable immediately, or a monthly payment, amortized at eleven and a half percent, adjustments to be made semiannually on the basis of the consumer price index.

It was the funniest damn blackmail demand he'd ever seen, and Brandon was disappointed when his visitor, who arrived promptly, failed to see the irony of it. He was in the midst of saying as much when the trophy came down on the back of his head.

Brother Verber was a mite disappointed himself, but only because the book he'd bought at a back-alley used book store in Farberville had no decent illustrations. Oh, it went on and on about rituals and incarnations of Satan and all your basic horrible devils and demons. There were diagrams of pentexes and hex symbols. There was a long, tedious chapter on the history of witchcraft in the medieval period, the only interesting part being the descriptions of witches burned at the stake or dunked in water until they admitted they was witches, at which time it was wienie roast time in the town square. Those ol' boys played rough.

But what he hoped for was a clear, concise recitation of how witches got naked and smeared sacrificial blood on their breasts and danced around until they collapsed in a sexual frenzy. Brother Verber needed to know all the details just in case the women across the street started doing it and he was called over to try to save them. He wasn't going to be able to save them if he didn't have an idea of what they were doing. And he surely needed to know what all they did once they were in this sexual frenzy, and if they had orgies with demons or waited in line to be serviced by a high priest in a goat mask. A drawing, or better yet an actual photograph of this wickedness, would be invaluable.

Brother Verber realized the back of his pajamas were getting sticky from sweat. The mobile home sat around all day building heat and was reluctant to do much releasing until way late. He opened a window and returned to the couch to study his book. Why, he wasn't at all sure he'd recognize a sexual frenzy if he saw one, much less some priest fellow with a mask and, one would hypothesize, an organ befitting his station and therefore alarming to the hussies waiting for it. Begging for it.

He mopped his face and took a swallow of iced tea. The heat was making it awful hard to concentrate on the material at hand. But he owed it to his flock, and those women across the street in the bank lot were likely to rip off their clothes any time now. Brother Verber intended to be ready when the time came.

Kevin Buchanon thought for a minute that he smelled smoke. He sniffed long and hard but decided he was imagining things and flipped to the next page in the catalogue. Those fellows at Pro Bass came up with the darnedest things, Kevin told himself, totally awed by the lures that duplicated the movement of live fish and came in five colors, including chartreuse and white pearl.

While he tried to think of a chartreuse-colored fish, he caught another whiff of smoke. Mebbe Mr. Bernswallow's visitor was smoking a cigarette, or even Mr.

Bernswallow himself, 'cause he was in a downright weird mood and liable to do weird things—like suggesting Kevin abandon his post and leave the bank unguarded just when all that confusion was going on in the parking lot.

Why, Kevin wouldn't do anything irresponsible like that. He was obligated to guard the bank, which he was doing by staying in the bathroom for an hour with the catalogue. It wasn't any overwhelming hardship, for sure, and fit right into his regular schedule. His ma had told him time and again that it was important to be regular. Kevin had taken that bit of wisdom to heart.

7

Earl Buchanon was the first to notice the strange glow coming from inside the bank. It was a reddish color, kinda like what there'd been the night he and some of the fellows went to the topless bar outside Farberville, and lucky they did because a week later it was locked up tighter than a seed tick on a groundhog's ass and liable to stay that way till kingdom come or the sheriff got run out of the county, whichever came first.

But that glow had come from the colored lights on the edge of the stage. Earl couldn't for the life of him figure out why they'd put those lights inside the bank. It wasn't like anybody'd guzzle two-dollar-and-fifty-cent bourbon and Cokes to watch Miss Una peel off her cardigan or to see Oliver's bony knees when he paraded around in those baggy plaid shorts. Earl didn't even want to think about that.

None of the women were taking any notice, he thought with a scowl. They were all too busy visiting like it was before prayer meeting on Wednesday night. Like the damn missionary society having one of their godawful tea parties. Like the veteran's auxiliary at their annual rummage sale.

Earl nudged Jeremiah McIlhaney, who was brooding

worse than a hen on a dozen goose eggs, and said, " 'Member when we went to that topless bar over near Farberville?"

"I seem to recollect something about it."

"And they had those lights that made the women look all rosy?"

"Yeah, they were rosy, all right. Just like cherry tomatoes waiting to be pinched." Jeremiah hitched up his crotch and smiled, but just for a second before resuming his scowl. "What's gotten into those women? The next thing we know, they'll be chewing tobacco and demanding urinals in their public bathrooms. Mark my words, Earl, some woman'll up and run for President one of these days. Can you imagine some fool woman boo-hooing to the damn Communists instead of nuking the holy shit out of the them?"

Earl glanced back across the street at the front window of the bank, just to make sure he hadn't been seeing things. "But at that topless joint they had spotlights with colors in them, right?"

"I wasn't looking at the damn fool lights," Jeremiah said, still staring across the road like he hoped Millicent would feel his eyes blazing into her and git herself home where she belonged, which was actually what he was doing, albeit without any measurable success thus far.

"Well, take a look over yonder at the bank window. It's got that same funny glow."

Grumbling, Jeremiah did as ordered, and about swallowed his chew. "Holy shit, Earl! That's not some topless-bar stage light, fer Chrissake! The damn bank's on fire!"

That caught everybody's attention and sent everybody

storming across the road like a pack of wild dogs. The women all spun around, no doubt thinking the boxer (shorts) rebellion was beginning, but the yells and jabbing fingers finally convinced them to look over their shoulders in time to see a lick of fire in the lobby.

All of them knew what sort of thing to shout—"Fire! Fire!" being real popular—but then they mostly stumbled into everybody else in the confusion. Earl tripped on the leg of one of the card tables and went face down in the gravel. The mason jar with the marigolds barely missed Elsie McMay, who was clutching her bosom and doing her best not to hyperventilate. Ruby Bee told one of the hippie women to run over to the Emporium and call the volunteer fire department in Emmet, but she was having trouble catching her breath too. Joyce Lambertino was a hairsbreadth away from hysteria. Estelle was staggering around like a buck-eyed calf, demanding that someone do something afore the whole durn town went up in flames like the great Chicago fire.

The only motionless person was Dahlia O'Neill, who could have passed for one of those marble statues in a museum, or maybe two or three of them. Her eyelids were going pretty fast, and her mouth was getting rounder by the second as certain things sunk in. At last she found her voice and screeched, "Kevin! Kevin's in there! You got to do something!"

Eilene Buchanon grabbed Earl's collar and yanked him up. "She's right! Kevin's the security guard. What if he's in there? You got to save him, Earl! You got to save Kevin!"

"Kevvvin!" Dahlia wailed, louder than a freight train

in a tunnel. "Kevvvin!" She thudded toward the front of the bank, paying no mind to the ground quaking under her feet or the way she knocked Truda Oliver into the side of the station wagon. "Kevvvin, I'm a-comin' to save you!"

The lobby was now filled with flames, and smoke began to roil into the parking lot. Right square over the front entrance a finger of fire shot up, and seconds later a good half of the roof was burning to beat the band. Ruby Bee gaped, then came to her senses and dashed after Dahlia, who by now had made it to the sidewalk in front of the door.

"You can't go in there," she panted, hanging on for dear life to Dahlia's massive arm.

"I got to save Kevvvin."

"You can't go in there. You're liable to catch yourself on fire. Besides, Kevin probably went out the back door as soon as he saw the fire. He wouldn't stay inside to act like some fool hero, would he?" Ruby Bee immediately regretted the question, meant to be rhetorical. Kevin Buchanon had done some of the county's all-time foolish things. If they gave ribbons at the county fair for out-and-out foolishness, Kevin would have a whole clothesline of blue ones. She dragged Dahlia back a few steps. "In any case, you can't go in there. Look, the front's burning like a fire in a cotton gin."

Carolyn skittered up to them. "Did someone call the fire department?"

Ruby Bee dug her fingers into Dahlia's flesh, just in case the girl tried to do something from Kevin's repertory, and said, "I sent one of the hippie women to the Emporium. Emmet's no more than six miles

away, and they ought to show up as soon as everybody
yanks on his britches and boots.''

"At least there's no one in there," Carolyn said.

"Kevvvin! I got to save Kevvvin!" Dahlia howled,
getting all worked up again. She tried to pull her arm
free, but Ruby Bee wasn't having any of that.

"Is someone in there?" Carolyn gasped.

Before Ruby Bee could answer, a minor explosion
sent a blast of heat into their faces. They stumbled
back, swatting at embers that stung like a cloud of
mosquitoes. "Nobody's in there," Ruby Bee said as
she brushed frantically at her good navy blue skirt.

By this time everybody had stopped squawking and
was gathered at one side of the parking lot. The building
was a goner; that much everybody agreed on. Whether
Kevin Buchanon was in there or not was open to
differing opinions. Earl said Kevin valued his hide
enough to get out, but Eilene wasn't convinced because
she was his ma and knew him better than anybody.
Millicent McIlhaney said in a real firm voice that she
didn't think for one second that he was in there. Darla
Jean McIlhaney, who'd been in high school with Kevin,
felt obliged to say she doubted Kevin had a quarter of
the sense God gave a goose and sure as hell could be
in there, slinging cups of water at the fire or spitting
on it. Jeremiah McIlhaney dragged her to one side to
tell her to mind her language if she didn't want to get
whumped upside the head. Darla Jean started crying,
which sent Millicent over to tear into Jeremiah for
acting like a bully when Darla Jean was just trying to
be helpful.

The Emmet fire truck pulled into the lot before the
McIlhaney family came to blows, although a lot of

time was wasted due to the station wagon being in the way, not to mention the cots and card tables. It didn't help when the volunteer firemen came roaring up in their trucks and tried to find places to park without blocking the highway more than they had to. Eventually things got organized and the firemen started ordering everybody back and pulling out hoses. In order to make up for her thoughtless remark, Darla Jean went up to Eilene and offered to search the parking lot behind the bank to see if Kevin might have come out that way and passed out in the ditch, because smoke inhalation could kill you jest as fast as fire.

Eilene started bawling. Earl was about to pat her on the back when Elsie McMay flew into him for making poor Eilene cry. The dark-haired hippie woman said loudly to no one in particular that men in Maggody were nothing but ignorant, pinheaded slime balls, and that didn't please Raz or Perkins or Jeremiah or any of the others who'd happened to overhear the comment.

After a few minutes of dialogue, the parking lot was as hot as the interior of the bank, although at a less tangible level. Over toward the sidewalk Dahlia was wailing, Ruby Bee was clucking, and Carolyn was wringing her hands and praying there wasn't any way she could be held liable if the village idiot had opted to broil himself inside the bank.

Mrs. Jim Bob sat on the edge of the sofa, a cup and saucer balanced on her knees. Her best tea service, the one with the lavender rosebuds, which she'd inherited from her great-aunt, was on a tray on a nearby table, along with an extra tea bag and a little plate of lemon slices. "You must do your Christian duty, Jim Bob," she said, well into the second hour of the lecture. "Arly Hanks has closed her eyes to the wickedness going on right here in Maggody, and you have an obligation to just go down there and tell her she's fired. Tell her we don't need that kind of police protection. Tell her we need a chief of police who believes in traditional values and patriotism and motherhood. I have never been comfortable with her as chief, because it's not a fitting job for a woman in the first place. She orders people around with an arrogance that defiles the laws of God. She just needs to get herself married and settled down to raise a family. Then she'd understand her true purpose in life."

Jim Bob was sprawled in the recliner, a half empty beer can balanced on his gut. The only thing on the table next to him was a dog-eared *TV Guide*. He surreptitiously checked his watch. "I don't know if I'm empowered to up and fire her out of the blue," he said. "It may say somewhere in the town bylaws that I have to call a special meeting or something like that." He held up a hand before she could leap back in. "I'm not saying I won't get together with the council and discuss Arly's future. In fact, I might just drive over to Larry Joe Lambertino's and see what-all he thinks. Roy's in town, although I heard someone at the launderette say old Harry Harbin's off visiting his daughter in Miami Beach. Ho's still hoping for parole, and Jesse's back in the home, gumming oatmeal and talking to hisself. It's gonna be right hard to get a quorum."

"I am not at all interested in your quorum," Mrs. Jim Bob said with a sniff. "I am concerned with those scandalous women what think they can do this dreadful thing across the street from the Voice of the Almighty Lord Assembly Hall. Why, they might start screaming their filthy lies in the middle of Sunday morning services. Brother Verber is scared out of his wits they're practicing witchcraft right where all the impressionable youth can watch them.''

Jim Bob gave her a hooded look. "I heard how he's all worried they're going to get naked and smear blood on their bodies. I heard he's real hot to trot over at the drop of a girdle."

There was a semipregnant pause. Mrs. Jim Bob selected a crescent of lemon and dropped it in her tea while wondering what-all he had heard. At last she clattered her spoon in the teacup and banged it down on the tray. "Well, of course he's worried," she snapped. "Wouldn't you be if you were a minister of the Lord and women right out of your own congregation engaged in that sort of evilness?"

"I'd be over there faster than a bat outta hell."

"I do not permit profanity in this house."

Jim Bob chugged his beer, struggling with the lever until the chair was upright, and did his best to suppress a belch (bodily functions ranking up there with profanity in terms of popularity in the Buchanon household). "Tell you what, I'll swing by Larry Joe's and discuss this Arly situation with him. That way we can present our conclusion to the council at the next meeting, if we can't get everybody together before then. Don't wait up for me; I may be late and I wouldn't want you to be too tuckered out tomorrow to go to the county extension club meeting. I know how dearly you relish those meetings."

Mrs. Jim Bob looked a little suspicious, but she didn't say anything, and Jim Bob stepped lively out to the garage. He didn't feel safe until he was driving down Finger Lane, and only then did he scrabble under the seat to find the half pint of bourbon he kept for emergencies. It did a lot to perk up his spirits, and he was lost in moist thoughts of cute little Cherri Lucinda as he turned onto the highway.

And saw the fire.

"Damn to hell," he muttered. Cherri Lucinda was always ticked off when he was late.

Brother Verber jerked his eyes open. It was no time for dozing, he told himself with a snort. He needed to focus all his mental and moral energy on how he was going to handle the womenfolk if and when they commenced their depravities. At the first hint of wicked ritual in the making, he would snatch up the Good Book—his best defense against any personifications of Satan—and march right over to them. They'd be prancing around a bonfire, he imagined, with blood dripping off their exposed bosoms and streaming down their bellies like dark red rivers. Sinful, curling, twining, ruby-colored rivers that flowed straight to eternal damnation, among other destinations.

Unless he could save them. With prayer—that went without saying. Yessirree, a hefty dose of fire and brimstone. With a stirring sermon about their evil, pagan, naked ways that were sending them on the express elevator to hell. Why, they'd all just hang their heads and beg for him to cleanse their flesh of sacrificial blood.

It occurred to Brother Verber that he might need

another weapon in his battle against the devil: a towel, so he could wipe away that disgusting blood and restore them to piety and remorse. He went over to the kitchenette and found a dish towel. As he went to put it by the door, he caught himself mopping his forehead with it. Mercy, it was hot. He opened the door to let in what breeze the good Lord might provide his humblest of servants.

The good Lord seemed to have been occupied elsewhere, but what Brother Verber saw more than made up for the slight. Beyond the corner of the Assembly Hall was the flickering glow of a fire. A bonfire. The heathen ritual had begun, and right while he was priming himself to save their souls and cleanse their bodies. He was so excited he nearly fell over the coffee table in his rush to his bedroom. It wouldn't do to berate the naked, frenzied women while wearing pajamas dotted with beribboned teddy bears. He'd laid out his clothes earlier in hopes the good Lord would set off the heavenly smoke alarm and send him into battle. He hopped around on one foot and then on the other to get his trousers on, silently mouthing his opening accusations and subsequent warnings of the black, gaping abyss in front of them that led to you know where.

Panting something fierce, he hurried into the living room, snatched up the Bible and the dish towel, and stumbled down the steps of the trailer. Surely he would be there in time. The good Lord wouldn't play any practical jokes on his faithful servant, who once a month sent part of the Sunday morning collection to little orphans in Africa or some place like that. Surely the good Lord was smiling down real kindly on someone with the courage to meet the devil worshippers and fight for their souls.

Once around the corner of the building, Brother Verber stopped for a second to compose himself, then bravely lifted his eyes to meet the wickedness square on. His face crumpled like a wadded-up tissue as he realized that the bank was on fire and all the women were standing around fully clothed.

He gazed up at the smoky sky. "I don't reckon I'll be sending five dollars to the orphans anytime soon," he said through clenched teeth.

To the person hunkered down behind the forsythia, it sounded about as peculiar as it gets.

Staci Ellen Quittle watched Bruno fail to pick up the one-three-ten split. She kept her eyes glued right on him, because he always wanted to discuss every last ball he rolled when they went to the bar afterward. Staci Ellen's parents didn't know she went to the bar, of course, in that she told them every Thursday that she and Bruno would go to the diner for cheeseburgers and Cokes after the match. She didn't like lying to her parents, but she didn't see that she had much choice, since she knew for a fact that Bruno'd slap her around and call her a prude if she didn't go and her pa'd slap her around and call her a slut if he found out she did go. And it wasn't like she drank beer, for pity's sake. Bruno always ordered her a Dr Pepper and didn't even ask her if she might prefer something else. And made her pay him back when they got in the car, saying it was a sissy drink, not worth his hard-earned cash.

Jeepers, Staci Ellen told herself as Bruno stalked

back to the plastic bench and glowered at her like she'd snuck down to the end of the alley and whispered something to the pins so they wouldn't fall, it really wasn't fair the way men kept telling her what to do and not do, especially when she was nineteen years old and a high school graduate and had a full-time job at the Women Aligned Against Chauvinism in the Office office and gave three quarters of her pay to her parents for room and board, leaving her with so little that she had to scrimp just to buy panty hose and shampoo and that sicky-sweet cologne that Bruno made her wear.

She nudged Wanda, who was droopy-eyed and yawning but nevertheless holding an equally intent vigil. "Does Vic tell you what kind of cologne you got to wear on dates?"

"Sure."

"Did he ever give you a bottle of it?"

"Why would he do that?"

"I was just wondering," Staci Ellen said with a small sigh.

As I drove into town, I was smiling at one of the jokes the amiable state trooper in Farberville had told me in exchange for my riotous account of the protesters et al. The joke was no more than midway on the knock-knock scale of humor, but my standards had plummeted at the state line a couple of years back. The first thing I noticed was that the pickup trucks were no longer in front of the Assembly Hall. This was good. The second thing I noticed was that Estelle's station wagon was no longer at the front of the branch parking lot. Very good. I hit three when I noticed that the protesters were not snoozing on their army cots nor playing canasta by lantern light, due to the unmissable fact that the lot was uninhabited by cot, station wagon, card table, and protester. Perfect.

"Thank God," I murmured, working up to a grin. The grin turned into a grimace when I caught sight of the bank building. The remains of the bank building, to be more precise. I slammed on the brakes, put the car in reverse, squealed backward thirty or so feet, and pulled into the lot. My headlights illuminated the skeletal frame that had once housed money and ledgers and plastic plants and lines of impatient customers, all those things that make a banker's world go round and round.

Most of the brick walls were standing. The roof had fallen in, however, and all the plate glass lay in glittery pieces. With the perspicacity and agility of a zombie, I got out of the car and went over to the sidewalk for a better view. The air was acrid enough to sting my eyes and lungs, and smoke still drifted from the unrecognizable remains of furniture. Miss Una's teller window was silhouetted against a blackened (Cajun?) wall. A plant had been transformed into a vile-smelling puddle of toxic slime. Everything smoldered.

I cocked my head and studied the scene, then cocked my head the other way and studied the scene, then got on an even keel and studied the scene, but I couldn't quite assimilate that to which I was devoting all this studiousness. I'd been on my innocent jaunt for only a few hours. In my absence all hell must have broken loose. Grinding my heel into a charred lump of something, I went back to the police car and sat on the hood.

When that failed to evoke any startling insights, I got in the car and draped my arms across the top of the steering wheel. It occurred to me that a run-down battery was not likely to provide additional enlightenment, so I started the car and drove down the road to that renowned mecca of insight and enlightenment, gossip running a close third.

The lights were on inside Ruby Bee's, and Estelle's wagon and the subcompact were parked out front. I hurried inside and discovered the embodiment of enlightenment, etc., on a barstool next to Estelle. Carolyn McCoy-Grunders was slumped in a booth, a glass of water and a large bottle of aspirin in front of her.

"About time you showed your face," Ruby Bee said. "I find it hard to believe you'd waltz out of town without bothering to tell your own mother where you were going."

"Did I miss my curfew?" I said, matching her tone with practiced ease.

"Did you see the branch bank?" Estelle said.

I nodded, making a face as I climbed up onto a stool. "I did indeed, and I was stunned. What on earth's been happening around here?"

I was given a lengthy account of the fire, with much interrupting and a few acerbic remarks about my absence in the middle of a catastrophy. Dereliction of duty was mentioned more than once, as was uninformed flesh and blood and gallavanting all over the county while Maggody burned. I was pretty well characterized as a modern-day distaff Nero when the two ran out of steam (some might use the term *hot air*).

Carolyn eased onto the stool next to me. "I still

can't believe it. One minute we were trying to make a few modifications in the guard duty roster, and the next minute we're watching the bank burn and coughing our heads off from the smoke."

"Did the fire chief determine the cause of the fire?" I asked.

"Someone said something about faulty wiring, and they jumped on that as the probable cause. You aren't implying the fire was set intentionally, are you?"

"You mean arson?" Ruby Bee squeaked.

"I don't think so," Estelle said, nibbling on her lip. "Right after the fire broke out, I happened to overhear Miss Una telling Lottie Estes that she'd been warning Sherman Oliver for years about the wiring in the storeroom. She said she smelled burning rubber every time she went back there to use the ladies' room—I mean the women's rest room."

"Then it started in the back?" I asked.

Ruby Bee snorted. "We were occupied with more important things than staring at an empty building. Elsie McMay took one look at the army cots and said she'd just remembered that her chiropractor didn't want her to sleep on army cots and she was going home to her orthopedic mattress that she bought last year when it was on sale at Montgomery Ward. Well, Estelle got her Stinger about half out and said she didn't believe a word of it. Truda had just volunteered to take Elsie's shift when the boys stampeded across the road, hollering that the bank was on fire."

"Is that right?" I asked Carolyn.

She propped her forehead on her hand. "That's a reasonably accurate description. Most of my organizational experience has been on college campuses.

I've never dealt with this mentality before, and I was more than a little bewildered by some of the arguments that were advanced. However, I had the clipboard and was standing in the middle of a group when one of the women's husbands, a particularly chauvinistic pig if I've ever seen one, bellowed something about the fire. It was approximately ten o'clock."

"She's talking about Earl Buchanon," Estelle confided in my nearest ear. "He stayed on the other side of the road, slouched against his truck and staring at Eilene to try to frazzle her. I'm proud to say she'd stayed as cool as springwater the whole time, or at least up until the time she liked to flip her wig worrying about Kevin being inside the bank."

I closed my eyes for a minute. "Shit, I'd forgotten about him. He wasn't in there, was he?"

"We don't know for sure," Estelle said in her best Vincent Price imitation.

Carolyn shook her head. "As soon as someone mentioned the possibility, I ran around back and opened that door to yell for him. I don't see how he could be trapped, with exits at both ends of the building and windows in each office. All he had to do is leave through any one of them when he first smelled smoke."

"Surely he would," Ruby Bee said, not sounding particularly convinced. "Poor Dahlia was plumb out of her mind with worry. She was all set to go in after him, but I convinced her the idea was preposterous. She did some howling and carrying on until the firemen got the fire out. Then she demanded they poke around for Kevin in the rubble, and one of them said that was the doddliest thing he'd ever heard of, that no one in his right mind could be so damn stupid as to get trapped in there. You won't believe your ears when I tell you what happened next."

"Dahlia donned asbestos boots and waddled in like Smokey the Bear?" I said.

Estelle poked me in the arm. "There's no call to make rude remarks about Dahlia's weight problem. It's because of a gland unbalance. One of them doesn't work quite right, and that's why the food just puffs up her fat cells like they were teeny tiny balloons. She showed me a magazine article that explains every bit of it."

"And we shouldn't judge women by their physical appearance," Carolyn added smoothly. "Personal worth must be judged by mind and performance, not by the sexist precept that all women should torture themselves by dieting in order to resemble inmates from a prison camp. That's an outdated and immoral myth pushed on us by Madison Avenue admen."

"Yeah," Estelle said sulkily. Ruby Bee sulked silently.

"I apologize," I said. "It must be the lateness of the hour and the shock of finding the bank reduced to the remains of a campfire. Please tell me what Dahlia did in the moment of crisis."

"She swooned," Ruby Bee said.

"All three hundred pounds of her?" I said thoughtlessly, thus winning all sorts of dirty looks and setting myself up for another lecture on my sexist leanings. I hurriedly said, "Was she hurt?"

"No, she was not," Ruby Bee said. "It happens that she swooned atop Joyce Lambertino, who was right behind her. It took four of the men to drag Dahlia off Joyce, and the little thing was out like a light for nigh on to ten minutes. One of the firemen said he'd done a course in paramedics and she most likely had a mild concussion."

"But no one has seen Kevin?" I said slowly. "Surely he would have been seen by someone, even with all the confusion of the fire truck and clearing the cots and tables from the lot. I'm not terribly fond of him, but I really don't want to think he was still in the bank."

Ruby Bee looked away for a moment. "His parents are half wild with worry, and poor Dahlia is probably bawling into her feather pillow right this minute. It's too horrible a notion to even contemplate."

"We'll find out for sure in the morning," I said, patting her shoulder. "There's not much point in sitting here fretting about it, and it's well past midnight. I think we'd better get some rest."

"I had an appointment at the branch tomorrow," Estelle said, dabbing the corner of her eye with a dishrag. "I don't suppose there's any use showing up for it."

"Bernswallow might be hanging around the lot," Ruby Bee said.

"But all the papers in the branch burned up. You know what I ought to do? I ought to get myself a lawyer and sue the bank for making libelous remarks about me."

Carolyn smiled wearily. "Slanderous remarks. Libel is written defamation. Slander is oral."

"That's what I said," Estelle said. "They remarked in a letter that I was delinquent on a loan I never took out. If that's not libel, I don't know what is!"

"Letters don't remark," Ruby Bee said under her breath, but not softly enough to get away with it.

Estelle flounced around to the cash register and yanked open a drawer to take out a letter. Flapping it so hard it cracked, she said, "I find this pretty darn remarkable, not to mention libelous. Implying I don't get the difference—*that's* slander."

I bade them good night and went out to my car. I sat for a while, feeling awful about Kevin Buchanon and even regretting having once told him I was going to jerk his head off and donate it to a local soccer team to use during practice. Hell, there aren't any soccer teams in Maggody—we play all-American games like football and baseball, not foreign sissy games.

I drove to my apartment above the antique store and did my best to follow my own advice and get some rest. Dahlia's pillow was not, as it turned out, the only sodden one in town.

8

At some point while watching the shadows on the ceiling, I had what amounted to an olfactory flashback. The charred, sodden rubble had created an unpleasant smell, but there had also been that acrid stench of a methane byproduct lingering in the air. Methane in and of itself is an easily recognizable odor, a product of the decomposition of organic matter in swamps and other fun places, or a result of the carbonization of coal. I'd dutifully memorized all that at the police academy, but not in a chemistry class. Not by a long shot. We'd been working on the procedures of arson investigation. Kerosene, for example, is a hydrocarbon that produces odor when burned.

When the alarm went off not too much later, I called my amiable state trooper. He listened to my story and agreed to alert the deputy state fire marshal, who worked out of the same office. Before I'd finished fooling with my hair he called back to say they'd be there in an hour.

I stuck in a last bobby pin and went in search of sustenance. Ruby Bee's was still closed, most likely out of respect for the Earl Buchanon family, so I settled for coffee and a few bites of a stale, sticky honey bun at the PD. I thought about calling the above mentioned family, but decided I wasn't ready to hear any bad news just yet. I did rouse myself to call Ruby Bee to find out if she knew anything and found myself bullied into admitting I'd requested an arson investigation. Things went from bad to worse, and she, Estelle, and Carolyn were in the parking lot when I got there shortly thereafter.

"Earl and Eilene haven't seen hide nor hair of Kevin," Ruby Bee told me in a mournful voice. "Dahlia's at the bar and grill. She wanted to come with us, but I put my foot down and told her not to go one inch outside until we got back."

"The poor thing's white as a pillowcase," Estelle added.

Carolyn stared at the remains of the bank. "I truly do not understand what happened last night. The firefighters seemed satisfied with their faulty wiring theory, but it's too much of a coincidence."

I said I'd had the same thought most of the night. We were rehashing the story when a white Chevy drove up and two men climbed out. Sergeant Plover, with whom I'd had interesting encounters in both the distant past and the more immediate past of twelve hours ago, introduced me to Sergeant Merganser. Merganser was a slight man with a nervous squint, perhaps from all the smoke in his eyes over the years. For those of you who don't remember, Plover was as tall as I and disarmingly armed with a crooked nose, blond hair, freckles, and a divorce. Our romantic entanglement waxed and waned, depending on whose nose was bent out of shape and who would rather eat snake eggs than apologize. We both had malleable noses and enough stubbornness to shame Perkins's pet mule.

Once we'd gotten through Ruby Bee's rambling account of the fire, the two circled the exterior and began picking their way into the blackened rubble, Merganser with a methane meter and a camera and Plover with a shovel, a trowel, and several shiny evidence cans.

Within a matter of seconds Merganser stumbled out, his face an unattractive green reminiscent of Ruby Bee's split pea soup. "You better call the sheriff and the coroner's office. We got us a body in there."

"Oh my God," Ruby Bee said, clutching my arm for support.

Estelle grabbed my other arm. "Is it . . . is it Kevin?"

"Couldn't say ma'am," he said. "All I know is we found a Caucasian male in there who's about as dead as you get from being roasted. Plover's checking to see if there's anybody else in there, but in the meantime we need backup."

I managed to get myself into the police car, and for once the radio worked. I told the dispatcher at the sheriff's office to relay the messages to the appropriate people, then sank back and dug my teeth into my lower lip to stop it from trembling. When I could trust my knees, I got out of the car and informed Merganser that everybody was coming.

Ruby Bee and Estelle were at the edge of the lot, talking to Raz in his rusted blue truck. As I watched, cars and pickup trucks began to pull up across the road and park. Gawkers wandered out of the pool hall and barbershop. The hippies drifted onto the Emporium porch. Brother Verber and Mrs. Jim Bob came out of the Assembly Hall and stopped halfway down the sidewalk. The women who'd been swapping recipes in the name of sexual equality the night before began to materialize, along with Hizzoner and Larry Joe Lambertino in Larry Joe's four-wheel wagon. Joyce sat in the back seat. Miss Una and Lottie Estes rolled up in the ancient Crosley and found a slot among the trucks. Johnna Mae, Putter, and the little Nookims stood on the corner next to the defunct feed store.

Pretty soon most of the town was there. A shudder went through the crowd when Earl and Eilene drove up, but for the most part nobody said a word. Merganser mumbled something to me and went back into the bank. When Harvey Dorf, the Stump County sheriff, arrived, he took me aside to get an explanation, then groaned and headed for the lopsided doorway.

I couldn't make myself follow him. Kevin Buchanon had always been a royal pain in the ass, and I'd been on the verge of ripping his ears off his head on more than one occasion. But despite all his infuriating idiocy, he was a local boy, an essential part of the crazy goings-on in Maggody. I was rubbing my eyes and trying to brace myself for the awful reality when the sheriff came back out and joined me. He was as pea green as the sergeant had been, but he had a puzzled look on his face.

"It's not the Buchanon boy," he told me in a low rumble.

"Are you sure?"

Harve ran a finger around his collar and gazed upward. "It's real hard to make a positive identification, Arly. The lower body's badly burned, but he fell under the desk and a section of the ceiling collapsed on that, so the upper torso was partially protected. I'm not sure who the fellow is. But I remember that Buchanon boy from last year when he stole my jeep and got hisself involved in that marijuana murder case. I had him to my office for a couple of hours to lecture him about playing policeman and hampering the rest of us. The fellow that's in there isn't the Buchanon boy."

I loosed a major sigh of relief and flapped my hand at Ruby Bee and Estelle. "Harve says it's not Kevin," I called loudly enough to be heard all the way across the road.

There was a visible release of tension on every face. Earl slapped Jeremiah McIlhaney on the back, and Eilene collapsed into Elsie McMay's arms and cried. Everybody blinked wisely and informed everybody else they hadn't believed for one minute that Kevin Buchanon was so all-fired dumb as to get himself trapped inside a burning building.

In the midst of all this owlish buzzing, an ambulance pulled into the parking lot. Harve asked me if I'd try to identify the body, in that I knew the residents better than he did, and I reluctantly nodded. We wound through the mess and stepped across a pile of bricks. I figured we were heading for Brandon Bernswallow's office, and indeed we were. I nudged Plover aside and took a very quick look at the body almost hidden under the charred desk.

"It's Brandon Bernswallow. He was the head teller," I said, fighting an urge to disgrace myself by tossing the honey bun on someone's foot.

Harve scratched his head. "The bank most likely closed at five o'clock yesterday evening. What in tarnation was he doing here last night?"

I started to tell him about the demonstration, but

Harve cut me off with a guffaw. "I already heard about that. Shit, it was all over the county five minutes after it started. That doesn't explain why this boy came back to the bank after dark."

Merganser gave me a hooded look. "Or why he didn't get his ass out the door when the fire broke out."

"Or where the fire originated," Plover contributed.

I could only shrug in response. Harve put a hand on my shoulder and guided me back to the parking lot, stepping aside as the ambulance attendants came past with a body bag. He kept hold of me while he told his deputies what to do, and after a minute I came to my senses and started acting like a cop. I did so under the watchful eyes of most of the citizens of Maggody, since no one had left—or had even indicated he or she might at any time soon.

Truda Oliver put down the receiver and went to find her husband, who was scraping off whiskers in front of the bathroom mirror. "That was Miss Una on the telephone," she said. "It seems they found a body in what's left of the bank."

The razor clattered into the sink. Sherman met her eyes in the mirror. "That Buchanon boy who cleaned up every night? I told Brandon when he hired him that the boy didn't know which end of a mop was up, but I feel badly for the family."

"No, it wasn't the Buchanon boy. It was Brandon." Truda waited for a minute as her husband turned paler than the shaving cream on his chin. "They need you to go down right now and sign a consent form," she told him. "Brandon's family will be notified by the authorities, so I guess you can wait until later to call them and express our condolences."

"Did they determine how the fire got started?" Sherman asked as he picked up the razor and began to ease it along his jaw. Despite his best efforts, his hand was trembling so hard he was likely to do some serious damage to his face. He tossed it back in the sink.

Truda handed him a towel. "Miss Una said she heard one of the sheriff's deputies telling another of them that the fire started in the area of Brandon's body, which was discovered in his office. She was downright perplexed, she said, because she'd assumed the fire was started by the faulty wiring in the back room."

"Do they know why Brandon was in his office last night?"

"I would imagine that's what they'd like you to explain." Truda picked the towel up off the counter and neatly replaced it on the rack. She left her husband in the bathroom and went to the kitchen to pour herself a cup of coffee. Her own hand was trembling so hard she couldn't get the cup to her mouth, however, and the coffee eventually turned cold, the nondairy creamer forming a delicate beige skin across the surface.

When Ruby Bee and Estelle got back to the bar and grill, they found Dahlia slumped in the booth closest to the jukebox. She looked up with a hangdog expression and said, "Tell me the unvarnished truth, Ruby Bee. I deserve to hear it, and I am ready."

"They found a body in the bank, but it wasn't Kevin. It was Brandon Bernswallow, that new head teller fellow what stole Johnna Mae's job and then fired her for no good cause."

Dahlia's jaw sunk low enough to produce a couple more chins. "Then where's my Kevin?"

"Nobody knows. Earl and Eilene haven't had a word from him, nor has anybody else come forward to say he's been spotted anywhere in the county." Ruby Bee went behind the counter and poured herself a cup of coffee, her mind racing faster than a snake going through a hollow log. "You know," she said softly to Estelle, who'd settled on a stool, "it's real hard to see this as an accident. I'd wager a month's worth of tips that someone killed Bernswallow and set the fire to cover it up."

Estelle pursed her lips. "I think you're on to something here, Ruby Bee. Bernswallow was not a popular figure, and he'd pissed off all sorts of people with his oily ways. Who do you suspect?"

Ruby Bee glanced at Dahlia, then leaned across the counter and whispered, "For starters, Kevin has disappeared. I find that mighty suspicious."

"You don't think Kevin Buchanon . . . ?"

"I'd sure like to know what he saw last night and why he vanished like a preacher on the day of reckoning."

Dahlia interrupted all this most fascinating speculation with a bovine moan. "I got to find my Kevin," she said, struggling to slide out of the booth. "He may be out in the woods somewhere, dazed and hurt. We got to get a posse to search the ridge for him."

Ruby Bee rolled her eyes for Estelle's benefit and went over to the booth to help Dahlia. It took a good ten minutes to get her out, in that she'd wedged herself in tighter than bark on a tree and the table had been bolted to the concrete floor years back, after it had been utilized in a spirited debate about the high school football team's chances for the conference title.

"Thank you for calling the Women Aligned Against Chauvinism in the Office office," Staci Ellen said in a monotone.

"This is Ms. McCoy-Grunders, Staci Ellen. Things have become incredibly complex, and it seems necessary for me to remain here for several more days. I need you to run by my condo and pick up some clothes. Bring my navy slacks, my khaki outfit, a few blouses, and that gray Cardin suit with appropriate accessories. If you don't get stuck behind a chicken truck going twenty miles an hour, you should be here in five hours. Bring whatever correspondence has come in and the stack of telephone messages. I'll set up a temporary office in my motel room and make arrangements for you to spend the night in one of the units. I may need you to stay here for a few days. I'll let you know when you arrive."

She spouted off some directions and hung up without bothering to say good-bye. Staci Ellen banged down the receiver. "Well, fiddle-dee-dee, Ms. Hotshot. What happened to 'How are you, Staci Ellen?' and 'Is it convenient for you to drive all the way up to Maggody because I need my gray Cardin suit and appropriate accessories? How's your personal life, Staci Ellen? How's the damn weather, Staci Ellen?' "

She broke off with a gasp, having never used a word like *damn* out loud except once when she was helping her little cousin Angelette snap together a plastic dollhouse and she pinched her finger so hard it bled.

Bruno used that kind of language all the time, of course, and she didn't even want to think what he'd say when she called to cancel their date to go watch stinky old drag races out on a county road. She'd wanted to go to the drive-in and cuddle up with popcorn, but Bruno wanted to time one of the boys from the body shop and see if his Camaro was as fast as he was all the time bragging it was.

It was just tough luck for Bruno and his big plans. She went into Carolyn's office and took the condo key from the desk drawer, gathered up a stack of mail and the lone telephone message, took her romance novel from her desk, and left, locking the office door with a vicious click. Maybe, she thought as she went onto the steamy Little Rock sidewalk and headed for the bus stop, maybe she just wouldn't bother to call Bruno. Maybe she'd just borrow her father's car and drive away without so much as a word to Bruno. Let him wonder where she was, for once. After all, he sometimes stood her up and then got mad if she dared mention it.

Staci Ellen had a heretofore unfamiliar look about her as she sat down on the bench to wait for the bus.

By midafternoon Sergeants Merganser and Plover were finished, and there wasn't any doubt in their minds or in anybody else's that we were looking at arson on top of murder. The misshapen kerosene can was hard to overlook, and it wasn't standard issue in bankers' offices. Papers had been wadded up, soaked with kerosene, and set alight. The perp would have had to hustle to the office door, but once it was closed he or she had plenty of time to exit the building in the orderly fashion of a grade school fire drill. Merganser was as proud as a new papa as he showed us the sharply delineated burn marks on the floor and the V-shaped mark up the side of the desk. I was almost surprised he didn't pass out cigars.

The body had been somewhat preserved because of the desk and a hefty chunk of the ceiling on top of that. It might take as much as week to get the results of the autopsy, depending on how badly backed up the medical examiner was, but we'd all seen the crescent-shaped bruise on the back of the corpse's head. A blackened trophy nearby was selected as the most likely culprit and carefully added to the pile of evidence, which would be delivered to the lab by a state trooper. Harvey and I agreed that we would conduct the investigation as if we already had the autopsy report in hand.

Most of the locals had departed in the wake of the ambulance, and the sheriff's deputies had run the more persistent spectators off with a few idle threats. Sherman Oliver had shown up and been properly appalled, although without any idea why Bernswallow returned to the bank after closing time, which had been about two seconds after the demonstrators pitched camp.

Plover gave me a wry look and said he'd get back to us when he could. He and Merganser loaded their equipment in the Chevy and drove off.

Harvey took me out of earshot of his deputies, whose tongues were notoriously waggly, and said, "So who-all had it in for Bernswallow?"

"Lord, Harve, half the women in town, for starters, including my nearest and dearest. A wonderful pool of suspects, all of whom were milling around a dark parking lot. I suppose any one of them could have picked up a can of kerosene, slipped inside the bank, bashed Bernswallow, doused a hill of paper, and struck a match. Since the door was closed, it took a while for anyone to notice the fire. The perp may have had a solid ten minutes before things started hopping."

"I find it hard to see Ruby Bee in that role," Harvey said. "How 'bout the Nookim woman who was the most outraged? Think she might have gotten herself so worked up that she went bonkers?"

I considered the distasteful theory. "She spouted off some, but I can't imagine her committing a homicide over a bank teller job. The WAACO woman had an ingenious scheme afoot and was liable to win at least some concessions from the bank. It doesn't make any sense for Johnna Mae to have crept into the bank and taken such a risk when she had Oliver between a rock and a hard place."

"How 'bout the WAACO woman?"

"I don't see that she had any motive whatsoever. She was relishing every moment of the demonstration. She'd gotten superb media coverage, and everything was progressing perfectly. Before the confrontation on the sidewalk, she'd never met Bernswallow. They didn't hit it off real well, but that doesn't mean she murdered him a few hours later."

"Tell you what, Arly, I'll send someone to sort through the bank records from the main bank in Farberville. Maybe Bernswallow turned down a loan application or threatened to foreclose a farm in the area." He made a great production of lighting a foul-smelling cigar, all the while shooting sly looks in my direction. Once he'd elicited a noxious haze of smoke, he added, "Why don't you start interviewing the witnesses, Arly? We might get lucky and find somebody who noticed Bernswallow creeping back into the bank or wondered where somebody else was a few minutes before the fire broke out."

My look was not sly. "And conduct the interviews by myself, I suppose? When I drove by on my way to Farberville, there were three dozen women in the parking lot, and almost that many honorable citizens glaring from across the road. The ambiance in a lot of households is on the cool side these days, as in January on Jupiter. If I pop in and start asking questions, I'm apt to find myself in the yard with a boot imprint on my fanny."

"I know, I know," Harvey said, sighing. "But you know how stretched we are in terms of manpower. I've got a whole dang roomful of outstanding warrants, subpoenas, and contempt citations for fathers who can't be bothered to pay their child support. While we're standing here right now, there are liquor store holdups, convenience store holdups, hunters blowing each other to smithereens four months before deer season opens—"

"This is a homicide. We're not talking about a goddamn heist or a jerk who can't remember to mail his two-hundred-dollar child support checks by the fifth of the month. Come on, Harve. For once in your stellar career, do something smart."

"I said I'll assign someone to tackle the bank end."

The argument went on in this vein, but eventually I conceded defeat and agreed to interview as many of the witnesses as I could. Harve had a trace of smugness on his face as he drove away. As I stood there mindlessly staring at the bank, Miss Una's Crosley chugged into the lot and spewed forth its operator.

"I heard about poor dear Brandon," she said in a hushed voice. "I'm horrified to think something like this could happen in our cozy little community. I must say I did not approve of the way some of our citizens took it upon themselves to act in an undignified fashion."

It occurred to me that the local grapevine might provide insight for those studying superconductivity. I mumbled something vague about the tragedy and asked her when she'd left the bank the previous evening.

"Why, it would have been around six o'clock," she said. "Mr. Oliver and Mr. Bernswallow decided to close early because of the unpleasantness outside. We balanced our drawers as quickly as possible and left through the back door."

"All three of you?"

"Now that I think about it, Mr. Oliver left first. He really has little to do with the daily operation of the bank. Once I'd tracked down a minor error on a deposit slip, I turned in my drawer and said I was leaving. Mr. Bernswallow was in his office at the time."

"Did he say anything that implied he might remain at the bank for the evening, or that he had a reason to return later?"

Miss Una blinked at me. "Heavens, no."

"How did he seem?" I persisted. "Was he still upset by the presence of the demonstrators in the parking lot?"

"Not really," she said slowly. "I was a bit surprised by his mood. He'd been very distressed earlier, and rightly so, but by the time I was ready to go home, he was in a most jovial mood, as if he were anticipating good news or a gift."

"But he didn't give you any hint of what it might be?"

"Our relationship was strictly business," Miss Una said with a sniff. "Johnna Mae and I had worked together for so long that it seemed permissible to take a personal interest, but I would not have been so bold as to make such overtures to Mr. Bernswallow."

"Had anyone come into the bank lately and seemed upset about something Bernswallow had done?"

"Raz Buchanon has been pestering me relentlessly over the new bank statement. He is not the only customer to have difficulties with it, but I would hardly say he was upset enough to commit such a dastardly act. Johnna Mae, on the other hand, was quite furious. I happened to overhear her conversation with Mr. Bernswallow the day he fired her, and she made some terribly nasty threats." Miss Una clutched the collar of her cardigan. "You don't think Johnna Mae would do such a thing, do you?"

"Of course not," I said firmly if also mendaciously. It was getting pretty hard to ignore the fact that Johnna Mae was hefty enough to have bashed Bernswallow with a blunt instrument, and angry enough as well. Thus far we didn't have an abundance of motives, and hers was harder to miss than a Roman candle on the Fourth of July. I told Miss Una that I'd drop by later for an official statement. She got in her car and chugged back down the highway.

I decided to postpone dealing with Johnna Mae for the time being and drove to Ruby Bee's on the off chance the official period of mourning for Kevin (and where the hell was he?) was over and I could get a decent meal.

The Closed sign was still on the door, but I went on in and sat down next to Estelle. Ruby Bee came out of the kitchen. "What do you want?" she asked in an odd voice.

A great deal of what Ruby Bee says and does is said and done oddly, so I let it fly right past me. "I was hoping to ward off starvation with a blue plate special. I'm not proud; I'll settle for pork chops, meat loaf, ribs, or anything else you're in the mood to serve."

Estelle jabbed me in the arm. "I'm surprised you have time to worry about your stomach when Kevin Buchanon is missing and that Bernswallow fellow's been murdered."

"How do you know he was murdered?" I said.

Ruby Bee grabbed a dishrag and began to wipe the surface of the counter. "Everybody in town thinks it was murder, Miss Closed Mouth. You and Carolyn both said it was too much of a coincidence that an accidental fire started the very same time we were in the lot. And when the body was found, well, that made it perfectly clear."

"I wish it were perfectly clear to me," I said, "but I'm too weak from hunger to think straight."

The dishrag stopped. "If I'm willing to slave over a hot stove just so you can satisfy your stomach, will you tell us what-all the sheriff and those investigators had to say?"

I seriously considered stalking out the door, my nose high enough to brush the cobwebs off the ceiling, but acknowledged to myself that the results of the investigation would be common knowledge within a day or two, thanks to the mach-seven grapevine. "How hard are you intending to slave?"

"I think I have a slab of leftover meat loaf with tomato sauce and a little dish of creamed potatoes."

"No cobbler?" I said in a wounded voice.

Estelle jabbed me again. "It is unseemly to listen to you blackmailing your own mother."

"She started it."

Ruby Bee marched over to face me across the counter and folded her arms. "I reckon there may be a piece of cherry cobbler in the ice box. I was planning on serving it to Carolyn when she finished making phone calls, but what she doesn't know won't hurt her."

"Where is she?" I asked curiously. "And for that matter, where's Dahlia?"

"Carolyn went to her unit to call her office and make arrangements to stay in Maggody until this awful tragedy is resolved," Estelle said. "Although I told her until my face turned blue that none of this was her fault, she insisted that she was in some way responsible because of the demonstration and everything."

"So she thinks the demonstration was the catalyst for the murder?"

Ruby Bee snapped the dishrag under Estelle's nose. "See, I told you it was murder, didn't I? Arly just said so."

"I didn't argue with you," Estelle said, sounding deeply offended. "If I recollect, I was the one who said the fire was set to cover the murder."

"Then you disrecollect," Ruby Bee huffed.

To my utter relief, they took their squabble with them into the kitchen, leaving me in dim, cool, quiet bliss. I was almost dozing when the door opened and footsteps clicked across the dance floor. Carolyn climbed onto the stool next to me. "I heard you're planning to stay around until the investigation is completed," I said.

"I feel bad. Had I not accepted Johnna Mae's case, none of this would have happened." She stared at her reflection in the spotted mirror behind the bar. "Maybe it would have anyway. Johnna Mae was deeply upset by the blatantly sexist, illegal actions taken against her."

"Everybody seems rather eager to cast Johnna Mae as the villain in the piece," I said mildly. "Bernswallow wasn't especially popular with a lot of people. Perhaps your rhetoric stirred another of the women to violence, or even a closet sympathizer from the far side of the road."

"I incited someone to kill Bernswallow and burn the building? I'm good, but I'm not that good. I will say I was surprised by the cooperativeness of the local women when I first arrived to organize the demonstration. On the campuses, I'm usually lucky to find a handful of women who'll stand beside me in the name of equality and justice. Too many sorority girls would rather worry about dates to fraternity parties than worry about the injustices that they'll face in the workplace after graduation." She stopped with a rueful laugh. "Sorry, the rhetoric sneaks out when I'm not alert."

"Can you describe what went on in the parking lot before the fire caught everyone's attention?"

"It was chaotic, but not dreadfully so. There was a lengthy discussion about the quality of the army cots, and several of the demonstrators were making barbed remarks about dedication and sacrifice. I believe there was a canasta game going on. There was another group exchanging recipes. It was fairly dark, and I'd be hard-pressed to say where anyone was at any given moment. When that ghastly man began shrieking about the fire, I was standing with Ruby Bee, Estelle, and Ms. McMay. Five minutes before that, I really couldn't say."

"Did you leave at any time between five o'clock and ten o'clock?"

"At one point I became rather overwhelmed by the intensity of the group and walked back to the motel to pick up a package of pamphlets we were planning to distribute today. I'd estimate that I was gone for half an hour."

"Did anyone else leave for a time?"

"I have no idea. Each of us certainly could have been away for a few minutes to use the washroom facilities at the Emporium or to make a phone call. Our sentries were watching for intruders, not escapees."

I thought for a minute. "I understand that it was dark and that everyone was wandering around chatting or griping or using the facilities. Was there anyone you couldn't find at a particular time?"

"When I went to congratulate Truda Oliver on her courageous stand, it took me quite a while to locate her." Carolyn slapped her forehead, although carefully enough not to jar loose any powder. "And Johnna Mae did say she was going home for a few minutes to make sure her husband had the children tucked in bed."

"What time was that?"

"I have no idea, Arly. You'll have to ask her."

Ruby Bee and Estelle came out of the kitchen, the former with a heaping plate of meat loaf et al and the latter with a glass of milk and a bowl of cobbler. The lovely above-mentioneds were placed in front of me, and I had my fork poised when the pay telephone rang in the corner.

"Maybe it's Dahlia," Estelle said as she hurried to answer it.

I looked at Ruby Bee, who was doing her best not to notice me. "Just where is Dahlia?"

Estelle saved her by covering the receiver and calling, "It's for you, Arly. Some deputy calling from Farberville. Says it's real important."

I put down the fork and glumly went to the telephone. "Arly Hanks," I said. "What's up?"

I learned what was up in no time flat. Estelle was hovering at a discreet distance, her earlobes aquiver, so I turned my back on her and hunched over the receiver while I asked questions and listened to answers that got grimmer by the minute. At last I hung up and started for the door.

"What about your supper?" Ruby Bee squawked.

"Let Carolyn have it. I've got some official business, and I can't put it off any longer."

Estelle put her hands on her hips and gave me an indignant look. "But you said you would tell us what-all the investigation turned up. I thought we had ourselves a deal."

I turned back and gazed at Ruby Bee and Estelle, who were on the militant side, and Carolyn, who was on the bewildered side. "I'm afraid there's some new evidence that implicates Johnna Mae. I'm going to talk to her now. On an empty stomach."

There was a comment about Miss Liar Liar Pants on Fire, but I didn't stop to argue the issue.

9

The same Nookim child was throwing the same tennis ball against the side of the mobile home, and it was making the same infuriating *thwack* with each encounter. I told him to stop. He looked at me sullenly, then hurled the ball again. I told him that it might take him all day to extract the ball from his mouth, which was what he was going to have to do if he continued. I then went to the door and knocked, although my shoulders were tensed in preparation for the *thwack* beside (or more probably, in the back of) my head.

Johnna Mae opened the door and gazed through the screen at me. She wore a tired, wrinkled housedress; her hair was limp and her makeup unable to disguise her yellowish pallor. "Hi, Arly," she murmured. "That was pretty awful about Bernswallow, wasn't it?"

"It certainly was, and what's worse is that we're almost sure he was murdered," I said evenly.

"I can't believe that. I mean, that's downright impossible to believe that someone would do something like that." She produced the proper expression of horror and incredulousness, but her voice had a funny edge to it and her eyes were darting every which way except at me.

"I need to talk to you, Johnna Mae, and I think"— *thwack*—"that we'd have more privacy at the PD."

"Stop that right this minute, Earl Boy, or I'll whip your rear end with a willow branch so hard you won't sit down for a solid year!" She shrugged at me, then called over her shoulder that she'd be gone for a few minutes. As we walked past Earl Boy, she slapped at him without much enthusiasm. There were three more thwacks before we made it to the car.

I thought about making chitchat while we drove to the PD, but I didn't have the heart for it and Johnna Mae didn't look all that receptive. She kept her face lowered, and every once in a while muttered something unintelligible under her breath. When we arrived I asked her to sit down and settled myself in my chair behind the desk.

"I'm afraid this will have to be official," I told her, and recited the Miranda warning. When I'd made sure she understood it, I continued. "The problem is that the sheriff had someone go over to the main bank and dig through the Maggody branch records. He was baffled by the number of small loans made to locals over the last few years. When he saw his brother-in-law's name, he called and asked why the hell he was borrowing money. His brother-in-law said it was the first he'd heard of it, and why would anyone think a bank would loan money to an unemployed backhoe operator with a cast on his ankle and monthly disability checks as income."

"Oh," Johnna Mae said so quietly I almost missed it. "That would be Clarence Pipit. I'm sorry to hear about his misfortune."

"This is more serious than a broken ankle, because

the ankle will heal sooner or later. The deputy made several more calls. The upshot was that the bank got its bookkeepers in there, and they started shifting through all the files. A vast percentage of the loans originating from the Maggody branch were bogus. A bank employee had filled in the applications for small, inconsequential amounts that wouldn't raise an examiner's eyebrow, approved the loans, and pocketed the proceeds. When a loan came up for renewal, another bogus application was approved and a portion of it used to make an interest payment and reduce the capital on the previous loan. It was a widening spiral, but one that didn't stir up much dust. Then, about two months ago, the payments on the loans stopped. The computer spewed out letters to the loanees, reminding them they needed to make payments."

"I didn't know I was going to need the C section," Johnna Mae said dully. "I thought I'd be out for a few days, not a whole six weeks." She ran her hand through her hair and sighed. "And when I got back, Bernswallow was the head teller. I didn't have the money to make payments on the loans, and I sure couldn't run any new loan approvals past him without him catching wind of it. There wasn't a thing I could do but just wait until the shit hit the fan."

"Or kill him, and burn the records to boot. Didn't you realize the main branch would have copies of all the paperwork generated in the branch?"

"Kill him? Me? I didn't kill him and I didn't start that fire, Arly. You got to believe that."

I rubbed my forehead. "I'd like to believe that, Johnna Mae, but I'm having a hard time. You were absent from the branch for quite a long time, long enough for some indignant customer to demand an explanation from the top honcho at the branch, which used to be you but became Brandon. One of the accused was so pissed she squawked about a libel suit. Surely one of the others stalked into the lobby and shoved the letter under his nose. Lottie Estes, for instance, the day I dropped by to see how you were?"

"I tried to explain it was a mix-up, but she demanded to talk to the head teller. There wasn't any way to stop her," Johnna Mae admitted in the same dull voice. "Bernswallow didn't say anything about it that day, but I knew the whole thing was right on the verge of exploding in my face."

"So Bernswallow stumbled onto the bogus loans, probably long before you came back to work." I rubbed my forehead some more, trying to massage my brain into a more cooperative state. "If that's what happened, and I'm fairly certain of it, he had three possible alternatives. One was to run screaming to the bank auditors, with a side trip to the police, and we all know he didn't do that. The second would be to adopt the scheme and operate it himself. The third might not exclude the second, but it would include blackmail." I looked up in time to catch her sudden twitch. "Was that what happened? Did he demand that you meet him in the bank last night so you could pay him for his silence?"

"Pay him with what? You know I don't have two dimes to rub together, Arly. Bernswallow knew it too. All he had to do was take a gander at my checking account to see it was a rat's whisker away from overdrafts."

"What did you do with the money you embezzled?"

"Bills," she said with a humorless laugh. "Doctor bills, utility bills, grocery bills, pharmacy bills, shoe bills, you name it. I didn't take more than a couple of thousand dollars, and I mean to pay it back soon as Putter's able to work again and we can save a little something every month. I was just borrowing that money. The bank's got assets in the millions of dollars; they weren't going to have a hissy-fit over less than three thousand dollars."

"It's still embezzlement," I said, feeling like the Grinch on Christmas Eve, "and it's a felony."

"But I didn't kill him and I didn't set the bank on fire."

"One witness has already told me that you left the demonstration for a few minutes, saying you were going home. All you had to do was go around to the back of the bank, slip inside and have the fatal meeting, and then hurry down the road to the Pot O' Gold."

"I didn't kill Bernswallow," she said, shaking her head. "I went home, kissed my three angels good night, and came straight back to the parking lot in time to see the fire truck roll in. You can ask Putter."

"I don't know what to tell you, Johnna Mae. I'm going to question some more witnesses, and the fire marshal sent all the evidence to the state crime lab. Maybe we'll find someone else's fingerprints on the surface of the kerosene can. Maybe one of the women will remember seeing someone lurking around the back of the lot. Maybe you're telling me the truth now; I'd prefer to learn down the road that you are. In the meantime, I'm going to have to arrest you on embezzlement charges and book you in the county jail in Farberville. The sheriff and I will then have to decide if we have enough evidence to file murder and arson charges against you."

She opened her mouth to say something, then closed it and gave me a weary smile. "You do whatever you have to, Arly. If you don't mind too awful much, can we run by the mobile home so I can say good-bye to Putter and the children?"

Compared to yours truly, the Grinch was a friggin' prince.

Mrs. Jim Bob sat in her Cadillac and fumed for a good five minutes. Brother Verber was acting downright possessed hisself with the possibility of witchcraft in Maggody, and she was getting a might fed up with it. She'd already pointed out more than once or twice that now they knew what the women had been doing in Ruby Bee's during those days when the place had been closed: they'd been planning the vulgar demonstration and that was that. Mrs. Jim Bob hadn't really believed her friends and neighbors such as Elsie McMay and Eilene Buchanon would actually do anything so all-fired evil; she'd just mentioned the possibility of witchcraft to . . . well, to make conversation.

But Brother Verber was clinging to the theory like a wad of gum on the bottom of a school desk. He was on his knees inside the Assembly Hall, arguing with the Almighty and not being real respectful, if she said so herself. His face was shiny and beet red, and his eyes were on the bright side for one supposedly engaged in pious prayer. All she could get out of him were distracted nods and a few words about Christian duty. As if she weren't one of the most dutiful Christians in the entire congregation.

Mrs. Jim Bob switched on the ignition and went to evince a little Christian duty by consoling Truda Oliver over the embarrassment of having her husband's employee fried to a crisp during the fire. As she pulled into the cul-de-sac, she was relieved to see Truda's car in the driveway. When duty beckoned, Mrs. Jim Bob did not shirk or make excuses, but she really did need to get home within the hour to make sure Perkins's eldest had dusted the venetian blinds and vacuumed under the love seat and seen that the children didn't get into trouble.

Truda didn't look real thrilled when she answered the door, but she managed a smile and invited Mrs. Jim Bob in for coffee and a piece of apple strudel. After they were settled in the living room, Mrs. Jim Bob politely inquired how Sherman was holding up in the face of this most humiliating tragedy.

"He's been at the main bank all day. They've discovered that the Nookim woman has been embezzling money for the last three years. Sherman's beside himself, of course, although nobody's blaming him."

"He was the branch manager, and therefore responsible for everything that happened at the branch," Mrs. Jim Bob pointed out as she nibbled the strudel with an appreciative smile, even though it wasn't as flaky as her own. "She might not have gotten away with it as long as she did if Sherman had paid more attention to what his employees were doing."

"That's true," Truda said, wondering how the strudel might taste with a pinch of rat poison. "However, he has remained in charge of the bank's portfolio, and the board is aware that that occupied a great deal of Sherman's workday. And he trusted Johnna Mae."

"I myself have always had some doubts about Johnna Mae Nookim's character. Her father, Dewey Buchanon, owned a dry goods store over in Hasty until he and his wife got terminal cases of influenza twenty years back—and a good thing they did. If they'd known Johnna Mae was going to up and marry a Nookim, they'd have locked her in her room until she came to her senses. Everybody knows the Nookims are nothing but white trash; you can tell by the way they all slouch around with long, greasy hair and never hold down a decent factory job or make any kind of effort to amount to something. Putter hasn't supported his family since I don't know when."

"Which is why Johnna Mae's salary was so important," Truda said in a sharp voice.

Mrs. Jim Bob overlooked it out of consideration for Truda in her humiliation. "Important so she could steal honest people's money from the bank. What's going to happen to her?"

"Elsie called earlier to say she'd seen Johnna Mae in Arly's car and that they were driving toward Farberville."

"To lock her up where she belongs," Mrs. Jim Bob said smugly. "Well, we should all be pleased that this whole sordid ordeal is over. Johnna Mae most likely killed Brandon and burned up the bank to cover her theft. She's not going to fret over her salary for a long time. That wicked outside agitator can take herself back to Little Rock, where all the women are uppity lawyers who have no idea how to conduct themselves like proper ladies. I wouldn't be at all surprised to hear they run around in trousers, smoke cigars, and swear like sailors. And as for those loud-mouthed demonstrators—present company excluded, of course, since you're one of my dearest friends—they've had their comeuppance and are all home in the bosom of their families where they rightly belong, fixing supper for their husbands and making sure their children are brought up to attend Sunday school and mind their manners around their elders."

Truda gazed at Mrs. Jim Bob, but she was mentally revising her strudel recipe to include a heaping teaspoon of rat poison. "I suppose so," she said at last. "There will be all sorts of headaches for Sherman down the road. He said there's been no decision about the branch. The building is destroyed. They may want to bring in a trailer, or they may just close the branch. If they do close it, we may retire down in Florida somewhere. Sherman knows some real estate folks who claim property values are real solid."

"How nice for you," Mrs. Jim Bob said, thinking how the strudel needed a tad more cinnamon and a lighter touch with the dough. "If and when the time comes, do let me know and I'll have a farewell luncheon for you. I'm sure all the members of the missionary society will have forgotten all about this incident and will be more than delighted to attend."

Truda wondered what a cup of rat poison might do to the strudel.

The Closed sign was still on the door of Ruby Bee's Bar and Grill, much to everyone's disgust. It had been nearly a week now, and the frito pies at the Dairee Dee-Lishus were hardly any competition for a piping hot blue plate special, which included not only a roll and two vegetable choices but also dessert. Even Jim

Bob was getting tired of microwaving burritos from the Kwik-Screw, and he scowled as he drove toward Starley City and the titillating promise of a romp with Cherri Lucinda, his itty bitty titty kitty, as he was fond of calling her when she consented to one of his more imaginative ideas and then didn't cry afterward.

Inside Ruby Bee's, Estelle and Ruby Bee herself were slumped at the bar, both praying they'd hear the telephone ring and Dahlia's voice announcing she'd found Kevin. Dahlia had packed a hefty bag of provisions, having decided for some reason that Kevin was apt to be lost in the national forest along Boone Creek. Hours earlier she'd put together the final bologna sandwich, slung the bag—a plastic garbage bag, to be precise—over her shoulder, and vowed to beat the bushes until she found her Kevin and snatched him from the jaws of a bear or waded out into the creek to snatch him from the jaws of a gar or whatever. She'd refused the halfhearted offers of company and thudded proudly out the door and into the waiting arms of Mother Nature.

When the door opened, Ruby Bee turned around to bark something at being closed but stopped as she caught sight of a young blond girl carrying two suitcases and a stack of folders and holding a collection of irregularly sized envelopes between her teeth. A streak of grease ran across one cheek like a dueling scar. She dropped the suitcases, put the folders on a table, and took the envelopes from her mouth.

"I'm Staci Ellen Quittle and I'm looking for Carolyn McCoy-Grunders," she said in a squeaky, breathless voice. "I'm her secretary from the Women Aligned

Against Chauvinism in the Office office. I was supposed to be here earlier, but I had a flat tire."

The girl looked so worried that Ruby Bee couldn't help but give her a maternal smile. "Carolyn's in number two out back, freshening up. Why don't you wait here and have a nice glass of iced tea?"

"Thanks," Staci Ellen said gratefully. "I never changed a flat tire by myself before. I must've read the manual ten times before I figured out how the jack worked, and I like to never get those bolts loose."

Estelle raised a well-drawn eyebrow. "But you're such a delicate little thing. I'm surprised a truck driver didn't stop to change the tire for you."

"A whole bunch of them stopped and offered to do it, but I told them I could do it all by myself, thank you." Staci Ellen scratched at the greasy smear on her cheek, then stared at her finger. "Wow, I must look awful. I don't know what my boyfriend would say if he saw me now."

Ruby Bee eyed the stack of folders threatening to slide off the table. "Carolyn must be planning to do some work."

"Oh, yes, she said there was a problem up here that might require her and me to stay for several days. She didn't tell me what exactly, so I grabbed all the folders on her desk and brought them along, just in case. The one involving the Maggody resident is on top."

The three women looked back in time to see the folders slither to the floor. Staci Ellen gasped. She jumped off the barstool and ran across the room to start gathering them up. "Ms. McCoy-Grunders is going to be furious with me. I just know it. She doesn't think

I've got a brain in my head. Now all the folders are mixed up and she'll start yelling at me."

Estelle and Ruby Bee went to the rescue. Pretty soon they had the folders fanned across the table and were putting all the loose papers in the appropriate places.

Ruby Bee nudged Estelle. "Look at this. This is Johnna Mae's letter to the WAACO office, stating how she was discriminated against for taking maternity leave."

"That's supposed to be confidential," Staci Ellen said with a nervous gulp. "No one is allowed to read the contents of the folder."

"We can't sort them if we don't look at them," Ruby Bee said. She placed her finger midway down the page and said, "Right here where it says how Johnna Mae was demoted and then fired, someone underlined Brandon Bernswallow's name in red ink. What do you think that means?"

Estelle made a clucking noise as she peered at the page. "It's on the peculiar side. There aren't any other names underlined on any of the other papers. I don't see why Johnna Mae would have done it. She probably doesn't even have a pen that writes red ink."

"This is confidential," Staci Ellen said, shooting increasingly frantic glances at the door. "Ms. McCoy-Grunders will flat out fire me if she catches you reading that. She'll say it was all my fault."

"It's not a bit your fault," Ruby Bee said as she put the page inside its folder. She and Estelle kept exchanging looks the whole time it took to sort through the remaining papers and get the folders all nice and tidy.

When they'd finished and Staci Ellen had returned to her iced tea, Ruby Bee pulled Estelle into the kitchen and closed the door. "I think we've got something here, but I ain't real sure what. I'd hazard a guess that Carolyn knows something about that Bernswallow fellow."

"She didn't mention anything."

"I realize that. That's what's making me suspicious."

"What do you aim to do about it?" Estelle asked, screwing up her face like something itched that she couldn't reach. "Are you gonna tell Arly?"

"I guess I ought to, but then she'll say something to Carolyn and Carolyn will bawl out that sweet little Staci Ellen and fire her. I'd feel terrible if I was responsible for that." Ruby Bee considered how terrible she'd feel if that would be the case and decided she couldn't do such a thing just yet. "We can't say anything to Arly until we find a way to do so without getting the girl fired. Maybe we could sort of hint around with Carolyn and see if she'll drop something we can repeat to Arly."

"Like how she knew him from before and just forgot?"

"It'd be real handy if she did," Ruby Bee said, sighing. Arly could turn real petulant when she got the fool notion in her head that certain people weren't candid with her, that certain people might just take a civic interest in assisting in minor elements of the investigation to make sure justice was done. Arly didn't even care if the certain people provided valuable information in the end. Her voice still got icier than a widow woman's bed in December. Ruby Bee knew this much from personal experience.

Estelle seemed to read her mind like it was the yellow pages. "You know perfectly well that Arly ain't going to like it."

"Arly ain't going to find out about it. This is going to be strictly between you, me, and the kitchen sink. Staci Ellen sure isn't going to say anything and lose her job. For once Arly's not going to get all hot and bothered because we didn't pass along a minor little doodad that most likely doesn't mean a thing. If and when we decide we need to tell her, we'll think of a way."

"I think," Estelle said pensively, "that this is what they mean on television when they talk about being in the fast lane, where you risk life and limb every inch of the way. And you, Rubella Belinda Hanks, don't even have a driver's license."

"I know that." With a snort, Ruby Bee went back to the bar to see if Staci Ellen wanted a fresh piece of lemon in her tea.

After I'd done the paperwork and abandoned Johnna Mae to the care of the county jail, I drove to the main bank on the square. A security guard directed me to the basement, where I found all sorts of harried people bent over old-fashioned ledgers and new-fangled computers. The head bookkeeper, Mrs. Gadwall, seemed on the greenish side as she admitted they'd uncovered well over two thousand dollars of bogus loans thus far and still had seven months' worth of records to go. A full-scale internal audit would begin over the weekend, and the federal bank examiners would descend thereafter. She sounded as if she planned to report to work Monday morning in battle fatigues and a helmet.

Sherman Oliver came out of an office and joined us. "This is a sorry mess, Chief Hanks. I trusted Johnna Mae Nookim to handle the day-to-day operations at the branch. I never thought for a moment that she would embezzle money from the very institution that considered her part of the family. Why, if she'd come to me and explained how desperate she was, I would have done everything in my power to help her. Now she's got herself in a deep well and there's not a ladder long enough to rescue her."

"I've booked her at the county jail. The county prosecutor will call you in a day or so for a formal statement. Our investigation will continue, of course, until we find out who murdered Bernswallow and set the fire."

"Then there's no way the death and the fire could have been accidental?"

"It doesn't look that way," I said. "The evidence has been sent to the state crime lab, and the body to the same place for an autopsy. Until we learn otherwise, we're operating under the assumption it was murder."

He closed his eyes and groaned softly. "But you're not sure?"

"No, we're not sure. But as long as I'm here, I'd like to ask you a few questions about yesterday evening and last night. Is there someplace we can speak?"

"My office is there." He led the way to a unadorned box with cracks in the walls and a mildewed blotch on the ceiling above his desk. "When I was a veep, I had walnut paneling and potted plants. Now that I do nothing but portfolio work, they've assigned me to the bowels of the building. No need to present any amenities to the public, you see."

I nodded and asked him when he'd left the branch the previous evening. He said he'd departed first, which confirmed what Miss Una had told me. I then asked him if he'd spoken to Brandon on his way out.

"Yes," he admitted, "we discussed which of us ought to call Bernswallow Senior and other board members to warn them of what would appear on the six o'clock news. Brandon said he felt he could convey the situation more delicately, and I concurred with the alacrity of a yellow-bellied coward. Despite the impending unpleasantness, he seemed quite chipper when I left."

That fit into my theory that Brandon was planning to blackmail Johnna Mae at some later hour. I was about to ask him if he'd had any hint that Brandon knew of the bogus loans when the telephone rang.

Oliver flinched as if it had tried to bite him. "Sorry about this. I told the receptionist upstairs to hold all my calls, but she rarely pays attention to my orders." The telephone continued to ring. He finally picked up the receiver, gave me an apologetic shrug, and said, "Yes?"

While he listened, I glanced around at the unattractive decor, which consisted of clippings and reprints of financial charts, a worn map of Arkansas, and a faded diploma that informed all perusers that Sherman Oliver was a graduate in good standing of a private college in Conway.

"I told you to cancel the order!" he snapped, regaining my attention. He caught my look and lowered his voice. "The damn examiners will be here by the first of the week. The one thing I don't need is this flimsy thing in the portfolio. Cancel it, and keep trying to unload what we talked about earlier. Call me at home."

He replaced the receiver. "Just one of those pesky bond peddlers. I deal with them all the time, but they're still annoying. They lose all perspective when they're on commission."

"Tell me about a bank's portfolio," I said. "I've never understood what a bank does with all that lovely money."

"It's very, very complex, and not especially intriguing. The banks keeps a reserve to cover all activities in all accounts, then utilizes any additional assets to invest in a variety of bonds in order to earn a profit for its stockholders. I select the bonds on the basis of maintaining a diverse yet conservatively profitable portfolio. I'm sure you find this tedious and confusing, my dear. Do you have any further questions about last night?"

"What did you do after you said good-bye and left the building?"

"I stopped at the edge of the parking lot to have a word with my wife. I was very upset about her decision to participate in the demonstration, and told her as much. We have been married for thirty years, however, and have always had the greatest respect for each other. When I realized I could not dissuade her from her chosen course of action, I wished her a comfortable night on her army cot and went home."

"Did you go out after that, or have any telephone calls?"

"I closed the draperies, took the telephone off the hook, locked the den door, and poured myself the first of what was to be a series of very stiff drinks. If someone came by and rang the doorbell, I was unaware of it. I was deeply upset by the events of the afternoon and evening, and I was hardly in the mood for company. I was sound asleep when Truda came home to tell me about the fire."

"You had no inkling until today that Johnna Mae was embezzling small sums from the branch?"

"None whatsoever."

"And you have no idea whether Bernswallow or Miss Una might have suspected as much?"

"No." He made a production of checking his watch, then stood up. "I have a meeting with the board of directors in five minutes. They are as interested as you in what has transpired at the branch. I'm sure they would appreciate promptness on my part."

Despite his pomposity, I felt a twinge of sympathy for him. I thanked him and went to the main room to find Mrs. Gadwall. She agreed to send all the final reports to the sheriff's office, as well as the findings of the auditors and federal bank examiners.

I thanked her, then left the bank and went to the state police barracks for something. Congratulations, sympathy, praise, a beer. Anything.

"Kevvvin," Dahlia bleated as she put her foot right on a cow patty, and a moist one at that. Sweat was more than streaming down her back; it was bouncing and cascading like that Niagara Falls place where honeymooners went. If'n she didn't find Kevin, she wasn't ever gonna have a honeymoon, she thought while she scraped her shoe on a rotten log. The bag was getting mighty uncomfortable, and the plastic against her back was making her even hotter.

She lowered herself gingerly onto the far end of the log. It creaked, but it didn't break, so she wiggled around until the bark stopped poking her rear too much, opened the bag, and took out a bologna sandwich. Ever mindful of her mission, she bleated Kevin's name one more time before stuffing half the sandwich into her cavernous mouth.

As she ruminated, she tried to think why Kevin wasn't answering her. She was pretty sure he was in the woods somewhere in these parts, because she had a real firm vision of him stumbling out the back of the bank, blinded by the smoke, and stumbling across the road into the woods behind the old feed store. Originally she'd envisioned that he'd stumbled across the highway to the national forest, but after some pondering, realized that someone would have seen him stumbling thataway and therefore he'd been obliged to stumble thisaway, across the county road alongside the bank.

Besides, everybody knew the national forest was about a thousand acres of thorns, scrub brush, prickly pines, snakes, chiggers, ticks, and who knows what-all. This side was more like twenty acres and backed on the pasture that eventually sloped to the subdivision with the cute cul-de-sacs. While she worked on a second sandwich, Dahlia assured herself that Kevin would have preferred to stumble around in twenty acres.

It seemed more sensible to sit and bleat than to get scraped by branches and risk twisting an ankle on a root. If both of them kept moving, why, they could miss each other for days and not even know it.

"Kevvvin," she howled as she took out a ham salad

sandwich and a banana. She figured it was real important to keep up her strength.

Kevin thought it was the best chocolate cake he'd ever eaten in his entire life, right down to the fudge icing decorated with pecan halves. His ma wouldn't let him have chocolate because of pimples popping up when he did, so he was right pleased when the issue wasn't mentioned. He was even more pleased when his request for a third piece was seen to briskly.

He flipped over to the page with the fillet knives. The stainless steel ones were the best, he decided, even if they were a sight more expensive than he'd thought.

10

"Registrar's office."

"This is Ms. Martin at the attorney general's office in Little Rock. We need some information concerning one of your graduates from the law school up that way," the woman said in a nasal whine that was almost impossible to understand. "And also about a business student a couple of years back."

"You'll have to submit your requests in writing. We require three copies of each, plus notarized authorizations from the students involved. All records and transcripts are sealed."

"Oh, we don't want to worry ourselves about a bunch of paperwork, do we? I don't want to know about their grades or how they deported themselves. I just want to know if they were there at the same time. Maybe if they had any classes together or something like that."

"Three copies, and the notarized authorizations from the students involved."

"But this is the attorney general's office. You have to tell me what I need to know or we'll persecute you. You do realize we can put anybody we want to in jail, don't you? And if we've a mind to, just throw away the key?"

The only thing the secretary in the registrar's office realized was that it was four o'clock, and she would be on her way to the beer garden in a manner of minutes. "Have at it," she suggested, already salivating over the idea of an icy cold beer sliding down her throat, while the band set up for the show and all her friends wandered by.

"Now listen here, Miss Snooty Pants, unless you want to find yourself in a whole passel of trouble, you tell me if Carolyn McCoy attended the law school up there and if she did, what years. And also if—"

The secretary hung up the receiver, grabbed her purse, and wished everyone a nice evening. It was still hot, but the beer garden was always shady and the beer always cold. A dynamic duo.

When I got back to Maggody, I stopped at the PD and made a list of all the women who'd participated in the demonstration. I then mentally ran over the trucks that had been parked across the highway and did my best to write down the names of the silent vigilantes. I counted for a minute; at forty-seven, I lost heart, stopping midway down the second page.

The PD was a damn brick oven preheated to broil. The air conditioner clearly had ceased working hours ago, either while I was talking to Sherman Oliver or sipping a soda at the trooper barracks. My Alaska pamphlets were on the desk. I found one with a vivid photograph of a glacier and fanned myself with it as I chose my first victim for the Arly Hanks third degree. The selection was based on the rumor that one of our good citizens had recently acquired the newest, flashiest, iciest air conditioner on the market, a veritable state-of-the-goddamn-art miracle. And away I went.

Raz Buchanon came to the door in a baggy stained undershirt and a baggier, stainier pair of khaki trousers. He gave me a spotty yet sincere grin. "Howdy, Arly. Hot enough for ya?"

"I thought you bought a new air conditioner," I said through the screen. "Why aren't you running it?"

"I did, and I is."

I waited politely while he sent an arch of tobacco juice toward a Tupperware bowl in the middle of the braided rug. "But then don't you think you ought to close the windows and doors?" I asked him.

"Why in tarnation would I do that? This ol' house gits hotter than a fiddler's elbow if I close it up."

We blinked at each other, equally bewildered. "But, Raz," I said, enunciating slowly and carefully so he could follow each word, "if you leave the windows and doors open, the air conditioner can't cool the house. You'll end up cooling the yard and running up a whopper of an electricity bill."

He chawed on that for a minute, then slapped his belly and cackled. "You got it all cattywampus, Arly. I never aimed to cool this house with that contraption. I put it in the little shed I built for my hogs. I got me one of those fancy show sows. Name's Marjorie and she's in the family way. When it got so dadburned hot, her poor ears and tail started a-drooping and she got a real sad look in her eyes. Finally I couldn't stand it no more and bought the air cooler for her shed."

"Sorry, I guess I wasn't thinking straight. I came by to see if you noticed anything out of the ordinary at the bank last night."

"There was a fire what burned it to the ground." He was idly scratching his armpit, but he was watching me real close.

"I'm aware of the fire. I just wondered if you saw anybody going behind the bank, or acting in a suspicious manner."

He switched to the opposing pit. "Earl Buchanon was mumbling and fretting something awful, and Jeremiah was carrying on the same way. Is that what you mean?"

"Closer, Raz. All the women were in the lot, and all the spectators were across the highway on the Assembly Hall lawn. Was there anyone else you might have noticed?"

"I seem to recollect someone." He scratched and chawed and spit for a minute, then grinned. "That Nookim feller was hiding in the bushes beside the Assembly Hall. I think mebbe he was waiting for Brother Verber, because I heard the preacher say something and there weren't nobody else in earshot."

"Thanks," I said, trying to hide a frown. I started down the porch steps, then stopped and looked back. "Why were you there, Raz?"

"My damn fool VCR is broken. There wasn't a single network show Marjorie and I could agree on, so we moseyed down to the far end of town to see what was happening. She stayed in the truck, of course, because of her delicate condition. She's right shy about it."

That is a direct quote. I swear it.

I drove past Ruby Bee's, noting that an unfamiliar car had joined Estelle's station wagon and Carolyn's subcompact, and turned left on the county road. I bumped across the cattle guard at the entrance of the Pot O' Gold and wound through the mobile homes to the Nookim residence. Earl Boy was not in sight, thus saving me from a major moral dilemma in that I'd locked his mama in jail but I still couldn't tolerate the thwacks.

Putter, dessed in the same apron and with the baby in his arms, watched me as I came up to the door. "What now, Arly?" he said without spirit. "Is there news about what they're fixing to do to Johnna Mae?"

"Nothing will happen until Monday, when she's arraigned. The judge will appoint an attorney for her, and he'll do what he can to get her out on bail."

"We can't pay an attorney and we don't have any money for bail."

"The attorney's services are free. Maybe your neighbors can chip in on the bail money," I said, sounding more optimistic than I felt. "But there's something I need to ask you about last night. What time did Johnna Mae come back here to kiss the children good night?"

"Hang on a minute." He disappeared into the dim interior and came back with neither apron nor wee Nookim. "I didn't look at the clock. She wasn't here more than five minutes before she said she had to get back to the bank and take guard duty."

"What'd she say about the demonstration? She told me on the way to Farberville that you asked how long it would last and was there enough kerosene to keep the lanterns going all night."

He tugged on his forelock and sighed. "Yeah, we talked for a little while."

"On the sidewalk, she told me, while you walked her out to the gravel road?" I prompted, not especially fond of myself. Mendacity always strikes me that way.

"Yeah, on the sidewalk." He stopped tugging on his

hair and gave me a narrow look. "Why are you asking all this? Are you trying to get at something so you can keep Johnna Mae locked up for the next fifty years?"

"No, Putter, I'm not. I'm trying to get to the bottom of what happened last night. You and Johnna Mae didn't have the conversation because you weren't here. Who baby-sat for the kids while you were gone?"

"Who says I wasn't here?"

"Someone saw you in the bushes beside the Assembly Hall. The witness theorized that you were waiting for Brother Verber, but I don't agree. What were you doing?"

"I was worried about Johnna Mae. I wanted to make sure she was okay."

"You don't have to tell me any of this," I said bleakly. "You don't have to testify against your wife."

"She may have borrowed some money without asking, but I know for a fact she didn't kill Bernswallow and set that fire, and I ain't afraid to testify about that."

"Then who did?"

His expression turned exceedingly blank. "I can't say right now. I had Earl Boy mind the young'uns while I slipped over to the Assembly Hall to check on Johnna Mae. I didn't want her to see me because she'd have been perturbed about the kids being left alone, even for a few minutes. It was kind of dark in the lot and it took me a while to spot her. I guess that was when she'd gone home. Once I saw her with that WAACO woman, I hustled straight back here."

"Do you mind if I ask Earl Boy what time his ma came home for a brief visit?"

"I already asked him, and he doesn't know. He says he went to sleep as soon as I left. When I got back, I carried him into the bedroom."

He was blinking like a toad in a hailstorm, and I didn't buy much of his story. As I left I told him to stick around, I'd be back later for a statement.

It didn't sound like Johnna Mae'd come home during her absence from the demonstration. The two had cooked up the story of the visit to cover whatever she'd done during that time. Putter wasn't going to tell me what he saw from his post across the street. He sure as hell wasn't going to tell me he'd seen his wife sneak around the corner from the back of the bank.

She was smart enough to have embezzled money for three years without raising any suspicions. She was hefty enough to have smashed a blunt instrument over Bernswallow's head. She was dumb enough to think burning the bank would cover the petty thefts, or at least confuse things so we might not stumble across them. She had motive, means, and opportunity.

I went to the PD to call the sheriff, but as I reached for the telephone, it rang. I picked it up and ungraciously muttered my name.

"This is Francis Merganser, Chief Hanks. Sergeant Plover made a friendly call to the crime lab, and they've agreed to do a rush job for us, at least on the evidence we sent this morning. I can't write up my official report until the middle of next week, but I can relate the gist of it now if you're interested." When I admitted that I was, he said, "I had the film developed at one of those one-hour places and I've been studying the prints real close. I think it's safe to say that the fire had two points of origin: one was that pile of wadded paper next to the desk and the other was a metal wastebasket off in the corner behind the desk. The former did all the damage; the latter didn't spread, since it was contained. All it did was leave a mark on the wall."

"Can you determine which was lit first?"

"I think we can assume that whoever set the bank on fire didn't fight his way through the flames and smoke to burn something in a metal trash can," he said, trying not to imply I was the all-time stupidest person he'd ever met. The implication was hard to miss.

"Good point," I said. "What about the contents of the wastebasket? Was there anything left?"

"The lab boys may be able to do some restoration. You ought to hear from them in a day or so. Your buddy Plover came down on them like a ton of bricks." Chuckling, Merganser told me to have a nice day and rang off before I could reply that I had other plans. Being told to have a nice day ranked just behind being asked if it was hot enough for me (hell no, I love being parboiled in my own sweat).

I called Harve and told him what I'd learned. We hashed it around for a few minutes, but we didn't get very far. Two different fires were hard to explain; it would have been more expedient to put whatever was in the metal trash can on the floor with the other paper kindling. We did agree there wasn't any big rush to file murder and arson charges against Johnna Mae and that it would be quite nice to hear from the state lab before the Monday morning arraignment. Harve then mumbled something about a budget meeting with the quorum court and told me to keep up the good work (darn, I was looking forward to a major screwup). Said phrase fit neatly behind the heat poser.

I took out my list and decided to see if Elsie McMay

had noticed anything worth noticing. I didn't think for a moment that I'd hear much, but I was fairly confident I'd be offered iced tea and the seat of honor in front of the fan.

"What's for supper?" Earl asked in his friendliest voice. "I was hoping you might make your special chicken and dumplings, but if you've got another idea, why, that's mighty fine with me."

"Heat up a can of chili," Eilene said, and not by a long shot in her friendliest voice. "I'm too worried about Kevin to cook."

"You know how he is, honey—too dumb to find his way home or to even realize how he's got you all worried. When he does drag his sorry excuse for a tail home, I'll take him out to the workshop and give him a horse dose of education with my belt. But there's no point in making ourselves sick by eating stuff out of cans. You're the best cook in the county. My mouth waters every time I think about your fluffy dumplings."

"Don't try to butter me up with that sweet talk. You can eat canned stuff or eat nothing at all. It matters not one whit to me, Earl Buchanon. My days of leaping to my feet when you say boo are over, and over for good. If you want a slave, go buy yourself one. I ain't for sale."

Eilene turned on her heel and walked right out of the room, leaving Earl standing there dumbstruck. He figured she would have gotten back to normal by now, since that smarmy feminist had caused the bank to burn and had therefore been obliged to slink away in disgrace and to leave all the women to act like wives instead of loud-mouthed Communists.

He called Jeremiah McIlhaney on the pretext of talking deer season and slyly asked how things were over there. Jeremiah seemed real proud of the fact Millicent was baking bread, but then admitted he'd had to promise to take her to the picture show all the way in Farberville *and* have gussied-up ice cream sundaes afterward. Earl curled his lip but didn't say anything to Jeremiah except it sounded like fun. He called Larry Joe and tried the same routine. Larry Joe's voice got squirmy, and he finally said Joyce was still ticked off so bad she was refusing to do laundry or cook or much of anything except announce she was going to watch some movie on the television set that night, right when Roy had planned to settle down in front of a football game with a six-pack and a bag of nacho-flavored Doritos he'd bought for the occasion.

Earl made some more calls, but the reports were pretty much the same. The women were still acting screwy and showing no signs of easing up. As far as he could tell, Eilene was going to stand at the living room window until Kevin came home. She didn't care if Earl starved to death, or ran out of clean underwear, or had to match his socks himself.

"What the hell is the world comin' to?" he muttered out loud.

In the living room Eilene heard his plaintive remark but she saw no reason to enlighten him.

Carolyn came into the bar just as Staci Ellen was reaching the best part of her story about Bruno's bowling team's so-called picnic, when one of the boys had flung a Frisbee at a wasp nest just to show how tough he was. Ruby Bee and Estelle both sighed as

Carolyn said, "Good, you're here. Give me a run-down on what's been happening at the office, then you can take the suitcases around back to our rooms."

Staci Ellen thought of all sorts of barbed remarks but decided there was something to the business about discretion and the better part of valor. "The mail's on the table. There were no visitors and only two telephone messages. I wrote them down exactly how they were dictated."

"I'm glad you're learning," Carolyn said as she riffled the mail. "Just tell me who called and the essence of the messages."

"The caller's name was Monty. He said an anonymous person sent his wife a letter detailing your affair with him, and also called the hotel in Las Vegas last night and left a lengthy message with the desk clerk. Then this Monty started cussing up a storm and calling you all sorts of nasty names like—"

"Never mind, Staci Ellen," Carolyn said abruptly, looking a little warm despite the fact she was below a vent. She gave Ruby Bee and Estelle a strangled smile and suggested Staci Ellen take the suitcases to their rooms. Immediately.

Ruby Bee dived in. "Is Monty your boyfriend?"

"No, he's merely a colleague who's delusional at times. He really ought to be disbarred and committed to a nice quiet place with padded walls and designer straitjackets," Carolyn said, regaining some if not all of her poise as she imagined Staci Ellen with her lips stitched up in a zigzag pattern. "Have you heard anything new from Arly?"

Ruby Bee poured Carolyn a glass of iced tea and one for herself. "There hasn't been a peep from Arly, but Elsie McMay said she saw Arly driving out of town, and that Johnna Mae Nookim was sitting in the front seat looking despondent."

"We think Arly was taking Johnna Mae to the county jail," Estelle contributed. There wasn't any reason Ruby Bee deserved all the fun, so she added, "This Monty fellow sounds crazier than a loon, but I'll bet you've got all sorts of boyfriends down there in Little Rock."

"I'm too involved in my work to waste time engaging in sexist mating rituals. If I wish to have a male companion for dinner or an evening at the theater, I simply invite him. All expenses are divided evenly."

"Isn't that nice?" Ruby Bee said, thinking it was the silliest thing she'd heard in all her born days. "Is that what you did back in college too?"

"I've never allowed a man to think he's entitled to sexual gratification because he's invested money in me."

"But things were different back in college, weren't they?" Ruby Bee persisted (to Estelle's disgust, since she couldn't get a word in). "Didn't you say you attended the state college?"

Carolyn's eyes narrowed. "I don't think I mentioned where I attended undergraduate school or law school. In the face of the complexity of organizing the demonstration and coordinating the media, it didn't seem relevant."

"So where did you go?" Estelle said briskly.

"I went to the state university."

Ruby Bee jabbed Estelle. "What an amazing coincidence! Isn't that where Brandon Bernswallow said he went?" She put on her most amazed expression.

"Wouldn't it be something if you two had known each other? It'd just go to prove it's a small world."

"A real small world," Estelle said, rubbing her arm.

Carolyn looked thoughtfully at them for a long while. "Then I suppose the world is a little bigger than you imagine it is," she said. "If Bernswallow was at school when I was, I never met him. He would hardly have been my type. Those fraternity boys are obsessed with alcohol and sex. I spent my time in the law library or in my apartment. I preferred lectures to toga parties. I think I'll call the jail and find out if Johnna Mae has been booked. If she has, I'll take Staci Ellen with me and go there for a conference with the county prosecutor. I still feel some responsibility for Johnna Mae, so I will offer to represent her gratis. I would imagine the level of legal expertise around here is well below the low-tide mark."

When Carolyn was gone, Estelle glared at Ruby Bee and said, "Well, that didn't accomplish anything, did it? You might have tried to be a little bit subtle, Miss Bulldozer. She was real suspicious after you started chirping your head off about small worlds."

"And you don't think they're a might suspicious in the registrar's office? First you hold your nose and talk like a June bug flew up it, and then you start spouting off all that foolish stuff. The attorney general doesn't put people in jail and throw away the key on his own say-so."

"Then just what does he do?" Estelle countered, seizing the offense.

Ruby Bee regretted her remark, but it was too late now. "Everybody knows what the attorney general does, for pity's sake. He's sort of like the head of all the attorneys in the state. Now, how are we going to figure out why Carolyn underlined Brandon Bernswallow's name in Johnna Mae's letter?"

"She's not going to tell us and Bernswallow couldn't if he wanted to," Estelle said, putting her elbows on the bar and cupping her chin in her hands. "Staci Ellen doesn't know. That woman at the registrar's office was as tight-lipped as Mrs. Jim Bob at a temperance meeting. I don't—"

"Wait a minute. You said Bernswallow couldn't tell us if he wanted to," Ruby Bee said excitedly.

"That's because he's dead. You don't think you can converse with the dead, do you? I remember you acted pretty strange when the psychic set up shop and rambled on and on about how sensitive and perceptive you were, but I presumed you were over that nonsense. Maybe I'm wrong."

"I acted strange? Who wore nothing but aquamarine for five months in hopes of meeting a foreigner with a mustache?" Ruby Bee gave Estelle a moment to huff and puff, then said, "What I meant was that we could go to the Bernswallow house to offer our condolences."

"You mean make an innocent neighborly call?"

"I'll bake something for us to take," Ruby Bee said, her eyes glazing over, "and they'll have to invite us in to visit. One of us can drop Carolyn's name and see if Brandon's parents recognize it. They might say Brandon and Carolyn used to date or have classes together."

Estelle nibbled her lip while she thought it over. "You know what? You ought to make Elsie's green bean casserole with the water chestnuts."

They started a grocery list.

*   *   *

"Kevvvin!" Dahlia called, staring so hard at the undergrowth her eyeballs hurt. "Where are yoooo?"

A turkey vulture who'd been watching her flapped away with a disappointed squawk.

Dahlia unwrapped another sandwich. Even late in the afternoon it was hot as it could be, and it wasn't any picnic having to sit on a hard, bumpy log and holler every few minutes. To make things worse, she'd seriously underestimated the number of sandwiches she needed to sustain her on her search for Kevin. She was already out of bananas, and she hadn't even been in the woods more than a couple of hours.

She opened the garbage bag and stuck her head in it to find out just how sorry her predicament was. Low on bologna sandwiches and down to two of the ham salad. Only one of those chocolate cream-filled cupcakes with the squiggly line of white icing.

She didn't know how she could have made such a bad judgment call. She pulled her head out to holler Kevin's name, then glumly returned it and tried to see if there wasn't another cupcake hiding in the bottom or lost in the sandwiches. There wasn't even a spare crumb.

Kevin surely would have heard her by now and come stumbling out of the bushes to fling himself at her, his dear little eyes brimming with tears of gratitude for her faithful diligence. He'd fall right into her lap and try to express all that gratitude by showering her with kisses and compliments. It occurred to Dahlia that it might be prudent to set the garbage bag on the ground behind the log, since there wasn't any reason to smash perfectly good sandwiches and that last cupcake.

But she let the bag remain in her lap, considering the remote possibility that Kevin wasn't going to stumble and be grateful because he just might not be in the area. He sure hadn't answered thus far, and you'd think he would have. And if he wasn't around, then he wasn't going to fall on top of her and therefore there was no reason to worry about him smashing her provisions.

Feeling a good deal brighter, Dahlia left the bag in her lap and began groping around for the cupcake.

"Maggody? Where the fuck's Maggody? I've never fucking heard of Maggody," Bruno growled.

Mrs. Quittle shrank back into the foyer, wishing Mr. Quittle were home to deal with the situation instead of galavanting off to all the hardware stores in Little Rock to find some gadget for his car. "I don't know where it is, Bruno," she managed to reply calmly.

"What the fuck is she doing there?"

"I really couldn't say. I know it has something to do with her job. She mentioned that her boss called and asked her to bring some clothing or papers from the office."

Bruno began to pound his palm with a fist. "You're telling me Staci Ellen broke our date to go to this fucking little town because that lesbian bitch wanted some clothes? I fucking can't believe it."

"I wish you'd stop using that word," Mrs. Quittle said as loudly as she dared.

"What word?"

"The . . . uh, the F word, Bruno. I realize I'm a bit of an old fuddy-duddy, but it disturbs me. That's not to say there's anything wrong with your use of it when you're with your contemporaries."

Bruno stopped pounding his palm and scratched his nose, trying to figure out which word was giving the old bag such a problem. It finally came to him. "Fuck? Is that the word? Hey, I don't mind, Mrs. Quittle. It's no big deal. I won't use any words that start with *F* if you don't want me to. Did Staci Ellen say when that fucking—excuse me. When the goddamn bitch is going to send her home?"

"No, she didn't," Mrs. Quittle said, wishing she could slam the door in his face but lacking anywhere near enough gumption.

"You know what the fuck—sorry—I ought to do? I ought to just take a ride up to that crummy town and bring Staci Ellen home. She doesn't have any business up there when she was supposed to have a date with me. What am I supposed to do, fer chrissake? Sit home and friggin' knit baby booties?"

Bruno strode down the walk to his bike, which was just shy of being the size of a Clydesdale. Letting out a sigh, Mrs. Quittle sagged against the doorframe and read the silver-studded message on the back of his black leather jacket. It encouraged her to have a nice fucking day.

"Same to you, you little fuckhead," Mrs. Quittle said very, very softly.

11

In the ensuing day and a half, I plowed through my list dutifully, if not enthusiastically. As I'd predicted, Elsie's tea was iced, her furniture well arranged, and she hadn't seen anything suspicious. Joyce hadn't seen anything suspicious, nor had Larry Joe. Millicent, her daughter, and her husband hadn't seen anything suspicious. The hippies hadn't seen anything suspicious, although they had seen a lot of incredibly disgusting chauvinistic behavior from the pigs across the street. I didn't ask if they'd met Marjorie.

I must have covered every road in the area running down—not literally—those on my list, and I did so in a car with a nonfunctional air conditioner, which did little to lighten my mood. The mood in the households that I visited wasn't much better; for the most part, the women were pissed and the men so far off balance I was surprised they were able to walk and chew tobacco at the same time.

I'd been past the remains of the branch bank a dozen times, but as I came up the county road from the Pot O' Gold and a futile conversation with Eula Lemoy, I saw the Crosley parked in the lot. Miss Una was stepping cautiously through the scattered glass and charred rafters, her hands up by her shoulders to avoid any inadvertent contamination.

I parked and went to what had been the entrance. "You looking for anything in particular?"

Her head jerked around. "Goodness, Arly, you startled me. I was just seeing if any of my little personal effects might have survived the fire. I kept a photograph of my kitties in a little gold frame in my money drawer. It's silly of me to think it might be intact, but I thought I'd look. And I had a postcard from my deceased brother, a real pretty scene of a garden in Germany that he sent to me, oh, it must have been more than forty years ago."

I offered to help. We moved a blackened board and a stack of gunky ledgers, and eventually reached the drawer below what had been her teller's window. Although the pseudomarble counter was unbroken, the fire had eaten through the bottom of the cheap cabinetry and we found only ashes and a melted picture frame.

"What happened to all the money?" I asked.

"Heavens, we don't keep cash in the drawers at night. We don't have much cash in general, but we lock it in the safe each day when we close. Mr. Oliver had the safe transported to the main bank as soon as the fire was out and the security men could get to it. It would have been terribly irresponsible not to have done so."

"What will all the branch customers do now?"

"They'll be obliged to do their business in Farberville for the time being, I suppose. I'm not sure what the tellers there will make of Raz and Perkins and some of the more trying customers. Raz, in particular, refuses to grasp the concept of depository charges." She picked up the corner of the picture frame, then let it drop. "This fire has made me realize it's time for me to retire and spend more time with my kitties. They get so lonesome during the day, the poor dears. I've managed to put aside a little money each month, and I may take a trip to visit my niece in El Dorado or perhaps take a bus trip this fall to admire the foliage. Do they allow pets?"

"They may. I suppose you've heard about Johnna Mae?"

Miss Una blinked mistily. "Such a terrible thing. Johnna Mae could be on the zealous side at times, but I always believed she had a good heart. She doted on her children and was a homeroom mother for I don't know how many years. All those homemade cupcakes and party favors."

"She's not on death row yet," I said irritably. "The embezzlement charges are filed, but she took such a small amount that the bank may allow her to make restitution and let it go at that."

"But she murdered Mr. Bernswallow."

"We don't know that for sure. I'm still tracking down witnesses, and we should have a report from the state crime lab by late this afternoon or early tomorrow. The kerosene can may have fingerprints on it. Some of the burned papers may be restored, so maybe we can find out what it was that someone felt obliged to do murder over. In any case, Johnna Mae hasn't even been charged with anything except embezzlement."

"I thought she had been," Miss Una said, sounding confused. As we walked back to the parking lot, she gave me a conspiratorial smile. "I must say this lab sounds so very mysterious. Imagine being able to find fingerprints on something burned, or to read charred papers. I do hope they'll succeed. How nice it would be for all concerned if Johnna Mae could return to her family and occupy herself with cupcakes and party favors once again."

I didn't point out that Johnna Mae would be more likely to occupy herself with chicken gizzards at a poultry plant in Starley City, with lots of overtime to pay back the bank. When we reached our cars, I asked Miss Una to call me if she thought of anything that might be relevant. She promised to do so and drove away at all of fifteen miles an hour.

I went back into the bank and found the corner where Merganser said the second fire had started. The can and its contents were at the lab, but the black vee on the wall was there if one squinted just a bit and leaned to one side like a well-known tower. Two points of origin. Two fires. Two arsonists? That didn't make much sense, but nothing had lately. I mentally replayed what Johnna Mae had said to me. She hadn't denied being blackmailed, and she hadn't denied going into the bank. On the other hand, she'd vehemently denied killing Bernswallow and torching the bank. If she was telling the truth—or at least not telling any lies, since she wasn't actually telling much of anything—then a second perp was involved. Putter, for instance.

I wasn't real pleased with my thoughts. As I started for the police car and my list, Estelle's station wagon cruised by in the direction of Farberville. She and Ruby Bee managed not to see me, but I saw them long enough to realize they were wearing Sunday dresses and hats. Which wasn't the most peculiar thing imagin-

able, since it was Sunday. Then again, the Baptist
church was in the opposite direction and services had
been over a good hour or so. They might have been
going to eat Sunday dinner at the cafeteria in Farberville,
I told myself as I glowered at the tailgate. I didn't buy
it, but there wasn't a whole hell of a lot I could do
about it, so I found my list and checked off Eula's
name in that she, as she so succinctly phrased it, hadn't
seen spit.

I was plotting my next brilliant move when Plover
drove up and parked beside me. "I was looking for
you," he said, giving me the benefit of his boyish grin.

"Everybody knows you can't escape the long arms
of the law."

"Let's find someplace cool to talk. I had a conversation
with one of the boys at the lab, and I think you'll find
it fascinating." He gestured for me to get in his car
and then had the decency to turn up the air conditioner,
aim all the vents at me, and offer no comments about
the sticky wet blotches all over my shirt. "I don't
suppose the PD is cool, knowing what I do about your
budget. How about a back booth at Ruby Bee's? Since
we're not on duty, I'll spring for iced tea."

I mentioned that the place was still closed, but that I
had no qualms about breaking and entering with the
key so slyly hidden on the top of the doorsill. I tried to
badger him into telling me all the fascinating stuff, but
he insisted on a weather monologue until we had
broken and entered, poured ourselves tea, and settled
in the back booth.

"I called in an old marker from a guy at the lab," he
began. "He worked yesterday and today on a couple
of the samples we sent down, and he sent back some

interesting tidbits." Plover paused so I could utter a breathless demand or a few choice words of flattery. I gazed stoically across the table. He sighed. "He managed," he went on, "to pull up a partial print from the handle of the kerosene can, and a beautiful set from the metal wastebasket. They don't match."

"So? Kevin Buchanon emptied the trash every night. I have a hard time seeing him leave a beautiful set of anything, but it's likely he did this once out of perversity."

Plover made an exasperated noise. "Shit, I forgot about him. Pick him up and bring him in to be fingerprinted. That way we'll know if we've got something."

"He disappeared the night of the fire. No one's seen him since, including his beloved Dahlia." I wrinkled my nose. "Now that I think about it, she may have disappeared too. Ruby Bee and Estelle acted strange when I asked where she was."

"Well, ask them again."

"They've disappeared, although perhaps only for an innocent visit to the cafeteria in Farberville. The one person who hasn't disappeared is Johnna Mae Nookim, unless she crocheted a ladder and escaped from the county jail. What's more, her fingerprints are already on file."

"I thought of that," Plover said, his voice on the smug side. "Hers don't match the set or the partial from the kerosene can."

I choked on a mouthful of tea. "They don't? Then whose are they?"

"An excellent question, Chief. I don't suppose everyone in town would line up and meekly submit to having their fingers rolled in ink."

"Things are still a bit tense," I said. "We could ask the other bank employees to be printed. What about Bernswallow? I can't see him dousing the office with kerosene, but he very well could have burned something in the wastebasket. No, save your breath; I have no theories why he would."

"We're not going to be able to lift any prints off the body. His upper torso was partially protected when the ceiling collapsed on the desk, but his arms and hands were severely damaged."

"The prints are probably courtesy of Kevin, but I suppose we'd better follow this up however we can. I'll ask Sherman Oliver and Miss Una to come by the barracks and have their prints taken for comparison. If you'll arrange for that, I'll go by the Bernswallow house and ask if there might be something I can borrow that has his prints on it. I need to drop by anyway to ask a bunch of awkward, painful, useless questions about his friends and enemies. Now I'll have to mumble something about why the medical examiner can't get prints during the autopsy. What an enchanting prospect."

"I'll arrange it immediately," he said. "Do you want me to issue an APB for Buchanon? I doubt I can talk the Mounties into galloping down from Canada to search the mountains, but I can have all the patrol cars keep an eye out for him. Do you have any ideas about why he vanished?"

"Probably as many as he has. We're talking about Kevin Buchanon, who's never been accused of having an ounce of brains. He's pulled so many goofy stunts in the past that I wouldn't be surprised if he'd upped and run away to join the circus. Or entered a monastery, or decided to be a pirate."

"And the girl?"

"Same scenario, I'm afraid."

He drove me back to my car. I stopped at the PD and called Oliver, who said he would go by the barracks on his way to the golf course, and Miss Una, who said it sounded utterly thrilling. I then squared my shoulders, kicked the air conditioner, and limped out to the police car to drive to Farberville.

Brother Verber licked his finger and turned the page of the witchcraft manual. It still was possible, if only remotely so, that the women of Maggody had formed a secret coven and intended to engage in their evil rituals once all the furor over the bank fire died down. After all, they'd clearly lost their minds because of that home-wrecking feminist woman from Little Rock, who'd had no problem converting heretofore obedient wives into wicked, defiant, sinful women's libbers one inch away from burning their brassieres. He'd said as much in his sermon, and he'd seen the stubbornness flash across their faces.

They were still up to something. The most obvious thing was magic, and not the sort of magic where pumpkins were changed into cartridges, either. Black magic. Devil worships. Evil.

Brother Verber found himself increasingly interested in how one went about all those depravities, but he reminded himself he was doing it only to protect those members of his flock who'd strayed right off the path of righteousness and were down in the ditch of despair. It occurred to him that it might be real prudent to familiarize himself with all the details, just in case they somehow managed to call up some demon from hell so as to have a disgusting, lustful orgy.

He stopped for a minute to ponder if he was having wicked thoughts by admitting there might be demons on call. No, it was all right because the Catholic Church had exorcism rituals, which meant they worried about it, and although Brother Verber was a far cry from being a papist, he had to respect them. Why, everybody knew the Vatican was wallpapered in gold and the pope flew all over the world in a private airplane. He concluded that it was not only proper but also real important to test some of the instructions in the book.

"A cloak of patchwork," he read aloud. He decided he could get by with his plaid shirt, which kind of looked like patches. "Thirty days of fasting." This was more of a poser. After some heavy breathing, he told himself he was only shooting for a little demon and therefore would fast the rest of the day and wouldn't touch the two pieces of fried chicken in the cardboard bucket until he had conducted his experiment. The book went on to say he had to mediate and pray for a hundred days, but Verber figured he did that all the time anyway and could count that.

The rest of it was a piece of cake. A dark, secluded valley, seven stones stacked up around which he was ordered to circumambulate, some mumbo jumbo he was supposed to memorize but would write on a little crib sheet, and a glass bottle with a cork to put his demon in. Brother Verber wondered if a mayonnaise jar might work just as well.

"Truda says she and Sherman might move to Florida," Mrs. Jim Bob said as she delicately scooped up a forkful of mashed potatoes. "I was a little bit surprised, I must say. They must be a lot better off than they let on."

Jim Bob eyed the piece of fried chicken, but he didn't have the nerve to pick it up under his wife's beady scrutiny. The lecture on table manners wasn't worth it. God knew she all the time screeched at the damn brats about not eating like wild animals, and it didn't matter, since they always ate in the kitchen where nobody had to look at them except for Perkins's eldest. Sighing, he picked up his fork. "He's a banker. Maybe he takes home a little extra every night."

"I don't care to hear such remarks, even if you're joking. Sherman and Truda are my dear friends, and I don't imagine they go around saying you steal money from the town bank account." She put down her fork to consider the Olivers' financial situation. "Truda has always run her home on a real tight budget. I know for a fact she buys her clothes at a discount house, because once I happened to open the closet door by mistake and saw the labels. Their house is . . . well, even Truda would admit their house doesn't hold a candle to ours. It has one and a half bathrooms, and the carpet's so stained in the living room that I'd be embarrassed to let anyone even see it. They haven't been on a vacation in years, except for that one time they went to Eureka Springs for the Passion Play and stayed in one of those bed-and-breakfast places instead of a real hotel. How much do you reckon bankers get paid?"

Jim Bob tried to anchor the chicken breast with his finger, but caught his wife's disapproving look and glumly let it slide into the peas. "Why don't you ask them to send over a financial statement and a copy of last year's income tax return? That way you'd know exactly how much money they have. Maybe you can sneak a peek at the mortgage."

"Don't be vulgar—and stop playing with your food. I have no desire to offend my friends by taking an unhealthy interest in their personal finances. I was merely wondering, that's all. If you're bored, we can discuss the sermon this morning. I found it a shade peculiar myself."

"Verber's sure got a bee in his bonnet about this devil worship," Jim Bob muttered. "He looked disappointed when none of the women in the congregation ripped off their clothes during the closing hymn."

"He is concerned about the subject. He has a moral obligation to warn everyone of their wickedness, even if they're not actually engaging in it as of yet." Mrs. Jim Bob's face turned the color of the tomato aspic on her salad plate. "I do wish he'd stop talking about bared bosoms and blood running down bellies to—ah, to vile places."

Jim Bob had enjoyed that part, although he'd dozed off toward the middle of the sermon and had himself a nice dream about Cherri Lucinda's vile place, which might well be the vilest of them all.

After a few wrong turns and dead ends, I found the street that curled up the mountain to the large homes overlooking Farberville. When I came around the corner, I stopped to stare at all the cars parked on both sides of the street and choking the long driveway. The Bernswallows had visitors. It would make things more awkward, but I presumed we could find a room somewhere for a quiet talk.

I parked behind a chocolate brown Jaguar, walked past four pastel Mercedes in a row, and turned at a lemon yellow BMW to trudge past a rainbow of Audis and an honest-to-goodness silver Rolls-Royce. Beyond the house was a four-door garage, and beyond that a clump of mundane battered little cars. The help, no doubt.

A couple came up behind me, the man in a dark suit and stiffly starched shirt and the woman in a mink coat. It wasn't more than a hundred degrees in the shade; I took a small yet simple pleasure in noting the flush on her cheeks. The man nodded soberly at me and rang the doorbell.

We were admitted by what I assumed was a butler, who took in my police uniform with a subdued wince. In a properly mournful murmur, he announced that Mr. and Mrs. Bernswallow were receiving callers in the living room and would we be so kind as to follow him and would madam prefer him to see to her wrap. She whipped it off and tossed it to him, and we trooped down a corridor to a vast living room packed sardine-style with people. Most of them had wineglasses in hand and mortuary voices.

I caught the butler's arm and asked how to find Mr. and Mrs. Bernswallow. He gazed at my hand until I removed it, then murmured that Mr. and Mrs. Bernswallow were seeing only a select few of their closest friends in the library. It was pretty clear he didn't place me in that category, so I told him I was there on official police business.

He clamped his lips together and led me through the crowd to a closed door. "I shall let master and madam know you're here and ascertain if they will speak with you." He tapped on the door and slipped inside.

I smiled at those staring at my uniform with varying degrees of curiosity and disdain. About the time I was going to offer one particularly sniffy woman the chance to find out if my gun was loaded (it wasn't), the butler came out to the living room, a bizarre expression on his face. What I saw over his shoulder propelled me into the library. With a bizarre expression on my face.

A silver-haired woman dressed in black was gaping in horror at a casserole dish on the table in front of her. A silver-haired man in a dark blue suit was sputtering wordlessly, his nose bright red and his chin dotted with spittle. His hands cut through the air, but he couldn't seem to find any words. At least not for Ruby Bee Hanks and Estelle Oppers, who were perched on a brocade sofa, their purses in their laps and their expressions as bright as children on Christmas morning.

When they saw me, the eagerness blinked out like a lightning bug's tail. "Why, Arly," Ruby Bee said, gulping, "whatever are you doing here?"

Bernswallow found a few words, to wit: "You—you rude, outrageous, pushy—I saw your faces on the local news, you—"

"My God," Mrs. Bernswallow moaned, "why is it such a ghastly shade of green? It looks like dog vomit. Oh, Charles, make them take it away. Call Perkins at once and tell him to remove this from my sight."

"Is Perkins the butler?" Estelle said. "I know a fellow out in Maggody named Perkins. Do you think they could be any relation?"

"Do something, Charles," the woman commanded in the same agonized voice.

"Now you see here," Bernswallow said, finding more words, "I don't know who you are"—he spun around and jabbed a finger at me—"or you either, but I demand that all three of you leave immediately. It is totally outrageous for you to come into this house under patently false pretenses and upset Mrs. Bernswallow like this. If you do not leave this instant, I shall have you arrested for trespassing and impersonating police officers. Furthermore, when our period of mourning is over, I shall instruct my legal firm to file a multimillion-dollar civil suit against all of you for harassment and emotional distress."

"Calm down," I said before he found an entire dictionary. "I am the chief of police in Maggody, and I'm here on official business."

"I heard one of them call you by name. Do you know these two trespassers?"

I shook my head, but Ruby Bee waggled her finger at me and said, "You know perfectly well who we are, Miss Officious Business. We just came by to offer our condolences and to drop off a little something for supper. You have no call to act like we're a couple of burglars here to steal the family silverware."

Mrs. Bernswallow shuddered. "Charles, I do believe I shall be ill if you do not remove this dreadful thing from my sight. I had the carpet cleaned only yesterday."

"Don't be silly," Estelle said. "You just take green beans, cream of mushroom soup, canned onion—"

"Charles! Do something right now!"

Mr. Bernswallow snatched up the casserole dish and shoved it at Estelle. "Mrs. Bernswallow is not interested in whatever may comprise the contents of this unappetizing mess. Please take it with you on your way out the door!"

Ruby Bee and Estelle marched over to the door, their noses bent so far out of shape I was amazed they could see where they were going. As they went through the door, Estelle looked back over her shoulder. "And water chestnuts," she advised. "They give it a nice crunch."

"And pimentos for a festive air," Ruby Bee added.

I sat on the sofa while Mrs. Bernswallow coughed and gagged and Mr. Bernswallow patted her back and muttered rather colorful remarks at the closed door. Once she'd regained her composure, he glared at me. "This is a most difficult time for us. What do you want?"

"I am very sorry about your son's death. I'm working with the sheriff's department and the state police to determine who was responsible, and I need to ask you a few questions."

His eyes bulged dangerously. "About that McCoy woman? Don't you people ever give up? That was five or six years ago, and I see no relevance to the tragic death of my son." Mrs. Bernswallow hid her face in her hands and began to sob.

The McCoy woman? I flapped my lips for a minute. "No," I said slowly, "I wanted to ask you if Brandon had any enemies. I also would like a list of any of his close friends who might have knowledge of anyone with a grudge." The McCoy woman? Carolyn McCoy-Grunders? I was dying to ask, but I didn't want to deal with hysterics from Mrs. Bernswallow and a fatal apoplectic fit from her husband.

Mr. Bernswallow relaxed. "No enemies that I can think of. After Brandon completed his degree, I arranged for him to take a position as a teller at a bank in a different locale. I subsequently arranged the head teller position for him at the branch, in order to diversify his experience and increase his skills in management. I had hoped to bring him into the main bank in a year or two, perhaps as a loan officer."

"Did he live in this house?"

"Recently, yes. He's only been back a short time, and he's been putting in hard hours at the branch. I don't think he's even talked to any of his old friends." Bernswallow looked away for a minute. "I was very proud of his diligence, especially in the last few weeks. He returned to the branch on numerous evenings to familiarize himself with the idiosyncrasies peculiar to this particular branch."

"I was concerned that he was working too hard," Mrs. Bernswallow said in a quavering voice.

"Nonsense," Bernswallow said firmly. "There's no such thing as working too hard. I've never wasted my afternoons playing golf or having martinis with my friends, which is why I'm the chairman of the board rather than a petty tyrant in the boondocks. If you want to succeed, you've got to put your nose to the grindstone and run it at full speed."

"You've had a report about the embezzlement," I said. "If Brandon had been working on the accounts at the branch, don't you think he would have caught on immediately?"

Bernswallow harrumphed. "The employee was very devious, and Brandon was only beginning to familiarize himself with the customers and their individual accounts. He hinted to me that there were several problems at the branch, but I felt it would do him good to handle them himself and therefore refused to discuss them with him. I wanted him to learn how to take charge, how to handle sloppiness and petty theft. That's what builds character."

I nodded and asked if I might look at Brandon's room. Mrs. Bernswallow promptly burst into tears. Bernswallow rang for the butler, ordered him to take me wherever I wanted, and sat down to console his wife. I trailed Perkins (surely no relation) down a back hallway, up an imposing flight of stairs, down a corridor lined with oil paintings of grim-visaged ancestors, and into a bedroom.

"Will that be all, miss? I really must attend to my duties downstairs," Perkins said, peering down his nose at me.

"I'll ring for you if I want a snack," I said, and waited until he was gone before turning to study the room. It had all the warmth and personal touches of a bank vault. The walk-in closets were stuffed with clothes, and the drawers with ironed underwear and socks rolled into perfect eggs. In the drawer beside the bed I found a half pint of bourbon, which I decided was as likely as anything to have fingerprints on its shiny surface. I eased it into a plastic bag and tucked it in my purse.

I went back into the closet, marveling at its size, and ran my hand along the top shelf. I felt a flat, rectangular shape, and pretty soon I was sitting cross-legged on the bed with Brandon's college scrapbook.

It was a truly tasteless journey down memory lane. There was an extensive collection of snapshots, some of snickering boys draped over each other's shoulders and clutching beer cans, but the majority were of women in various degrees of undress. Under each was an editorial about her sexual prowess or certain skills. Exclamations marks abounded. I studied each face as best I could and couldn't find Carolyn. However, some poses focused on areas of anatomy I wouldn't recognize her by in any case.

The fraternity had thrown elaborate parties on a monthly basis; the invitations ranged from formal to lewd. The accompanying snapshots proved that even formal could degenerate into lewd, that chiffon could be removed if eyes were crossed enough. There were a few newspaper clippings that described the arrival of campus security and the reprimands and threats doled out by the fraternity council and the administration. The fraternity had been disbanded when a coed brought charges of a gang rape in the billiard room. What a charming bunch of guys, I thought as I flipped through the pages.

The final photograph was of Brandon beside his loving cup, his mouth curled in a sardonic grin and his hand raised in a crude gesture. I found it ironic, to say the least. I replaced the scrapbook, made sure the half pint bottle was secure in my purse, and slipped down the back steps and through the kitchen. Outside, the breeze was hot, but it smelled fresh.

12

◆

I went by the state police barracks to see how many fingers had been smudged in the name of comparing prints. Plover said Sherman Oliver had come and gone, and that Miss Una hadn't shown up yet. I said that on the highway she was apt to peak at a maximum speed of twenty miles an hour, which meant it might take her well over an hour and a half to cover the seventeen miles (yes, I know, but we have to take into consideration chicken trucks, railroad crossings, red lights, and pit stops).

"Did Oliver's prints match?" I asked.

"Our office expert is off today. I put them on a transparency and stuck them on the overhead projector with prints from the state lab. I wasn't positive about the handle of the kerosene can, but I'm confident they don't match the full set from the wastebasket. Of course, I would never accuse a branch manager of emptying the trash."

"Let's see if head tellers work any harder." I produced the bottle of bourbon I'd taken from Brandon's bedside table so we could dust it. It was covered with lovely prints, and we transferred the loveliest ones to a plastic sheet. Neither one of us could find a swirl of similarity.

"So I went through the ordeal with his parents for nothing," I said, sighing, and related what had happened at the Bernswallow mansion. Once Plover stopped laughing, I asked him if he had any idea how to uncover this murky connection between the Bernswallow family and Carolyn McCoy, who must have hyphenated at a later date.

"What's odd is that Bernswallow Senior brought it up," I continued. "One would hate to be petty-minded and suspicious, but one wonders if the name had been first mentioned by a blood relative of mine."

He threw up his hands in mock surprise. "What's this? Are you accusing your own mother of meddling in an official police investigation while keeping secrets from you, her only child?"

I dialed the number of the bar and grill, but no one answered, thus averting for the time being what promised to be a tiresome conversation. I resettled in my chair and said, "Once I find Ruby Bee, I'll get out my shiniest cattle prod and elicit everything she knows in no time flat. Bernswallow made another odd remark about how he was chairman of the board rather than a golf-playing petty tyrant in the boondocks. I wonder if it was in reference to Sherman Oliver?"

"If it was, does it have any significance?"

"Well, it wasn't a particularly friendly characterization. He also said Brandon had mentioned several problems at the bank. I'm convinced Brandon knew about Johnna Mae's minor embezzlement and intended to blackmail her, but we've got two fires and two sets of fingerprints. Do you think we could have two candidates for blackmail?"

"I gathered from the reports that Oliver is hardly

ever at the branch. He piddles around at the main bank and the golf course, with an emphasis on the latter."

"He piddles with great deal of the bank's money." I gnawed my lower lip for a moment. "I don't know much about how the portfolio is handled, beyond the explanation Oliver gave me yesterday. I wouldn't think he could skim off any money. He did snarl at a bond salesman who called, though, about a 'flimsy thing.' And the bond salesmen work on commission, which means they might do all sorts of favors for the purchaser."

"Kickbacks, for instance?"

"Why not? Oliver seems to have free rein in what he chooses to purchase. He might well accept a small token of esteem in exchange for the bank's business. It's bound to be way under the table, and I don't know how we could find out. Unless one of us had an off-the-record conversation with someone at the bank."

"You're looking at me," Plover said, squirming. "Shall I have Bernswallow Senior over for beer and pretzels? He sounds like more of a Perrier and caviar man, and you know how much I despise fizzy water and fish eggs. I've got it—I'll take Miss Una to the drive-in movie and butter her up with greasy popcorn and coy little kisses. Remember the night we watched the late-late movie at my house?"

I assured him that I did not, although I may have turned a bit pink. "I hate to break your heart, my khaki-clad Romeo, but Miss Una wouldn't know anything about the portfolio. Bernswallow Senior's likely to be reticent, no matter how fizzy the water and fishy the eggs. I was thinking about Mrs. Gadwall, the head bookkeeper at the main bank. She might have a few learned comments about the contents of the portfolio. If she thinks there's a preponderance of flimsy bonds, we might be able to subpoena all of Oliver's bank accounts to search for large, inexplicable deposits." I frowned as something nibbled at a far corner of my mind. It stopped before any metaphorical light bulbs clicked on. "That's presuming he not only accepts kickbacks but also deposits them at his bank. Brandon might have stumbled across something and decided to blackmail Oliver. Blackmailing Johnna Mae wouldn't have paid for a used bicycle, much less a Mercedes."

"That gives Oliver motive. Does he have any sort of alibi?"

"He says he was in his den, with the door locked, the telephone off the hook, and a bottle of booze within easy reach. His wife was at the bank parking lot, busily playing Ms. Benedict Arnold by supporting the demonstrators. Maybe Brandon had already approached Oliver with the blackmail demand. In his cups, Oliver might have started brooding about all the treachery from his wife and his protégé and decided to show them both by bashing the protégé, torching the bank, and making the issue moot."

"If he murdered Bernswallow, nothing's moot," Plover said. "You do realize that even if we can determine that Oliver accepted kickbacks from bond salesmen, and that Brandon Bernswallow knew about it and intended to blackmail him, we still don't have a pot to piss in. No one saw him anywhere near the bank."

"Unless Kevin Buchanon saw something. Kevin's dim enough to have held the kerosene can while Oliver struck a match. Oliver then offers Kevin a three-month cruise as a reward, and Kevin starts pedaling for the port. For once, I'd actually like to talk to him, but I don't have the wherewithal to pedal in pursuit. Why don't you wait here for Miss Una, take her prints, and then see if you can chat up Mrs. Gadwall at her house? Ruby Bee and Estelle have had plenty of time to get back to Maggody by now; I'm going to swing by the bar and grill for a cozy conversation."

Plover murmured something about cattle prods and bruises. He ushered me out to my car and wished me luck. I asked him if it was hot enough for him, told him to keep up the good work, and suggested he have a nice day. He was still scowling as I drove away.

Carolyn McCoy-Grunders sat in the uncompromisingly uncomfortable chair graciously provided by the Flamingo Motel management on the off chance someone might want to do torturous things to one's back. Staci Ellen sat on the edge of the bed, which wasn't a whole sight more comfortable, a notebook in her hand and a resentful look in her eyes.

"In the matter of the café in Rose Bud," Carolyn said, scanning the complaint, "send the waitress a form and tell her to send it to the Equal Employment Opportunity Commission for a formal review. I loathe these minimum wage squabbles."

"You took on this one," Staci Ellen pointed out. "Now your client's in jail, charged with embezzlement and waiting to be charged with arson and murder, none of which might have happened if you hadn't gotten everybody fired up enough to go storming down the highway to the bank. If you hadn't organized the demonstration, maybe Johnna Mae'd just be looking for another job."

"Would you like to be looking for another job, Staci Ellen?"

"I may consider the possibility," Staci Ellen said snippily, immediately wishing she could take it back. Why, lately her mouth had been operating of its own accord, and her mind had been running in all sorts of crazy directions, like a chicken with its head cut off. She decided she might as well go whole hog. "I've worked at the Women Aligned Against Chauvinism in the Office office for two years, and I haven't ever had a raise. You spend all your time making sure women get treated fairly. Maybe it's time to look a little closer to home."

"My goodness, aren't we feisty today?" Carolyn picked up the next folder and opened it, oblivious to the mutinous glare coming from her secretary. "This file is a mess, Staci Ellen. All the correspondence is out of order. How many times have I told you the importance of maintaining the correct documentation sequence?"

"About seven thousand times, not counting this one. I guess that makes it seven thousand and one."

"My, my, my," Carolyn murmured, looking up, "you are in a remarkably bad mood today. Shall I presume you're in the grip of a particularly bad bout of what seems to be an omnipresent state of premenstrual syndrome?"

"No, I'm not. I'm just plain tired of being treated like a bubble-brain by everybody, including my father, my boyfriend, and my boss. I can do a lot of things, you know. I can make sense of those little squiggles you write in the margins of letters. I can write down obscene messages from your married boyfriend. I can even change a flat tire."

"I have a wonderful idea, Staci Ellen: why don't you take a nice long hike down the highway and see if you can find some helpless soul with a flat tire? I need to get some work done, and I'm really not in the mood to listen to you blither and bitch about this perceived mistreatment by the entire populace, present company included."

"All right, I will!" Staci Ellen snatched up her purse and stalked out the door, almost running into Ruby Bee and Estelle as they crept around the corner from the bar. She didn't stop to say excuse me, either.

Carolyn stared at the original letter from Johnna Mae Nookim. One corner was dog-eared, and there was a dirty mark that might have been made by a shoe. Furthermore, just below the red line she'd drawn under the Bernswallow slime's name, there was a smudge, as if someone had put a finger there. Carolyn's fingers did not leave smudges. She did not dog-ear correspondence, nor did she step on it.

It was peculiar, and frightening.

I went by the bar and grill, but Estelle's station wagon wasn't there. I went on to Kevin's parents' house to see if they'd heard anything. Eilene was sitting on the porch swing, which was as motionless as her face.

"No word from Kevin?" I asked.

"None, and Dahlia's granny called a while back to say she's been missing since yesterday. You don't think the two hatched up some fool scheme so they could run off and get married, do you?"

"It doesn't make much sense," I admitted, sitting down on the porch steps. "I don't want to alarm you, but I'm worried that Kevin saw someone or something involving the murder, and for reasons of his own decided to disappear. We've got some prints from the scene, and I need something with Kevin's prints on it for comparison."

"I'll fetch his cup from the bathroom." She went inside for a moment and returned with a yellow plastic cup. "He's had this since he was a little boy who had to stand on a step to brush his—" She stopped as Earl poked his head through the door.

He smiled ingratiatingly. "I was thinking you might like a nice cold glass of lemonade. I made it myself."

"I told you I didn't want anything to drink. Now there's probably lemon juice on the counter and sugar scattered all over the floor. After you clean it up, why don't you go watch one of your damn fool football games and leave me in peace?"

Earl ducked back inside, but I could hear him mumbling under his breath as he crossed the living room. I'd observed versions of the exchange in numerous households in the last two days. Someone was going to have to tamper some tempers, or we'd end up with fat-cat divorce lawyers licking their whiskers and a mind-boggling singles' scene at Ruby Bee's Bar and Grill.

I told Eilene I'd let her know if I heard anything, and she agreed to do the same and gave me the yellow cup. The screen door slammed before I was halfway down the driveway, and voices were raised before I reached the car. Although the topic was sugar, the words were far from sweet.

It was getting dark as I drove past said soon to be fern bar to look once again for Estelle's station wagon.

When that proved pointless, I parked behind Stiver's antique store and dragged myself up the back stairs to my apartment. If Plover had any astounding revelations, he would call me. If Ruby Bee and Estelle wanted to hide for a few hours and sweat bullets over my impending lecture, more power to 'em. If Sherman Oliver was on the telephone with a Swiss banker, *comme ci, comme ça*. If Kevin had Dahlia perched on the back of his bicycle, he could pedal all the way to Tierra del Fuego for all I cared.

I got in the shower and turned on the cold water.

It was getting dark as Staci Ellen marched down the edge of the road, but she didn't care one bit. Ms. Hotshot With a Hyphen was the meanest woman Staci Ellen had had the misfortune to meet in all her born days. She stopped and found a used straw to do a bit of calculating in the dirt. All six thousand, nine hundred and thirty-five born days, to be precise. But that wasn't right, since she was twenty-seven days into her twentieth year. She scratched some more, carried the one, and eventually arrived at the amended number of six thousand, nine hundred sixty-two born days.

And what had Bruno given her for her birthday? Nothing. What had he done when she hinted timidly, then hinted so broadly any dummy could get it, and finally out-and-out announced it was her birthday and she'd like to go to a real restaurant for dinner? Told her they were going to an industrial league softball tournament across town, and she could get a chili dog when they got there. If she had any money with her.

Staci Ellen threw down the straw and marched ahead. Ol' Hyphen hadn't bothered with a birthday card or suggested the afternoon off. Ol' Hyphen had barked at Staci Ellen something awful just because a few words were misspelled in a letter to the EOA. Nobody could keep *ence* and *ance* straight all of the time, for pity's sake, or *ede* and *eed*.

If she was going to succeed in life, she thought, she was going to have to stand up for herself and not let everybody knock her around as if she were nothing but a bowling pin at the end of the alley of life. She liked that analogy so much that she turned up the next alley she came to, her shoulders thrown back and her head held high.

So high, in fact, that she almost stepped on the kitty cowering in the weeds.

It was getting dark, but Kevin didn't bother to switch on the lamp beside the iron bed. He'd been trying to get interested in the wedgehead jigs in the Bass Pro Shops catalog, since according to the fine print below the picture they were supposed to be dynamite for walleyes and both largemouth and smallmouth bass, none of which he'd ever had any luck with. The lures looked like little one-eyed dancers in colored hula skirts, but instead of envisioning Hawaii or even a deep pool in Boone Creek, Kevin was thinking about Dahlia.

Her final words had been so gosh darn harsh, he told himself as he flopped back on the bed and banged his head on the iron rail. But he loved her, and he figgered she must love him because she let him do such wondrous things between her legs, even when she used to be the clerk at the Kwik-Screw and he'd been obliged to crawl under the counter. Or when they'd been trapped in the outhouse, with the moon shining through the crescent in the door, she'd snuggled his face between her enormous breasts until he couldn't breathe and had started seeing polka dots inside his eyes.

Kevin wished he could talk to Dahlia, if only for a moment so he could ask her if she still loved him as much as he loved her. But that would be dangerous, he reminded himself as he cautiously explored the growing lump on the back of his head. They would all be in terrible danger, and Dahlia in the terriblest danger of all. Why, he couldn't bear to live if the light of his life was snuffed out. This worst-case scenario made him so sad he ate the piece of lemon meringue pie without even tasting it.

It was getting dark as a mysterious figure darted across the highway and into the shadowy sanctuary of the old feed store. A bag clinked softly as the figure looked over his shoulder to make sure no one had seen him, looked ahead to make sure the moonlit coast was clear, and then cut across the back lot and entered the woods, being careful not to snag the cuff of his best plaid shirt on any thorny vines.

It wasn't getting any darker in the motel room, in that all the curtains were drawn and the only light came from a flashlight on the bed.

"I still don't hear anything," Ruby Bee hissed. She stood next to the wall that adjoined unit 2, her ear pressed to the bottom of a wineglass, the mouth of which was pressed against the wall. "I don't even think this works, if you want my honest to goodness opinion."

Estelle, who had been sitting on the chair, got up and rubbed her buttocks to encourage some circulation. "It does so work, Miss Doubting Thomas. They do it all the time on television when they want to hear what's being said in the next room. Maybe nothing's being said."

"Maybe not," Ruby Bee allowed, although she still had her doubts. "Go make sure she hasn't gone out. This thing's hurting my ear something awful; I'm not about to keep doing it if Carolyn's on her way to Little Rock."

Estelle made a face, but she went to the door of the unit and opened it a few inches. "Her car and Staci Ellen's car are right where they were five minutes ago," she whispered sourly. "The curtain's drawn, but there's a light on in there. Staci Ellen's bound to be in there with her, because we're in her room and it's as plain as the nose on your face that she's not in here."

"And you're convinced that any minute now Staci Ellen's going to ask Carolyn why she underlined Brandon Bernswallow's name in red ink, and Carolyn's going to stand right next to the wall and broadcast all her secrets in a loud, clear voice?"

"There is no need to get sarcastic."

"You'd feel a might sarcastic if your ear was flattened against the side of your head, maybe permanently, and all for no good reason."

"Nobody said surveillance was supposed to be fun. But if you want to be Miss Quitter, you go right ahead. Just go sit in your unit or at the bar and wait for Arly, who's no doubt got a real fine lecture written and rehearsed for when she finds you. You can explain why you told that butler fellow that we were under-cover police detectives and would arrest everybody in the whole darn house if we didn't get to visit with the Bernswallows." Estelle eased the door closed, took a deep breath, and took off again like a teapot on a back burner. "We go to all the trouble of leaving my car in Lottie Estes's driveway simply so we can continue the investigation, and now you want to quit just because your ear hurts."

Ruby Bee had been imagining what-all Arly would say, and the prospect struck a real sour chord. "I guess we can do this a while longer. I got five minutes left on my shift, and then it'll be your turn." Smirking under cover of darkness, she put the glass back against the wall and leaned into it. "Wait! I hear something. I think she's getting ready to do something, because she's walking across the room. Maybe she's going to call someone!"

Estelle cupped her ear against the wall, wishing they'd brought two wineglasses. Just her luck to be on break when things got interesting.

It was getting dark as Carolyn opened the door and peered into the motel parking lot. She'd thought moments earlier that she'd heard voices, but the parking lot was empty and the units on either side were dark. Which was of small comfort, because it meant either the room was haunted or she was losing her mind. A few months back her therapist had listed symptoms of stress disorder, but she hadn't mentioned hearing whispers emanating from walls.

She took a final look at the lot, then closed the door and sat back on the chair to scribble more thoughts about Johnna Mae's defense.

*   *   *

It was getting dark and the sandwiches were gone. Dahlia's rear end ached something awful, and her stomach was growling like an earthquake. Her throat was strained so bad from howling for Kevin that all she could do was croak his name every now and then.

Big tears rolled down her cheeks. If she ever found him, she thought with a sigh, she was going to wring his scrawny neck. Here she was, sitting for nearly two days on a rotten log in order to rescue him, and he hadn't shown the decency to come forward and get hisself rescued.

Mebbe the woman lawyer was right. Men were no damn good. Oh, they strutted around and bragged about all the fish they almost caught and said how they'd hang the moon for their girlfriends, but in the end they were nothing but ungrateful brutes who wanted slam-bam sex all the time. Dahlia's brow wrinkled like a bloodhound's as she considered her last thought. Kevin wasn't like that, not by a long shot. He was gentle and tender, just like in the movies.

"Kevvvin," she tried to say, but it came out sounding like the plaintive call of a lonely bullfrog deep in the swamp.

It was getting real dark when the blue flashing light came on behind him. Bruno snarled under his breath, but he knew enough to pull over and jerk the helmet off his head before the pig walked up to him.

"Driver's license and registration," the trooper said, resting one hand on his gun. "Are you aware you were going eighty-three miles per hour in a fifty-five zone?"

Bruno couldn't believe the pig was so fucking dumb as not to see the speedometer in plain sight on the bike's handlebars. He decided not to say as much, and fumbled for his wallet in his back pocket. His hand slid in and out real quick because his pocket was fucking empty of anything, including wallet, which contained both license and registration.

"Gee, I must have left it at home, sir," Bruno said through clenched teeth.

"Is that so? Will you please debike and come with me?"

It was dark enough to require a light, but Truda Oliver was enjoying the gloomy ambiance as she wandered through her house. In her hands she carried a metal box. It had once been locked, but a brief session with a hammer and a screwdriver had taken care of that minor annoyance. How chauvinistic to think women couldn't handle tools, she thought with a smile.

She went into the living room and shook her head. The stain on the carpet was still visible. Grape juice was impossible to get out. She'd tried to keep Mrs. Jim Bob's brat from running through the room with a glassful of potential disaster, but her lack of success was right there on the carpet. She'd hoped Mrs. Jim Bob would offer to have the carpet cleaned, but she might as well have hoped for Mrs. Jim Bob to engage in spontaneous combustion.

Truda opened the lid and stroked the tidy stacks of twenty-dollar bills. It was so fortunate that Johnna Mae had warned her that Brandon intended to blackmail Sherman, if he wasn't already doing so. Johnna Mae had suggested there might be a box of cash somewhere in the house. Truda had gone straight to the den, and now she had this lovely box of money. There was enough to recarpet the entire house. There was enough to put in a dishwasher so her hands wouldn't look so red and chapped all the time. There was even enough to have Perkins's eldest clean, and for years to come.

But Sherman wouldn't like that. He probably planned to use the money for a golf cart or a trip to one of those fancy golf resorts. He'd disappear every morning and not return until it was so dark he couldn't find his golf ball on the fairway, much less in the rough or in a sand trap. From what he said, he spent plenty of time in the last two places. Sherman was a duffer, and she was nothing but an aging golf widow.

Truda told herself she deserved better. Carolyn had told her that she had every right to finish her college degree, or to find a remote place and write the children's books she'd dreamed about for years. Carolyn had said all kinds of things in that vein, until Truda started believing them herself.

And now, as if via divine interference, she had the money to follow her dreams, to seek her destiny, to find total fulfillment. Divine in that somehow she'd known to search every nook and cranny of Sherman's den. Human in that he'd hidden the box where anyone with a crowbar could find it.

Truda went into the bedroom to pack her suitcase but turned right around and went back through the living room, detouring through the kitchen to get her purse and keys, and meticulously locked the front door on her way out. Who needed a bunch of poorly made dresses and cheap plastic accessories from a discount house? Truda Longspur-Oliver, as she decided on the spot to call herself in the future, was going to wear designer dresses and a full-length mink coat.

*   *   *

It was so dark that Sherman Oliver tripped over a branch and went sprawling face first in the rough. As he pushed himself up, his hand brushed something smooth and hard.

"I found my ball," he called to the other members of the foursome, who were almost invisible out on the fairway. "I'll play it from here."

"It's blacker than the inside of a Baptist church, old man. You wouldn't be able to see it if you made a hole in one. We're going back to the clubhouse for a drink. You coming?"

"Hell no." Sherman stood over the golf ball, which was as likely to be his as the last damn fool's, and swung back the club. Bunch of damn sissies, he thought as he chopped down on the ball. He moved a few inches to where the ball had bounced and chopped again at it. They were on the seventeenth hole, for Pete's sake. Bunch of sissies wouldn't even finish out the round.

It was dim in the basement. Plover beckoned to the waiter and asked Mrs. Gadwall if she wanted another martini. When she nodded he instructed the waiter, smiling across the table.

"You certainly know a lot about junk bonds," he said, turning on the dimples until his cheeks hurt. "I'm very, very impressed."

Mrs. Gadwall giggled.

It was seriously dark as Staci Ellen walked down the alley, the tiny kitty cradled in her arms. The moonlight helped, of course, and she was not some goofy girl who was afraid of the dark, or of a bunch of dilapidated fences and smelly garbage cans.

The sweet little thing mewed, and she scratched its little head. "I'll find your mama," she said gently so's not to startle the kitty. "You're too little to have come very far, and I can't just let you stay lost out here where some mean old dog might gobble you up in one bite. Gosh, though, I don't know how I'm going to find your mama out here with nothing but garbage cans."

She was still talking to the kitty when a bobbing light came across one of the backyards. She almost screamed before remembering she wasn't a scaredy-cat, no offense intended to her companion. It took her a minute to catch her breath and say, "Hello, there. Are you looking for a lost kitty?"

Miss Una gasped. It took her a minute to catch her breath, too, and say, "How ever did you know the purpose of my mission?"

"I found her back that way," Staci Ellen said. She joined the elderly woman at the gate and passed over the kitty. "I was worried sick about what to do with her. I knew I couldn't leave her out here by her lonesome, where some nasty dog might hurt her, but I didn't want to go across people's backyards and right up to their kitchen doors to ask."

"Oh, you are an angel. I've scolded Martin so many times about straying from the yard, but he is just as stubborn as he can be. Aren't you, you runaway rascal?" Miss Una rubbed her cheek against the kitty's head.

"So she's a he and his name is Martin? My father's name is Martin, Martin Quittle. He's not a kitty, though; he's more of a sign painter."

"Isn't that something? My Martin is named after President Martin Van Buren. There is a familiar connection, although it's convoluted after all these generations. Miss Quittle, I'd like to repay you for your kindness and courage. I would be honored if you would join Martin and me for a cup of tea. That way you can meet all my kitties."

Staci Ellen hesitated for a moment, wondering if Ms. Hotshot With a Hyphen was worried about her by now. She decided that she didn't care. "That would be very nice, thank you. Can I carry Martin? You know, the way his whiskers shoot out sort of reminds me of my father. Isn't that hysterical?"

Miss Una agreed as they went into the house.

Raz Buchanon squinted at the much creased bank statement, but for the life of him he couldn't find the damn fool charges listed anywhere. It seemed to him that if'n they took his money, they ought to have to say so right on the paper instead of just telling him about it to his face. He considered the wisdom of approaching Miss Una one more time and asking where the damn fool charges were, then threw the paper down and reached for his tobacco can. Weren't much sense in that, he thought as he scratched Marjorie behind the left ear, which she loved most of all.

Marjorie was ecstatic.

13

I called the sheriff Monday morning and we decided to hold off on any further charges against Johnna Mae, mostly because we didn't have any evidence and the DA was s stickler about such things. All we knew about prints on the metal wastebasket was that they hadn't been made by Johnna Mae, Sherman Oliver, or Brandon Bernswallow. Plover and I had compared the partial from the kerosene can with the prints of the above mentioned printees, and we hadn't found any promising similarities. I admitted that Kevin and Dahlia were still missing and I was becoming increasingly worried about them. I declined to discuss Ruby Bee's and Estelle's latest caper, because I knew how Harve would respond and the guffaws were more than I could face on an empty stomach. He said to hang on until we got some more goodies from the state lab, told me to have a nice day, and rang off.

I decided to play fast and loose with the PD budget and called the lab in Little Rock. I was transferred to four different departments and spent a total of nine minutes on hold, listening to saccharinized old Beatles melodies. When I finally got the medical examiner on the line, he told me he was up to his goddamn neck in corpses and I was going to have to wait my turn.

I was grinning at the image when Raz Buchanon stomped into the PD. His cheek bulged dangerously, so I hastily went into the back room and found a coffee can kept for such emergencies.

"Much obliged," Raz said as he let a golden thread of amber dribble into the can. "I want to ask you something, Arly. You may not know the answer, and I'd be mighty surprised if you did." He flashed his sparse brown teeth at me so I'd know my abysmal ignorance wouldn't offend him none.

"I'll give it my best shot, Raz. But if it has anything to do with show sows, you might have better luck at the co-op in Starley City."

"I don't reckon it does. It has to do with bankin' practices."

"Again, Raz, it's not my field of expertise. Why don't you take it up with Miss Una, or better yet, Sherman Oliver?" I gave him a smile meant to send him away, in that the growing redolence in the PD was affecting me in the same manner as Harve's brayish laughter. It was obvious to those with noses that Raz and Marjorie had been watching a lot of television together.

"Miss Una's got a sharp tongue these days. I dun tried over and over for her to explain things to me, but I never could make out what she was saying. And I don't care for that Oliver fellow. The sight of his knees in those baggy shorts is enough to make a growed man cry." He took a grubby piece of paper from somewhere in his denim overalls and put it on my desk. "I just want you to take a gander at this, Arly.

You see if you can find where it says I paid a depository charge."

"There's no point in me looking at it. I wouldn't recognize a depository charge if it bit me on the ankle. My bank charges a service fee if my account drops below a certain level, and they go berserk with overdraft charges if I screw up and write a few bad checks, but they don't have anything called a depository charge. Are you sure that's the right term?"

"Hell, no, I ain't sure," he said, scratching his head. He spat into the can and shrugged. "It's not that this charge is so all-fired much. It's the principle of the thing. I can afford this twenty-five- or fifty-cent charge when I deposit my Social Security and my veteran's disability, but I think they should have to put it somewhere on this paper so I can balance my check-book every month and figger my taxes at the end of the year."

"I wish I could help you, but I can't, especially in the middle of a murder investigation. If you can't understand Miss Una's explanations, why don't you go to the main bank in Farberville and let them have a turn? Ask to speak to a Mrs. Gadwall; she seemed pleasant."

Raz chawed over my suggestion, stuffed the paper back in his overalls, and asked if it was hot enough for me, or would be by noon, anyways. I assured him that it would be by noon, anyways, and sent him away before I dumped the vile contents of the coffee can over his head.

Having savaged the air conditioner until it produced a mild breeze, I sat in my shabby chair and once again played fast and loose with the budget by calling all

seventeen miles to the barracks. I survived a round of
"I'll see if he's in," and "He doesn't seem to be in his
office," and "Please hold; I'll transfer you" with my
customary grace and charm.

When Plover finally came on the line, I said, "Well?"

"Well what?" he drawled, clearly amused by his
quick wit.

"Well, did you have a chance to talk to Mrs. Gadwall
about the portfolio? This call's costing money, you
know, and I'm saving up for a new radar gun that
picks on European imports."

"I did indeed speak to the woman, and I now know
more about junk bonds and grade B, double B, and
even C bonds. She promised to study the portfolio this
morning, if she could handle it. It seems martinis give
her horrible hangovers, and she drank them straight
through dinner and well into the night. The bartender
was whelmed."

"I'm delighted to know you had an entertaining
evening," I said coldly. "I had a marvelous time listening
to Kevin Buchanon's parents squabble and then driving
by Ruby Bee's a dozen times to gaze at an empty
parking lot. And I mustn't forget a shower and a can
of soup. The crackers were on the stale side, but they
were passable. Anyway, I've got Kevin's prints on a
plastic cup, so you can send someone to pick it up. As
for Ruby Bee and Estelle, put out an APB and mention
that the two are armed and dangerous. Maybe some
weak-kneed rookie will shoot them, thus saving me
the cost of the bullets."

"You'd better spend more time on border patrol,
Chief; you're losing your residents at an alarming rate.
Maybe I can find a roll of barbed wire and we can set

up a blockade at both ends of the city limits. Only to keep folks from escaping, of course, since no one in his right mind would want to come in."

"Did I tell you how funny you are?" I waited a second, then said, "There's a reason," and hung up. I sighed, jabbed the back of my head trying to adjust a loose bobby pin, propelled myself up and out the door, and walked down the highway to Ruby Bee's mumbling under my breath every step of the way.

Estelle's station wagon wasn't parked out front—naturally, but I banged through the door and stomped across the dance floor, around the end of the bar, and into the kitchen, where I found Ruby Bee and a man in a grease-stained jumpsuit arguing about the estimate to fix the vent.

"Go away," I said to the repairman.

He looked at my expression and my badge and started for the back door. Ruby Bee grabbed his arm. "Don't take one more step, Peewee Thrasher. I've waited three darn weeks for you, and you ain't going anywhere."

"Yes, he is," I said, folding my arms and glaring.

"No, he ain't," Ruby Bee said, hanging on for dear life and glaring.

"Yes—he—is. You and I have important things to discuss. Had you been in residence last night, we could have conducted the discussion at that time. I not only drove by here several times, I also called your unit until well after midnight. You chose to lurk under a bush all night."

"This kitchen's hotter than a final-night revival sermon. I've waited three weeks to get the vents repaired, all the while slaving over a hot stove so folks like you wouldn't whine about how hungry you are. Peewee's here to fix the vents and he's gonna do it right now." Her face was turning redder by the word, and her voice was climbing toward double-digit decibels. The repairman's head was going back and forth as if he were at Wimbledon, and I suspected he wished he were—or anywhere but where he was, for that matter.

"We are going to talk about your presence in the Bernswallows' library yesterday," I said. "He'll have to come back later."

"It took three weeks to get him here and he is not going to leave without fixing the vents, even if he charges a poor widow woman an arm and a leg to do it!"

We were still snarling and glaring when the kitchen door swung open and Estelle hurried in. Ignoring the ambiance, she said, "Well, it's about time you showed your face, Arly. We've got a problem. I'd even say we've got us a tragedy in the simmering."

"What?" Ruby Bee gasped, loosening her grip on the repairman.

"I stopped by Carolyn's unit to see if she wanted a pot of coffee, and she told me that Staci Ellen's disappeared. She went for a walk late yesterday afternoon and never came back."

Ruby Bee released the repairman in order to point her finger at Estelle. "You swore she was in Carolyn's room, being quiet as a mouse. Would you like to see the red mark on my ear?"

"Staci Ellen's whereabouts are a tad more important than your sore ear," Estelle retorted. She looked at me. "Why are you just standing there like one of your porch lights is burned out? You've got to find Staci Ellen before something terrible happens to her."

I told Peewee to fix the vents. I then marched the merry pranksters out to the bar and said, "For starters, I have no idea who this mysterious Staci Ellen is. I gather she has some connection with Carolyn McCoy-Grunders, and that leads to yet another topic of discussion." Before I could elaborate, the front door opened.

"Good, you're here," Carolyn said as she came across the room. "Staci Ellen Quittle is my secretary. She's nineteen or twenty, short, bleached blond hair, blue eyes, not especially intelligent or articulate. She went for a walk around six o'clock. I didn't hear her return, but I did hear a noise in her room later in the evening and assumed she was there. When I went to wake her for breakfast, I realized her bed had not been slept in and the clothes she'd been wearing yesterday weren't there."

"Does she know anyone in Maggody?" I asked.

"She knows us," Estelle said, frowning. "Are you sure her hair is bleached, Carolyn? I happen to be in the profession, and I'd of said it was natural. Maybe a little lemon juice, but—"

"It doesn't matter," I said curtly. "Let's take a look at her room to see if she might have written down a name or a telephone number. Then Estelle and Ruby Bee can wait here"—I gave them icy looks—"in case the girl comes back, and you and I will drive around town and look for her."

We all went to Staci Ellen's room. I opened the drawers, but the only things I found were a battered romance novel, *The Golden Ecstasy of Lady Beatrice*, and half a pack of chewing gum, sugar-free spearmint. A few clothes were folded neatly on a chair, and the bedspread was slightly rumpled. A dry toothbrush and a tube of toothpaste were aligned by the sink.

As I came out of the bathroom, Carolyn pointed at a wineglass on the dresser. "Staci Ellen must have been back at some time last night, because this glass wasn't here yesterday. It's the most peculiar thing of all. I'm almost certain she doesn't drink, but even if she decided to have some wine, where would she get this glass? And where's the bottle?"

I bent over to sniff the glass. "There's no residue in the bottom and no odor. It's smudgy, as if someone held it and twisted it for a long time. I agree with you; it's damn peculiar. A state trooper is coming to the PD this morning to pick up a plastic cup to be fingerprinted at the barracks. I'll send the glass along."

"Oh, you don't have any call to do that," Ruby Bee said. "Staci Ellen didn't arrive in Maggody until yesterday—the day after the fire. There's no way this innocent glass could have anything to do with important matters like arson and murder."

"That's correct," Estelle added, nodding her head.

Carolyn frowned. "But something funny is going on. There is no rational explanation for the wineglass's being in Staci Ellen's room."

"Maybe she brought it along for you," Ruby Bee said with a bright smile. "Maybe she thought you'd want to have a glass of wine. She figured you would prefer a real glass to a plastic cup, so she popped it in her suitcase, just to be on the safe side."

"Wait a minute," I said. I looked so hard at Ruby Bee that she backed into the bed and sat down with a grunt of surprise. "Why did you say that Estelle swore Staci Ellen was in Carolyn's room being as quiet as a mouse? What's wrong with your ear?"

"I disremember saying any of that."

"No, you don't. Just where were you two last night?"

Ruby Bee looked at Estelle, who looked at the ceiling. "We were here and there, running errands and visiting folks. Nothing worth mentioning. We did come by here for a minute or so—or would you say a tad longer, Estelle?" When Estelle didn't say anything whatsoever, Ruby Bee gulped and said, "We thought Staci Ellen might enjoy a little drive around the countryside, so we dropped by to invite her. She wasn't here."

I advanced until I was standing over her. "But Estelle thought Staci Ellen was in Carolyn's room. That was a reasonable theory. Why didn't you knock on the door and invite them both to go on this little drive?"

"We . . . ah, we didn't want to disturb Carolyn. She's going to defend Johnna Mae, and she might have been concentrating on what kinds of legal shenanigans to pull."

"Why do you have a red mark on your ear?" I said.

"Who said I have a red mark on my ear? Don't you think you ought to be searching for Staci Ellen instead of badgering your own mother? The poor girl could be lying in a ditch somewhere, bleeding and bruised from being knocked senseless by a chicken truck or some fool kid on a motorcycle."

I looked at Carolyn, whose eyes were zipping from the wineglass to the witness to the wall at a very brisk clip. Before she could say anything, I said, "Well, I'm going to send this glass to be fingerprinted, but in the meantime, let's drive around and look for the girl." I carefully picked up the glass, took Carolyn's arm, and pulled her out the door and into the parking lot.

Once we were in my car, she said, "Why on earth would those two spy on me? Do you think Staci Ellen made some sort of arrangement to vacate the room for them? The women in this town are crazy, absolutely crazy."

I turned up Finger Lane. "Those two in particular are indeed crazy. They feel an obligation to assist in official police investigations, which usually means they get themselves into a major muddle and have to be rescued. I doubt Staci Ellen made any kind of arrangement, though, since they're genuinely worried about her."

"They were spying on me to assist in an official police investigation? Does that imply I'm an official suspect?"

"You came all the way to Maggody because of a complaint of insignificant proportions. You spent five days organizing a demonstration that ended with arson and murder. During the half hour preceding the fire, several women were unable to find you on the lot. You told me you went back to the motel to get some pamphlets, but no one can confirm this."

"Nor can anyone disprove it. My specialty isn't criminal law, but I took enough courses to know you need more than a few women with poor eyesight who couldn't find me for a minute in a dark parking lot. In any case, I had no reason to harm either the banker or the building."

"Perhaps not the building," I said as I turned around in Earl Buchanon's driveway and went back toward the highway, all the while keeping an eye out for a pedestrian with blond hair and a poor vocabulary. "However, you did have a problem with Brandon Bernswallow. You didn't come to Maggody because Johnna Mae Nookim was demoted unfairly; you came because you recognized her immediate superior's name."

Granted, I was fishing. I was fishing so hard I should have been driving a bass boat and wearing a canvas hat decorated with lures. I decided to go right for the gills. "I had an enlightening interview with Brandon's parents yesterday afternoon. They were overcome with grief, but they allowed me a few minutes alone with them in their library."

"How veddy polite of them," she murmured.

I stopped at the traffic light, turned left, and then left again on Coot Road. I was doing my level best to appear knowledgeable, but she wasn't spilling her guts out of guilt. She was, I noticed out of the corner of my eye, getting more tight-lipped by the mile. I tried to think of something brilliant as we passed the McIlhaney house, and I was still working on it when I saw Estelle's station wagon parked in Lottie Estes's driveway. It was partly hidden by the sprawling forsythia, but I had no problem recognizing the dent in the hood and the bumper sticker that inquired if you had hugged your cosmetologist lately.

I swung into the driveway. "Damn it, I told them to wait at the bar in case Staci Ellen came back. We left them not more than ten minutes ago; they must have hesitated all of thirty seconds before leaving. I'm going to the door. Do you want to wait in the car?"

"I wouldn't miss this for anything."

I went to the door and knocked loudly enough to provoke a riot in the morgue. Lottie opened the door a few inches, but it was enough for us to see that her hair was wrapped around pink sponge rollers and her face covered with white cream. "Why, Arly, how nice of you to . . . drop by like this, and you, too, Mrs. Grunders. I'm afraid I wasn't expecting any company this morning. I was feeling badly when I woke up and called the school to say I wasn't coming in. A touch of the stomach flu, I suspect. If you'll give me just a moment, I'll wrap a scarf around these unsightly hair rollers and wipe the moisturizer off. We can have a nice cup of tea and what's left of an apple pie I made this morning. Are you here to interrogate me? Elsie said it was not the least bit what she expected, but she is quite religious about watching those dreadful police shows on television. I fear she was anticipating a spotlight in her face and a crowd of surly men looming over her with rubber hoses."

"I'm looking for Ruby Bee and Estelle," I said weakly.

She blinked at me. "I haven't seen either of them since the night of the demonstration. We had a nice talk about the weather and swapped a recipe or two. I'm sure Mrs. Grunders remembers it well."

Mrs. Grunders managed a pinched smile and allowed that she remembered it well. I pointed at the station wagon. "If Estelle's not here, why is that parked in your driveway?"

She came out to the porch and leaned over the rail to look. "I swear, this is the first time I've noticed. I don't drive, you see, and Miss Una prefers to pick me up at the end of the sidewalk so I rarely pay attention to that area of my yard. She is most kind about taking me to town, because, if I may say so myself, I take great pride in being prompt. Occasionally I must wait for her, but I really don't mind too very much."

I apologized for disturbing her, and Carolyn and I went back to the car. The whole thing was so screwy that I started laughing—or maybe I had a screw loose. Carolyn began to laugh, too, and pretty soon we were edging toward hysteria. I sputtered out a synopsis of Elsie's third degree, right down to the lemon cookies and mint sprigs in the tea. Carolyn choked out the ingredients in the infamous green bean casserole, because she'd been forced to listen to a heated debate on the water chestnut issue that lasted more than an hour.

We finally ran out of people to poke fun at and our laughter faded. I wiped my eyes, switched on the ignition, and started to back out of Lottie's driveway. When it hit.

"Lottie Estes did not support the cause," I said. "She's a great proponent of stereotypic roles. If given half a chance, she'll lecture for hours about the importance of small appliances and needlework. Her idea of sex education is making sure everyone knows that girl babies wear pink and boy babies wear blue. Why on earth would she show up in the parking lot?"

"She might have been more comfortable across the road," Carolyn said, shaking her head. "Ms. Estes was definitely there, however; she was defending traditional ingredients with the intensity of Perry Mason. It's hard to place anyone at any given time, but I don't remember seeing her until after I returned from the motel room."

"Speaking of which, don't give me that crap about the pamphlets. You didn't need to walk down the highway at that hour. The pamphlets were to be distributed the next morning. Why'd you go to your room? If that's where you went."

"I needed to make a telephone call to the current wife of an ex-friend. He's . . . a fellow attorney in Little Rock."

"And his wife can verify this?"

Carolyn ruffled her hair and sighed. "I left a message at a Las Vegas hotel, so the call can be verified through telephone company records."

"Or through the hotel operator, which might be faster. Will she remember taking the message?"

"Oh, yes, she most certainly will. I dictated a few words she was unfamiliar with. Why do you think Ms. Estes crashed our hen party in the parking lot? Do you think she was there to spy on us?"

"Shit, I don't know," I said with a groan. I came to the end of Coot Road and turned back onto the highway. "I don't know anything. I don't know where Kevin and Dahlia are, I don't know whose fingerprints are on the wastebasket and the kerosene can, I don't know who-all Bernswallow was blackmailing, I don't know who killed him, I don't know who lit either fire, I don't know where Staci Ellen is, and I don't know what the connection is between you and Bernswallow."

"I thought you did," she said.

"The Bernswallow Seniors declined to discuss it," I admitted with another groan. "You're not going to tell me, are you?"

"Not while it might be construed as a motive for murder. Once this mess is resolved, perhaps we can share a gallon jug of rotgut wine and I'll tell you about it. In the very first year of law school, lawyers are taught the wisdom of not incriminating themselves."

I turned up Raz Buchanon's road, which hadn't been graded in a decade, and pointed out Marjorie's air-conditioned shed as we passed it. Then I asked her if she'd ever heard of a depository charge.

"There's no such animal," she said firmly. "I did several courses in banking law. The regulations on fee structure are complex and rigid."

"Raz was all fired up about it this morning. Not so much that he paid it, mind you, but that it wasn't mentioned on his statement and therefore caused grief at tax computation time." I slowed down to a crawl. "I wonder if all the branch customers pay this mysterious charge whenever they make deposits."

"And to whom?"

I stopped the car and looked at her. "To Miss Una, I'd guess. When Johnna Mae was head teller, she spent her time writing bogus loan applications. Miss Una sat at her window and did the mundane chores, including taking deposits and explaining the inexplicable to people like Raz. She's a prim Sunday-school-teacher sort, and authoritative enough to convince half the town the sun rises in the west every morning, or at least plant a seed of doubt about it. She wouldn't have any problem convincing some of the customers that they had to pay a fee to deposit money. We're not real worldly in Maggody, which is why Chase Manhattan hasn't opened a branch here. The majority of the citizens didn't make it to the eighth grade prom."

"So Miss Una's been pocketing a dollar or so every day for the last twenty years? That could add up to a neat sum for retirement," Carolyn said thoughtfully. "It doesn't implicate her in the murder, however, or even place her at the scene."

"But she was there. Lottie didn't walk down the highway in the dark to exchange recipes. I'd wager the cost of a new radar gun that Miss Una stopped at the end of the sidewalk and tootled her horn. Furthermore, someone said Miss Una mentioned the faulty wiring as a logical cause of the fire." I put the car back into gear and sent a cloud of dust into the air as I grimly drove toward the highway. "I'd thought originally that we had one blackmail victim. Yesterday afternoon I upped it to two, because it fit so well with two fires. What if we had three victims—Johnna Mae, Sherman Oliver, and Miss Una?"

"Isn't that a rather larcenous group of employees for one branch bank? A hundred percent seems a high figure."

"I know, but this was an obscure little branch in an obscure boondock of a town. Oliver was an absentee manager. Perhaps Miss Una and Johnna Mae had a quiet understanding not to see what the other was doing, a you-embezzle-your-way-and-I'll-embezzle-mine pact. Then Bernswallow appears and starts spending his nights studying ledgers and rummaging through files. He stumbles onto the bogus loan applications the minute someone comes into the branch with a letter about a missed payment. He digs harder and sees that Miss Una's drawer is usually off a little bit."

"So which one of them murdered him and set the fire?"

"Let's drop by Miss Una's house and ask her." I

drove down the road with the fury of a demon conjured up from the bowels of hell.

Staci Ellen wrinkled her nose as the acrid smell became harder and harder to ignore. It was beginning to make her eyes burn, but she didn't want to say anything to hurt her hostess's feelings, having been brought up to say something nice or not to say anything at all, as well as to wear white gloves to church and skirts that brushed the middle of her knees and not one inch higher. The sacrilegious notion that she'd been brought up with a lot of foolish rules struck her.

She smiled politely and said, "Do you think there might be a gas leak somewhere? I seem to be smelling something strange."

Miss Una rose and in an uncertain voice said, "Why, now that you mention it, so do I. You stay right here and keep an eye on Martin; I'll make sure the burners on the stove are off as tight as they can go. How about that very last piece of lemon meringue pie?"

Mrs. Jim Bob pounded on the door of the mobile home, but there was not one peep from inside. She'd already been inside the Assembly Hall. She couldn't for the life of her think where Brother Verber could be. As she'd told Jim Bob, who agreed and then some, the sermon'd been sort of strange. Brother Verber's hand had been real wet when she shook it at the door; she'd been grateful she'd had a tissue in her purse. He'd mumbled distractedly when she made a few constructive comments about the contents of the sermon and how she didn't think it was proper to have all those words about private parts and buck nakedness said right out loud in the house of the Lord.

He'd been so much stranger at the potluck and prayer meeting last night that she hadn't bothered to invite him to the house for coffee and pie afterward. She didn't want those words said in her home. Why, she'd have to call in some kind of spiritual exterminator.

But she dearly wanted to know where he was, and she was more than a little miffed about having to pound on his door and holler his name. Finally she gave up and went back to her car. Still frowning, she pulled out onto the highway and right smack into the path of the biggest, blackest, loudest motorcycle she'd ever seen in her whole entire life.

Mrs. Jim Bob closed her eyes.

14

I parked in front of Miss Una's white frame house. Before I could open the gate, she came out on the porch and waved. "Hello, Arly. How are you today?"

"I'm fine, thank you. I need to talk to you."

I reached for the latch, but as I did so she said, "I'm afraid this is not a convenient time for me to visit with you. I already have company, and it would be rude to entertain someone else. Please don't open the gate; last night one of my kitties escaped that way. I was sick with worry until he was safe at home again. I scolded him quite sharply, and you should have seen his little face get all wrinkled up and sad." Her face got all wrinkled up and sad for a moment, then relaxed in an impish grin.

"I'm sorry to interrupt and I'll be careful not to allow any kitties to get past me," I said, trying to maintain a normal voice in the face of her odd demeanor. Even from where I stood I could see the red patches on her cheeks and the asymmetrical twist to her mouth. Behind her half-moon glasses, her eyes looked way too bright. "What I need to ask you is very important, Miss Una. I'll have to insist on coming inside."

She dug into her apron pocket and produced a disposable lighter. Flourishing it at me, she said, "Please do not force me to flick my Bic. The porch and a good deal of the house are saturated with kerosene. It will go up like a tinderbox, which it is. As I mentioned, I have company inside, and I see no way either of my visitors could escape."

I discovered new dimension to the phrase "stopped cold in one's tracks." I not only froze, I felt an icicle pierce my stomach. "Your house is saturated with kerosene? Why?"

"So it will burn more easily. Kerosene is highly flammable, or should I say inflammable? Oh dear, I'm never sure which it is. In any case, should I make even a wee little spark, it will catch fire immediately."

"Then don't do it. Who's in your house?"

"I'm surprised at you, Arly. I'm sure your mother has told you time and again that it's unseemly to ask about other people's guests or take a personal interest in a lady's private affairs."

Carolyn had been waiting in the car, but she scrambled out and came up behind me. "Three to two odds Staci Ellen's one of her 'guests,' " she hissed.

"Is there a blond girl named Staci Ellen Quittle inside?" I called to Miss Una, who was squeezing the lighter so tightly her fingers were white.

"You're prying, Arly, and it does not become you. I was just about to serve a piece of lemon meringue pie to one of my guests, and I really must go now. I'll keep the lighter in my hand, so please do not try to come into my yard or do anything rash that will force me to flick my Bic." She gave me another impish grin, coyly fluttered her fingers, and turned to go inside, Bic and all.

"Wait!" I croaked. While she hesitated, I tried to think what the hell to do. She was manic. I didn't doubt for a second that her house was ready to become a funeral pyre, and that its occupants would fare no better than Brandon Bernswallow. Carolyn was jabbing me in the back and whispering all sorts of unintelligible things, which didn't do a whole lot for my concentration. I finally told her to cut it out and gave Miss Una a strained smile. "We seem to have an awkward situation. I promise not to set foot in your yard, but I'm not sure it's best for you to go back inside the house with your . . . guests. Why don't you let them run along home so you and I can continue the conversation?"

"We haven't had lemon meringue pie yet."

"Miss Una, why are you doing this?"

She gave me a startled look. "Because I have no choice, of course. Once you mentioned how terribly clever they are at this lab, I knew it was a matter of time before you attempted to barge into my house and ask me all sorts of stupid, snoopy questions. You're somewhat quicker than I had anticipated, but I was ready for you, wasn't I? Mercy me, I hear Martin and he sounds distressed. I must go inside now."

"Please," I said, clutching the gate so hard my knuckles hurt, "please don't go inside yet. Are you worried about the fingerprints? We don't have to take yours if you don't want us to. Why don't you put away that lighter and we'll figure out what to do next?"

Carolyn peered around my shoulder. "I'm an attorney, Miss Una. If you're charged with murder, I'll do everything I can to help you."

"Murder? Why on earth would I be charged with murder? I may have been naughty, but I didn't murder anyone." Giggling at the absurd notion, she went inside and closed the door.

I gaped at Carolyn, my jaw so slack I couldn't seem to get out any words. Finally I swallowed a very large lump in my throat and said, "What just happened?"

"I think this is what is known on the nightly news as your classic hostage situation."

"Right, and I'm supposedly trained in the proper way to handle it." I wrenched my hands off the gate and got back in the car. The radio worked, bless its rusted soul, and after a bit of fiddling I told the dispatcher that I really, *really* needed to talk to Harve and to get him out of the goddamn rest room before I drove over there and parked next to the goddamn toilet and snatched the goddamn magazine out of his hands with my teeth.

Harve stopped grumbling when I told him what was going on. He promised to send backup as quickly as possible and to make a personal appearance in fifteen minutes or so. He also agreed to contact the state police, who were better trained and better armed than the rest of us, the Emmet volunteer fire department, and the media. Harve was up for re-election in a couple of months. I thanked him in a shaky voice, letting my head fall against the back of the seat.

Carolyn got in the car with me. "So now we sit and wait?"

"Unless you've got any astoundingly good ideas, yes. All hell's going to break loose in fifteen minutes or so. I wish I understood what's happening. She's lost it, obviously, and is beyond any appeal to reason.

There're two people inside, one named Martin and the other unknown. She said she didn't murder Bernswallow, and oddly enough, I tend to buy it. However, she flipped out over having her fingerprints taken for comparison, which means she knows that hers match one set from the scene of the crime."

Carolyn looked at the house. "It's old and dry. The term 'tinderbox' is apropos, and I shudder to think about those trapped inside. Shit, I hope Staci Ellen's not nibbling lemon meringue pie as we speak. She may not have much going for her, but she tries. Who is this Martin person?"

I checked my watch—the minute hand was creeping very slowly—and contemplated the possibilities. "I don't know anyone named Martin. I've never known anyone named Martin. No one in Maggody is named Martin. The only Martin I can think of is Martin Van Buren, and I'd be surprised if he were in there eating pie. You may be right about Staci Ellen, but I'll put my money on Kevin Buchanon. He was inside the branch and might have run into Miss Una. Somehow or other, she convinced him to hide out at her house, in the upstairs bedroom on the right."

"That's a guess?"

"Well, I saw him at the window a second ago," I admitted. "Maybe we're doing the wrong thing by sending for the sheriff's men and the state police. If Miss Una panics, she's liable to flick her damn Bic and send all of them up in flames. Why don't you go down the road a hundred yards or so and stop the cars from screeching up here with sirens going and lights flashing? I'll try once again to coax Miss Una outside."

Wishing I'd stayed awake during cop shows, where

hostage situations are invariably resolved in time for a dozen commercials, I went back to the gate and called Miss Una's name. She came out to the porch and gave me a stern look. "What is it now, Arly? I was pouring a bowl of half-and-half for Martin; he's still traumatized by his misadventures last night."

"A bowl of half-and-half? Martin is a cat?"

"Well, of course. Did you think I would offer a bowl of half-and-half to a dead president, even if there is a familial connection? Martin is my prodigal kitty."

"Oh," I murmured, finally seeing the light, although it was a very small pinprick of enlightenment in a vast black sky. "Did you meet Staci Ellen while you were searching for Martin?"

"How very astute of you," she said, beaming at me. It would have been more encouraging if one side of her mouth hadn't been twitching like a spider on a hot skillet. "That's exactly what happened. She discovered a little lost kitty in the alley and was trying to find his home. I was so grateful that I invited her in for tea."

"And the two of you are still drinking tea this morning?"

"In a manner of speaking. We had a tiny problem last night when she asked if she might freshen up before returning to her motel. She opened the wrong door and met another guest. The two began chatting, and I'm afraid Staci Ellen told my guest several things I would have preferred he did not hear at the moment. I was obliged to lock his door and to tie the girl up so she couldn't carry tales. I promised her a piece of pie, so I really must go back inside and feed it to her. These modern girls are so helpless." She waved and turned around.

"Please," I said (okay, ululated like a coyote), "please. Don't go inside yet. I—ah, I need your advice about—about something. It's—it's—important." I was stammering so badly I wasn't sure she could understand me, but I had a legitimate reason. The window directly above the roof of the porch had been inching open. The opaque curtain was pulled aside, and a naked leg came through the gap. A second leg followed, along with lacy pink underpants.

"Advice?" Miss Una said doubtfully. "Advice about what?"

"Something important," I said, trying not to stare at the apparition coming out the window. I put my hands on my face and scanned my mental Rolodex. "About banks. Yeah, that's it. Do you think I ought to take my business to the Bank of Farberville, even though they may not reopen the branch?"

"I really don't feel qualified in that regard, now that I'm retired. However, I will pass along something. Please don't repeat this, but I've heard rumors that the portfolio has gone downhill over the years, and that many of the investments are dubious."

I took a quick look at the blond girl, clad in nothing but the pink panties and a matching bra, who was now out on the roof and moving cautiously toward the gutter directly above Miss Una's head. I gulped and said, "Did you hear that from Johnna Mae Nookim?"

"Goodness gracious, Arly, I am very impressed with your deductive powers today. However did you know that?"

Kevin Buchanon's face appeared in the window. He gave me a bewildered look, then climbed out onto the roof. His face was as white as flour, and his Adam's apple was lurching up and down so hard it looked as though it might shoot out the top of his head. I took some small comfort in the fact that he was dressed in his normal jeans and T-shirt. If he'd been nearly naked, too, I would have said good-bye to all concerned and driven away to check myself into one of those nice, quiet, stress-free environments and sign up for tole painting classes.

I gulped again. "I . . . I . . . I . . ." couldn't think of anything, obviously. "I thought she might have come over to your house after she talked to Bernswallow."

"After she killed Bernswallow, you mean? Yes, she did come over. She was shaking so hard I made her sit down and have a cup of camomile tea. I find it so soothing, especially after a long, hard day at the bank."

"After she killed Bernswallow," I repeated numbly. "Did she tell you that?"

"She told me that she banged him over the head with that trophy he kept in his office. I always found it on the pretentious side. There's nothing wrong with a small photograph or a postcard. That's the sort of thing that gives a bank a homey atmosphere. But, in my opinion, a big trophy like that is tooting one's own horn."

As I desperately tried to come up with my next stall tactic, Plover strode up beside me, blessedly wearing civilian clothes. "What the hell is going on?" he said in a low growl. "The sheriff's dispatcher said to get my ass over here, and the woman who flagged me down babbled something about kerosene and a hostage situation on the nightly news. Who're those clowns on the roof and what in God's name do they think they're doing?"

"Miss Una, have you met John Plover?" I called. "He's a friend of mine from Farberville."

"This isn't the time for social amenities," my friend muttered.

"Oh, yes it is," I muttered right back. "Smile at the loony lady, damn it. She's got a lighter in her hand and a house soaked with kerosene."

Miss Una was studying Plover. "I don't believe we've ever been introduced, but I've seen him somewhere. Why, isn't he a policeman of some kind, or a fire marshal?"

All this time Staci Ellen was waving frantically at us, gesturing at the gutter, shushing Kevin, and creeping toward the edge of the roof. What she intended to do when she got there was way beyond me, but I wasn't in top-notch form at the moment. Estelle would have said both of my porch lights were out.

"I used to be a fire marshal," Plover called to Miss Una, "but that was last week. Now I'm . . . I'm an insurance adjuster."

"Isn't that nice," she said. Her thumb danced above the top of the lighter, then eased away, thus allowing others of us to release a breath. "If you're finished with all these questions, I'll go back inside now."

"So Bernswallow was dead when you went to the bank," I said in a conversational tone.

"He certainly was. In order to look through his drawers, I tilted his chair until he slid to the floor, and he didn't say one word. I didn't touch him, of course, since that would have been most presumptuous, but I did ask him several times if he could hear me. Johnna

Mae was correct when she said he had compiled a list of my little depository charges, but she was quite wrong when she said he was alive. You don't think I would have started such a big fire if he hadn't already been dead and therefore wouldn't mind?"

"Not for a minute," Plover called, giving her a genial grin. He nudged me and I did the same, although without much sincerity.

We were making progress of a kind: she hadn't torched her house yet. Wow. I was about to ask Plover if he had any ideas how next to proceed when Staci Ellen slipped. She grabbed for Kevin, and at the last second caught his hand and managed to regain her balance a good centimeter from the edge of the roof and a ten-foot drop.

At which point the biggest, blackest, loudest motorcycle I'd ever seen roared up in a veritable cloud of dust and gravel. The driver cut the ignition, yanked off his helmet, and, his eyes bulging like balloons, shouted, "What the fuck are you doing up there—and where are your fucking clothes, you little whore?"

"Bruno!" Staci Ellen screamed, throwing her arms around Kevin so wildly that they both began to stagger forward.

Miss Una's head shot back and she blinked at the porch ceiling. "Goodness gracious," she murmured as she flicked her Bic.

The porch disappeared in a sheet of flames.

Carolyn came into the bar and flopped down in the booth across from me. "I just talked to the county prosecutor. Johnna Mae's going to face a truckload of charges, but not murder. The autopsy report came in this morning; Bernswallow died of smoke inhalation. She admitted to me that she did go into the branch to try to reason with him. When he refused to back down on his blackmail demand, she lost her temper and bashed him on the head. She swears he was alive when she panicked and ran to Miss Una's house to tell her that Bernswallow intended to blackmail all three of them."

I nodded. "Then we have the second player—Putter. He saw her run out the back of the bank and head for Miss Una's house for help. He went in and found both the unconscious banker and the blackmail note, burned the note in the metal wastebasket, and went home, convinced Johnna Mae had killed Bernswallow. Johnna Mae assumed he had killed Bernswallow and then started the fire to cover it up. They may not communicate well with each other, but they're damn loyal."

Carolyn frowned and shook her head. "In retrospect, I shouldn't have taken the complaint to begin with. I was upset about a different matter and not thinking rationally. I thought it might be a way to get even with that prick after all these years." She closed her eyes for a moment, then gave me a forced smile. "I was the victim of a gang rape at the fraternity house. I let myself get talked into going to a childish party, where a drunken brute dragged me upstairs and invited all his buddies to join in the fun. Brother Bernswallow's father had enough money and influence to have my charge dismissed as the rantings of a promiscuous, drunken slut who'd participated willingly and then changed her tune in the morning. The administration seized the chance to banish the fraternity, but they refused to pursue it any farther. Brandon didn't even recognize me."

I looked away to let her regain her composure. "You couldn't have known all the craziness that would happen," I said. "I still have a hard time picturing Miss Una calling Lottie Estes to suggest a jaunt to the bank to visit with their friends. While Lottie was engrossed in recipes, Miss Una took a can of kerosene, slipped inside to start the fire, and then ran into Kevin on her way out. Only Kevin would fall for the story she gave him. Lord, what a moron he is."

Carolyn and I sat for a few minutes longer. She finally said she needed to make a long-distance call and wandered away. I was still in the booth when Ruby Bee and Estelle came out of the kitchen.

"I told you it worked," Estelle said, poking Ruby Bee with a wineglass. "I think you owe someone an apology for being all snooty about it. The someone is waiting right next to you."

"Then I hope someone's ear hurts," Ruby Bee said. She came around the bar and over to my booth. "That's just awful about Carolyn and those fraternity boys. No wonder she was a might testy when she talked on and on about how men were no damn good. If I was in her shoes, I might feel the same way. The vents've been repaired and I'm going to take the Closed sign off the door. Do you want I should fix you a nice plate of pork chops and crowder peas?"

"I'm not hungry." As I crossed the dance floor, the topic of apologies and ears was renewed, and with a verbose vengeance. I kept on going.

Truda Oliver struggled toward the bus depot. The new suitcase holding her recent purchases—and the metal box, naturally—was heavier than she'd first realized, but the bus depot sign was in sight. She dropped the suitcase for a moment to catch her breath, then fluttered her hands over her hair and reached down for it again.

"Let me help you with that," said a man in a three-piece suit and muted red tie.

"No, thank you," Truda said firmly. "I can do it myself."

"And that's another reason why you ought to fire Arly," Mrs. Jim Bob said. "She's supposed to keep those unsavory Hell's Angels types from speeding down the middle of the highway and terrifying the good citizens of the community. I was so terrified that I just sat in the middle of the road waiting for my heart to stop pounding. I was absolutely speechless."

Jim Bob didn't believe that, but he had enough sense not to say so. In truth, he didn't have time to say anything, because she was off and running again, and liable to make him late getting to Cherri Lucinda's, who was less and less willing to listen to his excuses. The bitch.

"I sure could do with another beer," Earl Buchanon said, peeking at his wife out of the corner of his eye.

Eilene put down her needlework. "Then let's both hope you can find the way to the refrigerator. I think I'll ask Joyce Lambertino if she wants to go to a picture show in Farberville. We might even stop somewhere afterwards and have a drink."

"But, honey, it's a long way into town, and you and Joyce shouldn't drive all the way back home after dark. I don't want any wife of mine in a bar at night, especially with another woman. You two are liable to get yourselves in a bushel of trouble."

Eilene dialed Joyce's number.

In the booth next to the jukebox, Kevin gazed forlornly at the light of his life, the apple of his eye, the salt pork in his turnip greens. "But, honey," he said piteously, "I did it all for you."

"Ate chocolate cake and lemon merinque pie for me, you mean, while I was all by myself out in the woods to save you. If I'd of known you were sitting around on your behind with a catalogue for entertainment, I wouldn't have nearly starved to death or been scared out of my wits."

"But I was doing it for you. I told you how I came out of the rest room just as Miss Una was leaving. I'd been in there for a long time, partly because I didn't want Bernswallow to know I was there and partly because I started looking at the reels in the catalogue and lost track of time. They've got a new one with a magnetic cast control system—"

"Kevin!"

Her cheeks were puffing in and out real fast, so he decided not to mention that it cost less than sixty dollars and was guaranteed for a year. "She told me that I had to hide or some of those men would do awful things. She said they'd already set the bank on fire because of the demonstration in the parking lot, and that if I'd stay at her house for a few days, you all would be safe because you wouldn't be able to yell at me and get everybody riled up."

"That's the dumbest thing I recollect you ever

saying," Dahlia said mercilessly. "There I was on that rough old log, out of sandwiches and my throat so sore I couldn't hardly get out more than a croak, when this crazed madman comes creeping up on me."

Kevin gasped. "He didn't—do anything to molest you?"

Dahlia folded her arms and put them on the table, where they spread out like Virginia hams. "You'd better get it in your thick skull that I can take care of myself, Kevin Fitzgerald Buchanon. There I am, sitting in the pitch black, minding my own business, and thinking I might ought to just let the bears eat you, when this madman starts trying to pile up rocks like they was wood blocks. Then he prances around and mumbles all kind of foolish nonsense in what sounded like a foreign language. After a while, I got wearied of it and got up and asked him what in tarnation he was doing. Well, that's when I realized how plumb crazy he was, because he jumped so high he banged his head on a limb and then ran off into the woods, a-stumbling every which way and spouting out more gibberish. It was the funniest darn thing I've ever seen. Mebbe I ought to send it in to *Reader's Digest.* I reckon they'd pay me money."

"You don't need to worry your precious head about money," Kevin said with all the tenderness he could find within his being. "I told you I'd always take care of you, my dumpling."

"Then why don't you explain one more time how come you were clinging on to some skinny-minnie girl dressed in nothing but her underwear?"

"I had to take off my dress to climb out the window," Staci Ellen said, and not for the first time. "Once I'd wiggled free of the clothesline, I saw Miss Una out on the porch with that cigarette lighter in her hand and heard her saying all that crazy stuff. I was scared she'd see me if I went to the kitchen, so I crept upstairs. I couldn't let that peculiar fellow in the bedroom get burned up, so I let him out and told him to shut up and let me think for a minute. I finally decided to get above Miss Una and then jump down on her and grab the lighter right out of her hand."

"You couldn't grab a lollipop out of a baby's hand," Bruno said, sneering at her. "Not even if the baby was sleeping."

"You might be surprised what-all I can do. Anyway, I was about to leap on her when you showed up and ruined everything. If I hadn't shoved that fellow off the side of the roof and then jumped after him, both of us would have been burned up along with Miss Una and—" Staci Ellen stopped to wipe a tear. "And sweet little Martin."

"Who the fuck is Martin?" Bruno growled.

Staci Ellen gazed across the table. "That's none of your business. Furthermore, I don't care for your tone of voice and I don't like the way you use bad language around me. I'm real sorry that you got that speeding ticket and had your motorcycle run over by the fire truck, but nobody invited you to Maggody, so it's your fault. From now on you're going to treat me with respect. I'm going to say where we go on dates at least some of the time, and I'm going to wear whatever kind of perfume I choose. If I want a cocktail instead of a Dr Pepper, you're going to order it and you're going to pay for it."

Bruno's eyes bulged but finally receded back into

their sockets without exploding. "So whaddaya want to drink?"

In that Staci Ellen had never ordered a cocktail in her life, she was stumped for a minute. "I know," she said at last, "I want something sophisticated, not one of those sissy girl's drinks with an umbrella and a fruit salad on the rim of the glass. I think I'll have a Perrier and soda, thank you." Remembering a scene from a movie, she flipped her hair back and put his cigarette between her lips. "Make it a double."

Sherman Oliver sat in the den, drinking whiskey and wondering when Truda would get home so he could tell her about the burglary. And getting fired. And how he'd come real close to making a par on seventeen, and would have if the ball hadn't stopped one inch from the cup.

Brother Verber sat in the darkest corner of his closet, the witchcraft manual in his hand. He'd heard the demon pounding on his door a while back. Just remembering how the hulking creature had risen from the ground and croaked something vile was enough to put him right smack back in a cold sweat. When the demon had persisted trying to get into the mobile home, Brother Verber had cowered so hard he'd ended up with a crick in his neck, which fit in real well with the lump on his head and the soreness in his ankle from sprawling in the dark. He figured the demon would be back for him, and the only thing between him and true evil was the manual and the mayonnaise jar.

There had to be a section on how to send demons

back where they belonged, but he hadn't been able to find it, mostly because it was real dark in the closet and he didn't want to risk opening the door. Somehow, requesting a little assistance from the Almighty seemed inappropriate, considering the awful truth that he'd raised the demon all by hisself.

But for a good and righteous cause, he amended as he let the manual slip out of his hand. Everything he'd done was to save the mortal souls of his flock, to prepare himself to meet their impending depravities and do battle with the devil, if and when he was called on to do so. He'd been real convinced the women were going to get naked and do all those wicked, lustful, depraved things.

Brother Verber opened the closet door to let in a small ribbon of light. By positioning the book just right, he could take one more look at the drawings of all that depravity. You never knew.